LEAF AND BONE

AFRICAN PRAISE-POEMS

Edited by
Judith Gleason

ILLUSTRATIONS BY
STÉPHAN DAIGLE

PENGUIN BOOKS

PENGUIN BOOKS
Published by the Penguin Group
Penguin Books USA Inc., 375 Hudson Street, New York, New York 10014, U.S.A.
Penguin Books Ltd, 27 Wrights Lane, London W8 5TZ, England
Penguin Books Australia Ltd, Ringwood, Victoria, Australia
Penguin Books Canada Ltd, 10 Alcorn Avenue, Toronto, Ontario, Canada M4V 3B2
Penguin Books (N.Z.) Ltd, 182–190 Wairau Road, Auckland 10, New Zealand

Penguin Books Ltd, Registered Offices:
Harmondsworth, Middlesex, England

First published in the United States of America by The Viking Press 1980
This updated edition published in Penguin Books 1994

10   9   8   7   6   5   4   3   2   1

Acknowledgments for permission to reprint copyrighted material appear at
the end of the chapters.

LIBRARY OF CONGRESS CATALOGING IN PUBLICATION DATA
Leaf and bone : African praise-poems / edited by Judith Gleason.
p.   cm.
Originally published: New York : Viking, 1980.
ISBN 0 14 058.722 5
1. Laudatory poetry, African—Translations into English.
I. Gleason, Judith Illsley.
PL8013.E5L38   1994
869—dc20   94-596

Printed in the United States of America
Set in Elante
Designed by Kate Nichols

"Ruhmen, das ist's!"

    —Rilke, *Sonnets to Orpheus*, I, 7

Members of the Writing Group, *egbé akòwe*
adept at translating lives into wind, into rain
piecing shards of memory into earthenware jars, basins
leaf-catchers, resonant chambers
Gentle voices, capable of stilling the roar of traffic
having once seated yourselves companionably in this room
from everywhere—Brooklyn, Narrows and Charlottesville,
upstate/downtown, I beg you, return now to welcome
to sustain in answering chorus: *hmmm hmmm a-eeee*
these longtime traveling across hectic frontiers
language-tossed, customs-shorn
irrepressible praise-poems.

Contents

Introduction

Praise-poems (*amazina*; literally "names") are composed to honor a generous patron's or the author's own valor in battle. Highly refined literary-rhetorical skills, composition, and good delivery of *amazina* are included in the speech training of young boys of good family. The naturally alliterative character of Kirundi is reinforced by conscious selection of assonant words in the construction of praise names and figures of speech. There are slight though perceptible modifications in wording and number of verses presented as the authors repeat their steadily increasing store of *amazina* on appropriate occasions. For some, virtuosity earns wide fame. An elderly man with a long history of bravery and gifts of cattle may fill three or four hours with his chanted recitation. The *amazina* in fact are repositories of Rundi history. . . . Clever cow thieves, the most dreaded members of the community, may compose *amazina* in self-praise: since the punishment for stealing cattle is immediate crucifixion if caught in the act and since precautions against stealing are elaborate, a cow thief who lives to tell the tale has earned the right to *amazina*.[1]

The praise-singer would install himself in our goldsmith shop, tune up his kora, which is our harp, and begin to sing my father's praises [in Malinké]. I would hear recalled the lofty deeds and the names of my father's ancestors from earliest times; as the

[1] Ethel M. Albert, " 'Rhetoric,' 'Logic,' and 'Poetics' in Burundi: Culture patterning of Speech Behavior," *American Anthropologist* 66 (6: 1964): 49–50 (slightly abridged).

couplets were reeled off, it was like watching the growth of a great genealogical tree that spread its branches far and wide and flourished its branches before my mind's eye. The harp played an accompaniment to this vast utterance of names, expanding it and punctuating it with notes that were now soft, now shrill, accelerating the singer's rhythm, increasing his flatteries as the trinket took shape, and praising my father's talents to the skies. . . . Indeed, the praise-singer participated in the work. He was no longer a paid flatterer; he was no longer just the man whose services anyone could hire; he had become a man who creates his song under the influence of some very personal, interior necessity.[2]

I greet you readers lolling about on a summer's day
    may copper beech or mottled sycamore continue to shade
    may insects fail to prevent your concentration
To you nocturnal readers curled up in your chairs or flattened
       out
    on the bed, greetings; may sounds of your partner's TV
    neighbor's tape deck, buses grinding their gears
    all muffle themselves in your immediate vicinity
And you, bending over table or crouched by shelf in shop or
    library
Headstrong child of the wind, close associate of hunters
    I greet you for browsing through these leaves.

Though generalizations of continental scope are risky, certain aspects of African cultures may be said to share common characteristics. For example, African music wherever played is notably polymetered, with all parts articulating unique rhythmic sequences; and wherever sung, it is characterized by call-and-response disposition of voices whose phrases slightly overlap. And were one to ask if there is any form of verbal expression distinctively and pervasively African—that is, a form of oral literature in which continental similarities outweigh ethnic differences—the answer would be the subject of this book: praise-

[2] Camara Laye, *The Dark Child*, translated by James Kirkup (London: Collins, 1955), 26–34 (abridged).

poetry, regularly performed in households and public spaces in all African languages one can think of.[3]

Though praise poems must be pronounced and heard in order to have their intended effect, saturated listening surely is their creative genesis. Competence begins with an ability to join in the choruses.[4] Inadvertently the putative praise-singer picks up snatches of matter along with the manner, until gradually attention grows more focused and memorization of traditional phrases in various combinations more conscious. There follows a search for clarification of cryptic statements and amplification of curious formulations from experts, perhaps an apprenticeship—formal or informal—until creative use of traditional material comes to include invention of new material within a conventional format. Thus, revision and refinement of texts in the light of their reception by local connoisseurs, as well as a cultivation of the confident art of improvisation (including topical commentary), contribute to acceptably stylish utterance of whatever subspecies of the praise genre, which everywhere bops along to an unpredictable cutoff. Praise-poetry's vividly particularized segments are conspicuously analogous to those of strip-weaving on a narrow loom, whose lengthy warp threads extend variously—across the shed, the courtyard, along the edge of the dusty street—before being wound around

[3] For an early study, with detailed commentary on a variety of texts, see Judith Gleason, "An Example of African Verbal Art: The Praise Poem," in *Introduction to Sub-Saharan Africa*, Edgar S. Efrat, ed. (Lexington, MA, and Toronto: Xerox College Publishing, 1973), 198–228. There are several excellent studies of particular traditions, whose titles are given in the notes to individual chapters.

[4] The process of gradually acquired competence described briefly here is an abstraction based on a variety of experiences and readings over the years and incorporates a range of philosophies, from Aristotelian mimesis to John Dewey's notions of experience. Bourdieu's theory of *habitus* would probably be relevant too; but I can't say I've explored it thoroughly enough to include here in any formative sense. The concept of "saturated listening" can well apply to acquisition of verbal and musical skills cross-culturally. For a long time, scholars of African performance traditions were unaware of the negative feedback loop provided by local "connoisseurs," until Robert Farris Thompson provided dance evaluations in *African Art in Motion* (1974). Since then, Henry John Drewel for Gelede masquerading, John Miller Chernoff for African ensemble drumming, Robin Horton for drum-praise identification, and Karin Barber for *oríkì* chants have given us an especially lively sense of how virtuoso performances may be polished within parameters of cultural expectation by constructive criticism. I would here like to thank Toña Velez, fellow student of Cuban ritual dancing and chanting, for discussing the nature of her intensive apprenticeship with me.

and weighted down at the always portable end by a solid rock of silence.

Molecular praise-poetry's heaviest segments consist of names—emblematic and anecdotal, terse as riddles. As incorporated into growing organisms of poetic discourse, such epithetical proper nouns reflect and keep verbal pace as the poetry develops. Although customs vary from group to group, in general it may be said that names given to a newborn child are both existential and essential. The first type reflects conditions of entry into the familial world: as a twin, as a sibling following twins (both categories being mystically regarded), after a series of infant mortalities, as a boy after a run of girls, under unusual conditions or in a special place on a certain day, in the midst of memorable parental circumstances (straitened, unusually prosperous, in the midst of a journey, a drought, a war) or simply the quality of joy with which a baby is welcomed. Essential names denote a spiritual force known to have interceded in the baby's conception or the identity of the ancestor "come again" to form part of the infant's complex soul.[5] Certain unusual features (born wrapped in a caul, for example) or initial manner of self-presentation (feet first) may denote character and/or spiritual affiliation and thus form part of the given name. A praise-name drawn from a repertoire of traditional epithets proper to the clan into which one is born, or in recognition of a totemic alliance (determined by divination), may also be bestowed, thus linking the newborn to the past and providing a distinguishing impetus toward self-realization.

Songs and chants of self-presentation and arrival mark the passage from youth to adulthood. Here follow two examples, the first from a 1954 novel by Mopeli-Paulus, which contains a dramatic memory of adolescent self-praising in a Sotho community. The youths have been secluded together for weeks, during which time they have been circumcised, instructed in traditional law and custom, toughened physically, and, to speed the process of identity formation, required to compose orations on their own behalf. The protagonist, a young schoolteacher (older than the others), once forbidden by his Christian

---

[5] See commentary on naming procedures relevant to the appellations Abatan and Ambari in Chapter II.

preacher father to participate in the initiation proceedings, now defies the old man.

The youths of Makong and the surrounding villages had now been away at *mopohoto* for more than two months and were about to return home. Everyone who belonged to Makong or had already arrived there was crowded near the *khotla* and the Chief's cattle kraal, standing on walls, peeping through the reed fence of huts, or on tiptoe in the open courtyards bounded by low walls of smooth mud. There they are! The procession appears, and surrounding the band of boys is a crowd of men singing the *mokorotlo* [a "grumbling" warlike song and dance], one leaping out here and one there to the *tlala* [inspired solo performance] stamping and dancing, crying praises, sticks in their hands, while another and another give honking blasts on ox horns. The air is thick with praises: Cattle! Cattle! Calf of the Beast! "Letlaka, [calls the boy's instructor] come out and praise!" The young teacher stands still in the space before the Chief. He holds his knobkerrie out at full length before him, and his eyes are fixed on the end of it, as in a clear, strong voice, he praises himself:

> The Vulture of Ramalana refuses to cut his crest
> He denies those who would cut it
> Save only those who are men!
> Save only those of Kali and those of Khiba.
> He gathers together the ends of Joseph's blanket
> He is the shrewd one of Manini and Maleshoane
> Who left home when the bells were ringing
> Ringing the call to church in the morning.
> Father, hold fast to the book and pray!
> Your [true] servant is the one who fights for you
> When you are old, he will hold you in his lap—
> Son of the Moruti who now comes into the *khotla*.[6]

[6] A. S. Mopeli-Paulus, *Turn to the Dark*, written in collaboration with Miriam Basner (London: Jonathan Cape, 1956), 110–113 (abridged).

The second example, from Karin Barber's exemplary 1992 study of praising in a Yoruba town, shows young women preparing themselves to chant their own praises on the way from youth to adulthood as they move from one enclosure (their father's compound) to another (that of the groom's family).

All through their childhood they accompany their mothers and older sisters on festival and funeral parades; they participate in the oral performance that underpins family rituals within the house. . . . By the time they are adolescent they are able to hold their own in the performance of the genre that is the special preserve of young women, *rárà iyàwó*. On the "bride's day," the day before she goes to her husband's house, each bride is escorted by a party of younger girls from her compound. As the bride chants her laments and farewells, they provide a sympathetic chorus. . . .

SOLO   Duduyemi [Blackness-Suits-Me], dark as the
threatening rain
On this day I see my mother
May good luck attend me today.
CHORUS On this day the chorus supports you resoundingly
The chorus raises your song on high
It's the chorus that holds sway today
This day the chorus supports you resoundingly
May good luck attend me today. . . .

[T]wo or three months before the date of their wedding, young women would go into intensive training. They would go to an older woman in the compound—often there was an acknowledged expert all the girls in that house would consult—and ask to be taught the "real thing": *oríkì orílè* of greater length and complexity than they had formerly known, and those of other lineages, for instance their maternal grandparents'; and elaborate and copious laments, reflections on marriage, thanks to their relatives and so on. They would do this learning privately, with a view to surprising everybody on the day. . . .

On the one hand, it [*rárà iyàwó*] is a set piece, performed on the day when the bride is shown off to the world as the prize her future husband has won. Its function is to display her, not to make other people's heads swell. . . . But on the other hand, it is the bride's one moment of action and expression. In its simplicity of diction, its clarity of structure, and its luminous, lucid imagery, it achieves a poignancy that no other chant does.

In all her subsequent performances of *oríkì*, the woman directs her attention not to herself as she steps out on to the stage of adult activity, but to other actors on this stage: above all, to the important male centers of social and political power in her compound and town; to the influential dead and other spiritual beings; and to the collectivities that constitute her father's and her husband's *ilé* [lineage], past and present.[7]

Thereafter, at every subsequent stage of life, upon the completion of each level of spiritual initiation, upon the assumption of increased public responsibility, in recognition of noteworthy accomplishments —even of pranks or curious incidents, narrow escapes (as the cattle thief's from justice)—more praise epithets are added to one's verbal curriculum vitae,* whose strongest components include standardized litanies of lineage harking back to legendary founder and place of origin—chants always accessible to those who at times of sickness, on the eve of stressful encounters, or by courtesy at the beginning of each new day require strengthening. In Bambara, *fasa*, the generic word for "praise," literally means "tendon." By extension, the term includes all spoken or chanted literary compositions tending to stimulate physical and moral vigor, thus to maintain its tonicity.[8] Who verbally massages the weary muscles of our soul? Who keeps track of the tonic? Knows when and how to voice it? Chiefs retain professional

---

[7] Karin Barber, *I Could Speak Until Tomorrow: Oriki, Women and the Past in a Yoruba Town* (Washington, D.C.: Smithsonian Institution Press, 1991), 97–98 passim, 116.

* Although they are not numerous, exceptional women who acquire status by excelling in activities outside the home will acquire praises accordingly. And those who become initiated priestesses—mediums of the spirits—thereby complete themselves, in my view; so that when praise-songs for the sacred beings with which they have aligned themselves are sung, as modest earthly representatives of such forces, these women rejoice accordingly. (See discussion of *bori* praise-session that follows.)

[8] Dominique Zahan, *La dialectique du verbe chez les Bambara* (Paris and La Haye: Mouton, 1963), 133.

praise-singers to do the job which in ordinary households falls to the lot of qualified women.

Thus, everyman's river rapidly can be traced to its sources and the past brought succinctly to bear upon the present. Heroic poems, whose substance is panegyric, contain discontinuous segments of history, reframed to focus thematically (rather than chronologically) upon a single protagonist with reference to enduring societal values.[9] So intently may the praiser bear down that whatever the occasion, social identity of the praisee, or length of the collaged composition, its abrupt units—yoked into reiterative structures, accumulating and releasing energy in the course of insistent recitation—galvanize inherited and idiosyncratic characteristics, reinforced by associatively appended snippets of proverbial and narrative lore, with the awesome result that the object of such a barrage of sententious particles experiences overwhelming self-possession.

Everywhere in Africa, being richly, bulkily clothed demonstrates status—acquired in part along with one's inherited, chosen, or gradually acquired social role, in part by personal accomplishment. Resounding praises, verbal counterparts of such festive clothing, reify status internally. Thereafter, extreme self-possession compels release as benevolent action, for a swelled head is susceptible to internal combustion. Once debited, a praise must be discharged. To begin with, an unsatisfied praise-specialist might turn to cursing; and those attending the praise-session might walk away bad-mouthing its stingy recipient. (Ego) inflation generates mishap, enemies, bouts of delusion, and eventual fall from grace. Bestowing remuneration upon the praiser not only releases some of the pent-up vital force, but also signals ensuing generosity more broadly exercised. For to be praised is to be called to validate position by performance, one of the results of which secures attentive adherence of those followers (including impoverished hangers-on) by means of which status socially resounds from town to town throughout the continent.

The vast majority of women in Africa, though they arrive at public

---

[9] Harold Scheub, A *Review of African Oral Traditions and Literature*, commissioned by the ACLS/SSRC Joint Committee on African Studies for presentation at the 27th annual meeting of the African Studies Association, October 25–28, 1984, Los Angeles, California, 12–14.

occasions superbly dressed, may not direct much attention, verbal or otherwise, to themselves in adulthood. But when the others they praise are spirits, they become more than themselves in the profoundest way imaginable.

In the course of a 1957 account of Hausa praise-singing, M. G. Smith presents us with wedding festivities on a double screen; for such occasions are celebrated simultaneously in two compounds. Over at the groom's place professional *maroka* (praise-singers) have been busy since afternoon in the entranceway, drumming and singing praises of his *gida* (lineage), particularly of its male head.

> Descent, age, generosity, relations of solidarity with important persons, and other prestige-giving conditions are referred to time and again; and gifts received by the *maroka* on behalf of the principal addressed [the groom] are followed by singing the donor's praises also.[10]

Meanwhile, over at the bride's compound, women who have finished cooking the feast begin to gather after dark for a *bori* ceremony at which they will call the spirits to bless and join in the celebration of the marriage.

> [O]ne or more of the female *maroka* present will sing the praises of individuals in the assembly, stressing their fertility, generosity, descent, family connections, seniority, and other desirable qualities. Indirect references are also made to female bond-friend and client relationships, which are expressive of status as conceived among females, and these references are designed to stimulate the person addressed to give freely. . . . Gradually the *kidan kswaliya* changes to *kidan ruwa* played to call the spirits at female gatherings.* Calling the *bori* then begins, the *marokiya*, who is often a prostitute, taking the lead. . . . To call a particular spirit one keeps playing through its series of praise-songs until it pos-

---

[10] M. G. Smith, "The Social Functions and Meaning of Hausa praise-singing." *Africa* 27 (1957), 33 – 34.

* That is, huge gourds (hollowed out to provide a resonant chamber) overturned on the dry sand are now overturned in basins of resounding water. In both instances they are beaten with "hands" made of flexible sticks.

sesses one of the [initiated] persons present, usually one who is already dancing.[11]

In such situations, from Hausaland to the Zarmaganda, from the sands and acacia scrub of the Sudan to the mangrove swamps of the Niger Delta, a woman on the verge of possession will be borne down upon by the praise-singer until the spirit, pleased by what it hears, descends to take over its chosen medium's body. What emerges is a grand being outside the pale of everyday social existence. The *bori* and related *zar* cults summon strangers, exotics—mostly male and of sultanic rank, who insist that they be costumed accordingly and who speak at least snatches of their own foreign languages. To women who regularly entertain the "other" in this dramatic modality is presented the possibility of reframing and reintegrating their socially constructed personalities in a liberating way.[12] Though the local power structure excludes women, the world to its farthest reach, including the forces of nature, is open to their religious imaginations. And the artistic prostitute who sings those spirits into the Hausa bride's compound, she has also chosen to maintain an ironic (outsider's) perspective on weddings.

Because praise-predications ferment inner life, they are symbolic actions, cross-culturally paradigmatic of the animating artistic process.[13] But not all the qualities ascribed to the praised one are complimentary by our standards. Some may strike a foreign reader as grotesque, frightening, even scurrilous. African artists are vitalistic, and their invigorating predications are apt at times to present an aggressive texture, which can be read as laudatory or as cautionary. For words, like leaves, have two faces: one side rough, the other smooth. Even as striking images arouse feeling and excite the imagination, they are also intended to temper outrageous impulses leading to de-

---

[11] *Ibid.*, 33.

[12] See Janice Boddy's *Wombs and Alien Spirits: Women, Men, and the Zar Cult in Northern Sudan* (Madison: University of Wisconsin Press, 1989).

[13] Leopold Stein (following Ernest Jones) makes a useful distinction between a metaphor, which tries too hard to accomplish something beyond its oversublimated emotional strength, and a symbol—seemingly passive, but saturated with emotional strength. Leopold Stein, "What Is a Symbol Supposed to Be?" *The Journal of Analytical Psychology*, 2 (1:1957), pp. 76–82 passim.

structive behavior. (See individual praise of Mnkabayi, page 15; clan praise of the Diara, page 39; and spirit praise of Ogun, page 175.) Not all praise-singers are content to purvey flattery to the powerful. Those with a social conscience must upon occasion turn confrontational and censor oppressive leadership and misconduct.

> I came across ancestors at the top of Xhalabile's mountains
> They said we were subverting the country by our great desire
>   for power. . . .
> What have these white officials done for you?
> Is it worth the heritage of your forefathers, your rights, your
>   children's future?
> Your embittered and wretched fellow men stand before you.
> When their voices reached Jonguhlanga [praise name for the
>   bard's patron Chief Sabata], he responded surprisingly.
> He does not drink European liquor, he swims in it.[14]

The praise-singer's exaggerations are often extremely funny and have a variety of intentions, as when in the course of a brilliant and lengthy (488 lines) eulogy for an elderly hunter, the eulogist, expatiating on the theme of inheritance, presents the spirit of the deceased and all within earshot with the following sequence:

> When the Gabon viper dies, its young inherit
>   its poison-injecting assignment
> And when the palm kernel oil maker dies, to her daughters
>   must go her legacy of palm kernel oil manufacture
> When the bathroom dies, its successor inherits
>   urine and the noise of waterfalls. . . .[15]

Chuckling over these outrageously symmetrical situations, one may discover oneself imbibing a delightful dose of philosophical meta-

---

[14] Excerpt from a recitation by Meliklaya Mbutuma, *mbongi* (official bard) to the Thembu paramount chief, Sabata Dalindyebo, in the Transkei, March 1963 (English version slightly edited). Archie Mafeje, "The Role of the Bard in a Contemporary African Community," *Journal of African Languages* 27 (1957), 216, 218.

[15] S. A. Babalola, *The Content and Form of Yoruba Ijala* (Oxford: Oxford University Press, 1966), 292.

praise: for are not African eulogies strengthening blandishments from which the potent essence of the praisee is extracted—like poison from the viper, oil from the hard-to-crack palm nut's unctuous kernel? What has been bequeathed to offspring and colleagues of the feisty old hunter (himself adept at uttering praise-incantations with which to stun animals into submission) is no more material than lingering smell and sound of an abandoned urinal.* What remains for them to invoke and draw upon is temperamental—precisely those aspects of personality reflected through the gritty, prismatic verses of his eulogist.

Implicit in the act of praising is the assumption throughout Africa that every person, human group, tutelary spirit, animal, plant, or body of water, as well as certain manufactured things, has a praiseable core that words can elicit, revitalize, and nudge toward behavior beneficial to the human community. Just as in musical performance, well playing the part enriches the whole, so in all life's modes, including the composition of paratactic sequences of praise utterance. Equally implicit in the act as in the format of praising, then, is the notion of interrelationship of multivarious discrete phenomena.

Among all clusters of relationship the most crucial is that of human community (which is why it seemed appropriate to begin this introduction with greetings to a putative community of readers of this book, these poems). Taking time out to accomplish a ritual exchange of salutations, even in a perfunctory manner, is obligatory civilized conduct. Members of a household, casual acquaintances, even strangers passing along the road, in honoring the custom help generate that pervasive atmosphere of trust upon which social harmony depends. Only an identifiably ill-intentioned person would slink off rather than engage in this rudimentary stitching together of the social fabric. Greeting is like preamp tuning that may or may not amplify into full-blown conversation, common endeavor, or transaction. (Those who

---

* The deceased hunter's personal effects and venatic equipment do not get handed down, but are praised and ceremoniously carried off into the bush at the conclusion of the funeral. See notes to Chapter V.

have spent time in African communities are well aware th
to pick up a modest repertoire of greetings and appropriate
in the local idiom reinforces alienation, whereas even a mu.......
competence in this regard inevitably draws one in.)

Prior to praising, then, is this indispensable and always highly for-
mulaic speech-event, reiterated throughout the day, on into the night.
What follows is a composite, hypothetical exchange:

> Greetings for the early morning.
>> Yes, early morning it is, greetings.
> Did you pass the night in peace?
>> In peace only.
> And the road you took during the night?
> Nothing bad along the way.
> How is everybody at home?
>> In health, thankfully. . . .
> May you go well until we meet again.

Later on, one might stop and greet somebody for supporting upon
his or her back the rigors of the hot sun, or for the work he or she is
performing. In rural Mali, one should salute the smith with his patro-
nymic, followed by "You are with the stone and the fire."[16] A sick
person might be saluted for enduring pain, a vendor for attracting
customers, an elder for being pleasantly seated among cronies; and so
on until bedtime, all recognized intervals of temporal experience hav-
ing been crisscrossed with verbal encounters—each a pause embroi-
dered with chains of mutual inquiry and collectively woven into an
ephemeral talkative cloth of which each participant falls to sleep hold-
ing onto a residual fragment.

What happens when praise-poetry performances become translated
into printed poems? Those that would seem to have suffered most in
the process are those originally drummed. Talking drums "talk" by

[16] Germaine Dieterlen, *Essai sur la religion Bambara* (Paris: Presses Universitaires, 1971),
79.

reproducing the rhythmic periods and tonal inflections of African languages—a process that involves varying the pitch on a single drumhead or using a set of distinctly tuned drums in combination.* The most flexible praise-drum is carved in an hourglass shape. Its two heads are subsequently laced together with thongs upon which pressure can be applied by the elbow as the drummer strolls about producing intelligible melodies whose register encompasses almost an octave.[17]

Since they must speak circuitously (with redundance) in order to be understood, "talking drums" are natural progenitors of poetry. For example, in the Kele language of central Africa, the words for "manioc" (*lomata*) and "plantain" (*likondo*) have similar tonal patterns. Therefore, to make his message plain, the drummer indicates the first by a stereotyped phrase meaning "manioc remains in a deserted garden," and the second by "plantain, which is propped up when ripe." Here are the sounded equivalents in a two-toned system:

Low (pause) low low low high low low (pause) low (pause) high low. Low low (pause) low low low low low.[18]†

I shall never forget the first time my presence as a visitor was announced by sweet-talking pressure drums. My bicycle had broken down, and I had been picked up by a truck full of exuberant Yoruba Baptists. As we roared in second gear through the gates of the (then) Timi of Ede's palace (presumptuously, I thought, but could do nothing about it), the bedraggled official drummers in the entryway struck up this news. I shuddered at such additional and unavoidable publi-

* The lips of a hollowed wooden slit drum are of different thicknesses and therefore produce contrasting tones suitable for "talking" in a two-toned system.

[17] William Bascom, notes to *Drums of the Yoruba of Nigeria* (Ethnic Folkways, FE 4441, 1953), 4.

[18] This material is from J. F. Carrington, *Talking Drums of Africa* (London: Carey Kingsgate Press, 1949).

† Among the Kele all men have a drum-name by which they may be summoned across considerable distances. A man's drum-name will include an expression of personality, like "spitting cobra whose virulence never abates," followed by the most characteristic part of his father's drum-name and, finally, by the drum-name not of his mother but of her village.

city, but I was new to Africa then and so eager to pass muster as to have swallowed my sense of humor. Nor did I realize that such an announcement, a convention, had nothing to do with the personal identity (in our sense) of the visitor but rather reflected the status of the Timi, who turned out to be not only a charming man, but an acknowledged expert on African drumming!

Back to the printed words on these pages. Once the sounds, accompanying gestures, praiser's gaze, and all participants in the lively process have been lost, how much meaning vanishes with them? In the dire words of Dan Ben-Amos:

> The social features of folklore are not merely background for a text or supplementary information which elucidates and explicates obscure references and describes performance situations. They are integral components of folklore communication. They have symbolic significance for both speakers and audience and affect the perception and conception of an expression much the same as the words themselves. The ideas, beliefs and attitudes that members of the community bring with them into a communication event of folklore are an essential part of the verbal statement that a speaker makes.[19]

Obviously, most readers' experience of these praise-poems will be of literature rather than of culturally saturated events. And either they will "work" in this (literary) mode or they won't. However, in translations from one culture to another, some explanation is essential, especially in the case of praise-poetry, stylistically characterized by rapid-fire allusions that only an insider truly gets. So, relying on imagination, common human concerns, and feelings to rush forward to fill the inevitably vacated folkloric-space, I have added extensive commentary after each group of poems so that there may be consecutive experiences: first the poems themselves, then supportive information, I hope followed by a second reading.

[19] Dan Ben-Amos, "Folklore in African Society," *Research in African Literatures* 7 (2: 1975), 193. See also Richard Bauman, "Verbal Art as Performance," *American Anthropologist* 77 (1977).

Lifted from their original contexts to keep company with others of comparable theme, anthologized poems are expected to generate reflective, residual meanings by contrast and comparison. The categories in which these various praises were originally stored, having taken shape in the course of exploring the field, were subsequently maintained as proto-chapters and subjected to seasonal winnowings. The field is vast as sub-Saharan Africa itself; and though adequate geographical and linguistic distribution were just concerns in the beginning, the intent was never cadastral, and eventually choices for inclusion were made with an eye to patterns that were already forming. As a result, certain gaps and disproportionate inclusions occurred.

For example, though east Africa is well represented by its cattle poetry, with which human personality is reciprocally identified, central Africa remains underrepresented, even though the two longest poems in the book are by Luba artists. Nor are the bards of Mali given full voice. This, ironically, can be attributed to proliferation of epic cycles in both areas.[20] As a "supergenre that encompasses and harmoniously fuses together practically all genres known in a particular culture,"[21] and which functions like a collective praise, investing its auditors "with a power of action totally oriented toward affirming the identity that authenticates and unifies them,"[22] the epic tends to monopolize creative energy of both artists and scholarly collectors.* (Because of length, no epics could be included here.)

---

[20] See the marvelous map of "The African Epic Belt," John William Johnson, *The Epic of Son-jara* (Bloomington: Indiana University Press, 1986), 61.

[21] Daniel Biebuyck, "The Epic as a Genre in Congo Oral Literature," *African Folklore*, edited by Richard M. Dorson (New York: Doubleday [Anchor Books], 1972), 266.

[22] Christiane Seydou (translated by Brunhilde Biebuyck), "A Few Reflections on Narrative Structures of Epic Texts: A Case Example of Bambara and Fulani Epics," *Research in African Literatures*, Vol. 14, No. 3 (Fall 1983), 312–331, 322 (reiterated p. 330 and *passim*).

* For example, Youssouf Tata Cissé of Mali and Paris, who collected a formidable amount of prose and poetry from the late traditionalist Wa Kamissoko of Krina, has given editorial priority to epic material while a 774-line *fasa* ("praise") of the national hero Sunjata remains in manuscript. Sudanese epics consist of narrative episodes interspersed with praise-poetry and proverbial sequences that move the group to cohesion despite migrations, resettlements, and social friction (Seydou, footnote 22). Among the various Bantu-speaking groups of central Africa, the epic would seem to have a double origin: (1) from extended clan praises and lamentations, including (depending on per-

The first imbalance began innocently enough. As the categorical granaries were filling up nicely, all due deference apparently having been paid to geographical and linguistic distribution, in the quiet of nights I began to hear a subliminal dialogue going on between Sotho *lithoko* and Yoruba *oríkì*, which, being made of air, paid no heed to boundaries. Once given permission to be heard, the conversation intensified, found other avenues of starker give and take, until only by coopting it as subtext could reasonable editorial control once again be asserted. As a result, though examples of praises in Zulu and other southern Bantu languages have been included, Sotho praises of people, animals, and things predominate. Oracular verses are not classified *oríkì* by the Yoruba, but with apologies to the *babaláwo* who chant them and conclude their recitations by praising Ifa, their higher power, because the Basotho do consider their divination poetry to be a species of *lithoko*, the dialogue between these two expressive cultures in the predictive mode of poetic discourse continues.

Animal praises abound to form a little book-within-a-book especially for children, whom I hope will be thereby encouraged to compose their own. At the conclusion of the nineteenth day of his conversations with Ogotemmeli, having learned that whenever a person is born, at the same time a series of animals (of graduated species) comes into being, each related to its predecessor as totemic twin, Marcel Griaule says that behind every man he met in the narrow Dogon streets he "seemed to see the shadows of an eighth part of all the living creatures of the world."[23] So behind each praise-poem printed here are an octave of might-have-beens.

Already, as early as the seventies, some of these hardy praise-poems began to reproduce themselves in an American idiom. In 1970, when I began teaching a seminar in African humanities to practicing teachers enrolled in the School of Education at New York University, I was particularly concerned about presenting the material in ways that would stimulate their pedagogical inventiveness in the classroom. The

---

formance context and character of the bard) proverbial wisdom, topical commentary, and arousement to battle like the Luba *kassala,* and (2) Pygmy epics of the mythic and the marvelous.

[23] Marcel Griaule, *Conversations with Ogotemmeli* (Oxford, England: Oxford University Press, 1965), 129.

poems, having been wrenched from their original performance situations, came to life again—with a difference. *Karaw* masks were constructed out of plywood and held by their spokespersons according to Dominique Zahan's description.* Dogon animal masks fashioned from shoe boxes danced upon their creators' faces to live drumming as classmates praised them, partly in translation, partly in their own words. (The funniest one, with streaming, wild hair made of "secret" celluloid tapes, was called "Water-gator.")

The most valuable exercises in the long run, because they were the most inwardly transformative, were re-creations of Yoruba invocations of the Orisha. After being exposed to a range of praises culled from Pierre Verger's collection, each student was asked to choose one divinity, to seek symbols of its power from our urban environment and from his or her own imagination, and produce a poem to be recited before the group in the course of a celebration for all the Orisha. One student exuberantly chose three. A month after the course ended, he wrote that those *oríkì* (or *pipè*) were "the heaviest thing" he'd done as a poet. "I have never been able to use Greek or Hebrew mythology this way for sustained depth or human resources." Later he published them as a trilogy.[24] Here I would like to quote a few lines from each in his memory.

ESHU
    Eshu makes nothing.
    Stick your finger up the sea of a mystery
    and there he is—winking at you
    from atop a skyscraper.

OGUN
    Outlaw. That you are.
    First to come, first to go.
    Across that river lies life.
    Over those mountains is humanity.
    Ogun goes first. Restless hunter, he prepares
    to drink the blood of births and endings.
    His the first hand to pick up the first gun.

---

* *Karaw* are spatula-shaped. For a fuller description, see notes to "Voice of the Karaw," Chapter VIII.
[24] David Rosenthal, *Eyes on the Street* (New York: Barlenmire House, 1974), 31–35.

YEMOJA   In the darkest blue of the deepest pools
you rest, and take your pleasure.
Goddess of the soft skin
Agèd mother looking on
You have known all seasons and blessed
them—
both the beginning and the end.
In secret places you find your spirit's deepest
calm.

After that I wanted to go to the children themselves. In a third-grade classroom, I was able to take the boys aside, explain to them what self-praising in Sotho was all about, read them a few examples, and ask them to compose their own *lithoko*, eventually to be presented amid stomping and clapping by the group as a whole. Here is a sample of what happened.

Praise to André (Pegus)
Grate grandson of Pegassus the fl[y]ing horse
Has arms instead of wings
The third Pegus
Leader of fl[y]ing things
And leader of all horses.

Praise to Minard for great long legs
in highest math group and reading group
Ten feet tall
Skinny as an ox horn
Had one brocken shoulder bone when baby, very painful.

Praise to Rico Williams, chess player
Grandson of Henry Northern and Mrs. Northern
wich have power of the Sun and Moon.

The following day Rico brought in an amplification, which his mother, delighted with the project, had helped him compose.

> Praise to Rico
> Great grandson of Henry with the Northern name
> Palm tree of many branches
> planted in Wilkesbarre, Pennsylvania
> Cross-roads of Sioux and Ashanti
> God's trombone for half a century
> on the holy air waves.

The kids from that class are twenty-nine or thirty years old by now. Rico serves as his class representative. His name appears every year in the alumni bulletin. Given the signs that Rico liked to keep in touch, I boldly looked him up. Although his memory of our praise-event was rather vague, he courteously agreed to come and see me. We had a good talk. Like his grandfather, a preacher who had his own radio program, Rico has entered the field of communication as script-writer for a technical television program that specializes in detailed financial reporting.

"Do you still play chess?"

"No, now it's golf," he said.

"What's the connection between chess and golf?"

"[In both cases] there's no limit to how far you can go with it."

When he was twelve or so, his mother took him on a trip to Ghana.

"How about the Sun and Moon? How did you happen to put them into your praise-poem?"

Rico laughed. "I guess I've always been interested in mythology."

In a recent provocative essay, Olabiyi Yai of the University of Ife argues that critics, teachers, and translators of oral poetry will always fall wide of the mark if they do not immerse themselves in the culture of the source language, and, further, if they do not undergo an on-site apprenticeship in a chosen genre so that eventually they may translate by re-creating the text (a process traditionally inclusive of hermeneutics) in their own "target" language—and, still further, they must do this not in writing but in oral performance.

> In our model, improvisation is basic and the translator-performer
> may even add "lines" of his/her own making to the "text" which

is never closed, once he/she is inspired by the mood or the muse of the genre.[25]

May such an awesome opportunity in the future present itself to all so inclined. Meanwhile, with apologies to the hunters' bard:

> This road has run along as far as it's going today
>   take over from me, reader
>   find your own way through the thicket
>   throw the bones, recall the absent to mind
>   refresh your body with mint tea, with an herbal bath
> Soft breeze is drummer for the "wrap up" leaf
>   we're wrapping up now
>   said and unsaid
>   obvious corpse and sustaining secret
> Let the leaf continue to dance on its own
>   for leaf and wind are equals.[26]

New York City, August 2, 1993

[25] Olabiyi Yai, "Issues in Oral Poetry: Criticism, Teaching and Translation," *Discourse and its Disguises: The Interpretation of African Oral Texts*, edited by Karin Barber and P. F. de Moraes Farias (Birmingham: Center of West African Studies, Birmingham University African Studies Series No. 1, 1989), 69 and *passim*.
[26] Adapted from and improvised upon lines quoted by S. A. Babalola, *The Content and Form of Yoruba Ijala* (Oxford, England: Oxford University Press, 1966), 57.

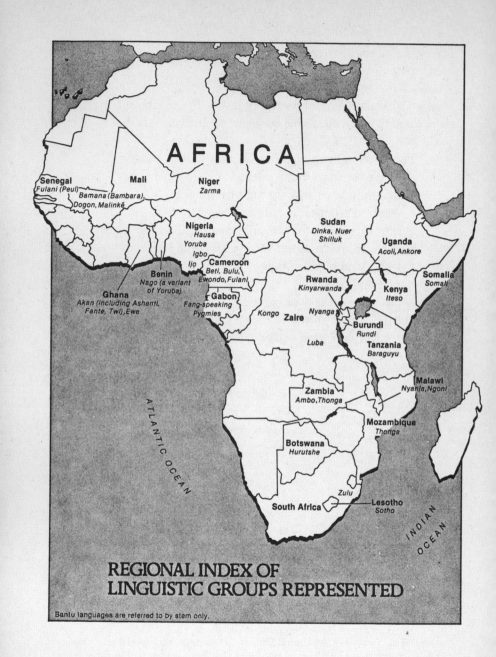

REGIONAL INDEX OF
LINGUISTIC GROUPS REPRESENTED

Bantu languages are referred to by stem only.

A Note on Translations

With few exceptions (and these are specified), the texts drawn from
are bilingual, consisting of the African-language transcription of the
performance and a European version—French, Flemish, or English.
Occasionally there were two European translations, a word-by-word
version and a "literary" version. The African-language source has been
indicated in parentheses at the conclusion of each selection. The
French and Flemish I translated, aided by the collectors' notes and
by study of the African-language text. Here and there I have tampered
with the original English renderings, to rid them of Victorianisms, lax
vocabulary, or awkward syntax and to move the sound, rhythm, and
tone closer to that of the imagined original. English versions I admire
and therefore have left intact are those of Ulli Beier, Okot p'Bitek,
Daniel P. Kunene, Karin Barber, and Terese Svoboda.

PRAISE OF THE WORD

The word is total:
it cuts, excoriates
forms, modulates
perturbs, maddens
cures or directly kills
amplifies or reduces
According to intention
it excites or calms souls.

—A bard of the Bambara Komo society,
quoted in Louis-Vincent Thomas and René Luneau,
Les Religions d'Afrique noire, textes et traditions sacrés

Leaf and Bone

I : *Speaking the World:*
Dogon Praise-Mottoes

ARM AND HAND

Arm, shoulder is big
Arm, separates at the elbow
Fist is small
Fingers lengthy
Palm is striated
Fingers, each with three phalanges.

HOE

Iron hoe says *hu*
All day; iron palm
Finger tip
Hole in the handle fits
Iron in: hafted like man and woman
Bent neck
Slenders to the grip
Poor man works with it
Rich man works with it
Who has a hoe hangs on
Even an orphan grows
By dint of:
Sun, fatigue, content.

WOMAN

Worn stirring stick.

YOUNG GIRL

Young girl sways
Eye of the dawn star
Gleaming neck
Breasts no bigger than
Ewe's udder
Firm as a cake of indigo
Belly flatter than
Fulani's sandal
Hips a hand could
Span the measure of.

ACACIA BUSH

Bad bramble
Bush-spirit's home
Razor-fruited
Leaves worse than useless
Touching, it touches you
Tearing clothes—
How sweet the root!

MILLET BEER

Millet beer numbs, slumps
While its genius dances.

LEBE

Great Serpent froths space, clouding it
Great Serpent glides about
Inscrutable traces, morning and evening
Gliding everywhere, mist.

TO THOSE RECENTLY DEAD

Bush! Bush!
Gratitude for yesterday, wizened worker
Gratitude for millet, for water
Gratitude for meat, hunter.

TO THE ANCESTORS

Clearers of thornbush,
    Receive our morning greetings,
You who graded clefts in the cliffs,
    Receive our morning greetings,
You who laid the cornerstone,
    Receive our morning greetings,
You who placed the three hearthstones,
    Receive our morning greetings,
And you, women, who carried long-stemmed calabashes,
    Receive our morning greetings.

TO GAZELLE MASK

Greetings, goat of the bush,
Full of the beans you have eaten,
An able man shoots—
Blood flows on the ground.

All eyes are upon you—
Hare stares
Turtledove watches.
Good bush, shake your legs
Good bush, shake your body.

TO MASK OF THE SMITH

Master of the forge, greetings
Come to the sound of the drums.
Gong is your iron song
Make it speak well
All ears are listening.

TO MASK OF THE YOUNG GIRL

Senior mask, yet freshest of all
Old and good mask, good mask and young
With fine legs
With legs that are agile, agile, agile!
The woman has returned to the village,
     placed the fibers in a storeroom
The woman has brought back the costume
     an old man puts it on
[Now] the mask belongs to all men.
Good legs, good arms, beautiful eyes—
Everyone is watching you
Shake those whisks well,
All men are watching you
Greetings! Greetings!

BLINDNESS

Morning darkness, evening darkness
Always, always.

OGOTEMMELI

Flicks away rooted obstacles.

COMMENTARY

Although all personal praises by implication honor the head, the other parts of the body are "spoken" in dance. Since one's head (as the carrier of ancestral and divine principles) both is and is not one's own, the self in some societies makes of the head an altar, and in the interest of spiritual hygiene, worships it. The Igbo even make an image of the right arm of accomplishment as a spiritual being and venerate that. But only the Dogon, so far as I know, have verbal tributes to various anatomical propensities. What does a Dogon farmer mean when he carefully describes the articulations of his arm in praisewords concisely moving from shoulder to phalanges? So cut off are we, as adults, not only from the cosmos but from our own bodies that the first poem in this collection must seem exotic indeed. Yet in this very recognition—that it is we who are exotic, we the outsiders—lies the seed of transformation.

Sometime between the tenth and twelfth centuries A.D. the Dogon people, rather than convert to Islam, left their mountainous home in Manden (upper Guinée). Carrying a bit of earth from their altar to Lebe (ancestor-snake), they migrated to the cliffs of Bandiagara, whose inhabitants either fled or had to be dislodged. After that, although nominally subjugated by various intrusive groups (the Sonrai, the Bambara of Ségou, the Fulani of Macina), the Dogon were able to keep their culture intact because nobody else wanted to take up residence in their escarpment. Gradually, from neighbors like the Bozo, the Fulani, and the Bambara, the Dogon absorbed compatible ideas, all the while continuing to elaborate what they had resolutely brought with them: a remarkable cosmology based on "correspondences," magnificent art forms, and—played out in this poor theater of theirs, maintained by the simplest of technologies—a courteous, integrated way of life. For the men, that is—the Dogon "golden age" was never, so far as I can see, matriarchal.

We begin with this brief harvest of *tige* (praise-mottoes) to introduce the reader to a quality of mind that many consider paradigmatic of traditional (animist) Africa uncorrupted by extraneous influences. At least so the Dogon were in the thirties when the famous "mission Griaule" arrived to study them. Now, alas, the Malien ministry of tourism conducts all comers—from Cannes, Köln, or Kansas—to their cliffs and arranges to have them perform "picturesque" dances.

Praise-words for the Dogon are like water. Like rain upon millet seeds, they cause self-esteem to germinate and realize tendency in action. Through all beings flows that vital energy the Dogon call *nyama*. Strain—contention, fatigue, illness—is attended by a decrease of this energy, which good words and participation in ritual recharge. A dead person's (or animal's) *nyama* is dangerous, being a sort of incorporeal outrage, and must be deflected. Hence the institution of the Society of Masks, whose praises are not only blandishments to the dancers who wear them but reaffirmations, in mythical shorthand, of the death-defying purpose for which art was first executed.

The source of most of these *tige* is the beautiful annotated collection by Solange de Ganay: *Les Devises des Dogons* (Paris: Institut d'Ethnologie, 1941), a pioneer work. The three praises of masks are to be found in Marcel Griaule's magisterial *Masques Dogon* (Paris: Institut d'Ethnologie, 1938). Ogotemmeli's praise is to be found in Geneviève Calame-Griaule's *Ethnologie et langage* (Paris: Gallimard, 1965, p. 480). I have also found her *Dictionnaire Dogon* (Paris: Klincksieck, 1968) most helpful in the preparation of these translations, together with the numerous publications of Germaine Dieterlen.

ARM AND HAND. This may be recited to increase one's own strength or to encourage another in a heavy task. The anatomical articulation is equivalent to "verbal" articulation: a definition of social relationships. (de Ganay, *Les Divises*, pp. 60–61)

HOE. This *tige* is formally recited to one's own implement at the beginning of the agricultural year. It may also be called out as encouragement to someone else engaged in hoeing. In this case, the hoer's individual *tige* would be shouted also. When a man dies, his hoe is ritually broken and disposed of, away from the village in a southerly direction. (Ibid., pp. 145–146)

WOMAN. A Dogon woman does not merit individual *tige* but is honored thus, for her hard work, generically. (Ibid., p. 46)

YOUNG GIRL. This generic praise is a combination of Solange de Ganay's version (ibid., p. 46), collected in Sanga, and that of Geneviève Calame-Griaule (*Ethnologie*, p. 479), collected in Pèguè, a nearby village.

LEBE. This is the name of the mythical ancestor, incarnation of telluric powers, whose death and resurrection in the form of a Great Serpent symbolize the vegetative process. This Serpent may assume any dimension and insinuate itself anywhere. Nights, it always goes forth from its cave to lick the body of its human representative and priest, the Hogon. The traces it makes are comparable to partially realized graphic signs by which Dogon initiates represent cosmological processes, configurations whose conception is prior to their realization (as "plot" to "drama" in Aristotelian poetics). (de Ganay, *Les Devises*, p. 102)

TO THOSE RECENTLY DEAD. Recited during the course of funeral celebrations, this praise accompanies the individual *tige*. (Ibid., p. 69)

TO THE ANCESTORS. Passage from one place to another in Dogon country often involves steep ascents and descents, aided by natural rocky steps, which are in this poem assumed to be the work of the ancestors. But if they moved mountains, so they also stooped to install the three stones upon which Dogon cooking pots are set. Ancestral women are credited with carrying water and are thus praised by implication for their wombs. (Ibid., p. 84)

TO GAZELLE MASK. The real world of the Dogon has its counterpart in the dancing world of masquerades. Headpieces carved in wood represent animals; those composed of braided fibers (helmets or cowls) represent various human prototypes. (The superstructures atop the wooden masks represent mythic events, cosmic principles.) Each mask is associated with a story of origin. This antelope is a *wilu*. Griaule does not report its story, but by analogy with other antelope-mask stories and from evidence given in the praise-poem itself one may deduce it, roughly, as follows: A gazelle came out of the bush, invaded a farmer's field, and consumed some beans. (This action would have its esoteric counterpart in the rebellious activity of the cosmic power the Dogon call "pale fox," who came to earth on a vessel shaped like a bean-sieve.) Outraged, the farmer shot the *wilu* and neutralized the outraged *nyama* of the dead animal by installing its skull on his hunter's altar. But when the man himself died, all the force contained in the altar dissipated and the force that had animated the *wilu* attacked the murderer's son. So, following his diviner's advice, the young man fashioned a *wilu* mask, into which the animal's *nyama* was ritually coaxed. Now the son donned the mask with impunity and proceeded to take part in his father's funeral. Imitating the movements of his father's animal antagonist, the son managed to frighten the old man's outraged energy-ghost away from the village of the living into the bush, and beyond, to await reincarnation. (Griaule, *Masques Dogon*, p. 801)

TO MASK OF THE SMITH. The mask of the smith is dressed in ordinary work clothes. " 'At first,' said Ogotemmeli, 'the smith did not have all the tools that he has today. . . . The red-hot iron was held in the bare hand; and that is something one can still see today, when smiths come together for funerals. As they chant the dirges for the dead, they pick up red-hot iron in their hands in memory of the practice of the first smiths' " (Marcel Griaule, *Conversations with Ogotemmeli* [Oxford: Oxford University Press, 1965], p. 85). Behind this myth lies another. With the sound of forging metal upon the earth is associated the first dance: undulations (like swimming motions) performed by the Great Serpent as he burrowed underground to resurrect Death's first victim—the first victim, that is, of aggression with murderous intent. (Griaule, *Masques Dogon*, p. 558)

TO MASK OF THE YOUNG GIRL. Known to the Dogon as *Bede*, this mask commemorates a young girl who was killed by a lion. (Perhaps the story recalls a historical battle with a Mande-speaking group.) The killing of the lion in reprisal occasioned the first hunter's altar as well as the first mask of the braided-cowl type, designed to ward off death from human beings. But to this story, in its praise-poem context, is joined another. The Dogon say that these early defenses against death (mask and altar) originated with a previous people, the Andoumboulu (small red people, like the Pygmies). It was a Dogon woman who first discovered the secret embodied in the red-dyed dancing-skirt fibers worn by Bede's impersonator. She stole them and used them to terrify men. But her husband found out where she stored the red fibers and appropriated them on behalf of his own sex. Since then, only the exceptional woman may have anything at all to do with the masks. This is a tale of pollution and counterpollution, of the apotropaic power of blood-red. (Ibid., p. 523)

II : Praises, in Various Modes, of Various People

AMBARA, THE INTERPRETER

Ambara
Abundant cloud
Pushed up through hollow bamboo
Fatigue
Banished brothers
Men of mud
Cutter of the road.

(Dogon)[1]

ABATAN, THE POTTER

Abatan
Hunter gives us one to indulge
Child whom we favor
Child of the hook like someone pecking a tree
Child from Udofoyi
Child of the ax-handle sculptor

[1] The names in parentheses refer to the languages in which the praises were originally uttered. In certain cases names have been simplified—a prefix or suffix has been dropped so that the name corresponds to the familiar designation of both language and people. For example, the Dogon speak Dogonso. The Yoruba speak Yoruba. The BaLuba speak CiLuba, but only Luba will be given in parentheses. This procedure is justifiable because in Africa, ethnic affiliations are established on the basis of linguistic affiliations.

Child of facial marks like the three stars guiding night hunters
Child of the diviner who entered the house to become its lord
Child of the small snake under dead leaves
Uninitiated is unaware.

(Yoruba)

ZAILA, THE BUTCHER'S DAUGHTER

Zaila from a distant town
Zaila from a distant town
Whoever sees Zaila gives a thousand cowries
Even if it breaks a poor man
Or he gives her five hundred.

(Hausa)

ONGIYA, FRIEND OF OKOT P'BITEK

I am the one who knocks down—
Listen to the sound of the pot as it falls;
You are the one who knocks down
Cooking pots in the house of the mother-in-law;
Your hair is white with ash
You are the disturber of the cooking pot.

(Acoli)

GIRL FRIENDS OF KEMPUMBYA

O companions, those of my life who support me
Goddesses of the drum, come sing the chorus;

(*Kakyabashenyi*)
She doesn't sit pat as though she were placed there
She doesn't shame her husband's kraal;

O companions, those of my life who support me
Goddesses of the drum, come sing the chorus;

(*Kenyonyozi*)
They brought her a giraffe-tail bracelet from Bwera
The "spotted one" excelled them all;

O companions, those of my life who support me
Goddesses of the drum, come sing the chorus;

(*Kyomugyemu*)
They brought her white cloth with bold red-sun pattern
Which put that "deep purple one" back in fashion;

O companions, those of my life who support me
Goddesses of the drum, come sing the chorus;

(*Mbibi*)
Bride-wealth cow accomplished its mission
"Branded with stripes" brought back "big-eyed" Mbibi.

O companions, those of my life who support me
Goddesses of the drum, come sing the chorus;

(*Kijajaare*)
Her legs, plump as though molded, she lifted
Skirt gathered above her knees, she led forth cattle;

O companions, those of my life who support me
Goddesses of the drum, come sing the chorus;

(*Ihangwe*)
Beads of sweat gleam upon her face
She is as ripples upon an expanse of water;

O companions, those of my life who support me
Goddesses of the drum, come sing the chorus!

(Ankore)

GEORGE AMAKIRI, HEAD OF A CANOE HOUSE

The crocodile with a cavernous mouth
The crocodile with a cavernous mouth

What is sweeter than yam?
A thing sweeter than yam, what is it?
Is meat sweeter than yam?
A thing sweeter than yam, what is it?

Okrika and Ogoloma
Threw a challenge to Kalabari
Kali kulukulu kalika, Kalabari threw it back.
The people of Bonny, jealous of the wealthy
Strong as fish, threw a challenge to Kalabari
Kali kulukulu kalika, Kalabari threw it back.

The white man, son of the sea that blows *wule wule*
Threw a challenge to Kalabari
Kali kulukulu kalika, Kalabari threw it back.
The Ibo, heads flattened by heavy loads
Threw a challenge to Kalabari
Kali kulukulu kalika, Kalabari threw it back.

Bearer of weighty burdens.

(Ijo)

FAKOLI KOROMA, A YOUNG HERO

If you cannot find me at Lake of the Spirits,
Look for me at Lake of the Priests,
If you cannot find me at Lake of the Priests,
Look for me at Lake of the Spirits;
Me, Fakoli, big mouth in a big head
(Like the hunting eagle)
Me, Fakoli, of the five freed chiefs

Me, a free man who dies
Rather than be ransomed
Me, crest of the tree [of knowledge]
Me, backbone and magic
Me, spine and seer.

(Malinké)

MAYGARI, TRUCK DRIVER
For Pat Simpson

I've begun a song, I've invented praises; now I'm going
    to write it down, carefully arranging the letters
Song of the truck driver of Garoua, a saintly man
    Song to be sung to the world so I may narrate his virtues.
Maygari is our chauffeur, European-style; it is he who
    clothed me in an embroidered gown;
Maygari, son of Figuil; the noise of his motor:
    prayer and greeting.
Maygari, seated in the cabin, has astounded me; the voice
    of his motor can be heard as far as Fort-Lamy.
At the sound of his motor I seem to hear the meat-for-sale
    drum of the butchers; when he shifts gears
      he begs Allah's pardon.
At the sound of his motor I seem to hear the royal trumpet
    north and east resound, are full of it;
Then the motor beats out a dance rhythm; and the guards,
    even the commandant, clap their hands.
The smoke from the truck is as fragrant as sandalwood
    Its twin tires leave a postmark on the sand.
Driver who could manage even an airplane, who surpasses Maygari?
    No one . . . from Paris to Bangui. . . .
Fortune is with you, never fear, Maygari; at night, no lie
    I've dreamed of your good fortune.
As the noise of the motor praises, the son of Figuil Hamman
    Maygari drives in peace. . . .
Reduced to the little fruits of the thorn three, your adversary
    prays for gourds to eat;

Allow me to curse your adversary, Maygari; Allah has decided
    you are going to live in peace;
Who leans upon Allah, may tread down all obstacles, even a
    mountain; understand my words, Maygari, they are not
    mere rumor. . . .
Certainly Maygari presented me last Friday with an embroidered
    gown of the finest brocade; and as for money, he's given me
    one hundred "dola" . . .
Praise Allah, I have fashioned these praises; and when the song
    was complete, I wrote it down, carefully marking the
    characters in ink.

—Bouba Malam Jarida
(Fulani, Adamawa)

MNKABAYI, ROYAL WOMAN

Father of guile!
Cunning one of the Hoshoza people
Who devours a person, having tempted him with a story;
So she killed Bheje among the diviners.
Morass of Menzi
That caught people and finished them off;
For example, Nohela, "The fire that burns on every hill"
Morass caught him and he disappeared.
Beast that lows on Sangoyana hill
Lowing, its voice pierced the sky
And shattered the ears of Gbabalanda
Son of Mndaba of the Khumalo clan.

Girl who matured and her mouth dried up
So then they criticized her among the old women.
She who allays anxiousness for people—
Anxiousness they catch and she looks at it with her eyes.
Opener of all the main gates so petitioners may enter
Opener of the narrow side gates as well.
Daring to sip for others the Cobra's venom.

The Mhlzthuzi river will flood at midday.
Little mouse, scratched tracks here and there at Malandela's
Thinking the people of Malandela
Would widen these tracks into paths.

(Zulu)

MCAYI, THE DAUGHTER OF VUMA

She is of a roundness that rolls to and fro
She is generous to strangers as well as to family members

She is the strong woman who inspires men.

She is like a snake coiled at the gate
Who denies entrance to cows and their calves.

She is the smartly dressed woman in a combination of two colors
As her body fights between the striped and the plain white.

She is as tall as the legs of children.

Can mealies be boiled on rocks
While fire is kindled by wild buck?

Even the mamba feared, slipping away cautiously from the treetops.

Her cornfields are ploughed near her lover's home
That he might see and choose her.

She out-tricks tricksters:
Let those who think they can tame her try!
Not even with grinding stones!

O my uncle, the cattle shy from the bride
They fear she is a wild beast

They fear the bride
They fear her; behold, here comes the mighty one!

(Zulu)

SHAKA, WARRIOR-KING

Rampageous son of Ndaba!

The joke of the women of Senzangakona's kraal
Joking as they sat in a sheltered place
Saying that Shaka would not rule, would not become chief
Whereas it was the year in which Shaka would prosper.

Fire of the long dry grass, son of Senzangakona
Fire of the long dry grass, fire of scorching
Fire that burned the owls on Dlebe hill
And on the hill of Mabedlana, eventually.

He who traveled across to Ndima and Mgovu
And women who were with child gave birth too easily;
The newly planted crops they left stunted
The seed they abandoned among the maize stalks
The old women sitting in abandoned courtyards
The old men abandoned along bush paths
The roots of the trees staring up at the sky.

—Magolwane
(Zulu)

SUNJATA

Kani Simbon [Fond Hunter]
Kani Niokon Simbon [Fond Hunter's Sworn-friend]
Lafolo Simbon [First Hunter]
Lawale Simbon [Hunter Way-back-when]
Jata, the exile
Jata of the crippled limbs

Jata of the crippled limbs
Jata, irreproachable victor
If the Manden thrives,
May God grant you numerous descendants
If the Manden crumbles,
May God grant you numerous descendants
Son of Maghan, the handsome, who divined in a cave.

Hunter, Lion, apprentice of the ancestral Cat.
To remain where Hunters' altar is placed
    is not appropriate for the weak.
Water of the depths cannot be compared
    to water flowing along a bed of gravel:
Water flowing along a gravel bed is clear.

                            (Malinké)

THE KING OF OYO

Kabiesi!
Child of death
Father of all mothers
King of all kings
You carry the blackness of the forest
Like a royal gown.
You carry the blood of your enemies
Like a shining crown.
Be merciful with us
As the silk-cotton tree is merciful with the forest
As the eagle is merciful with the birds.
The town rests in the palm of your hand
Weightless and fragile
Do not destroy it:
Our fate rests in your hand
Wield it carefully
Like your beaded scepter.
The enemies who want to destroy you
Will destroy themselves.

When they want to roast maize
They will set fire to their roof.
When they want to sell water
There will be drought.
The sieve will always be master of the chaff.
The water lily will always float on the lake.
Child of death,
The hairs on your chest are as numerous
As the words of a talkative woman.
You grab the heads of your enemies
And push their faces into boiling water.
You lock the door in front of their noses
And keep the key in your pocket.
Child of dcath
Father of all mothers
King of all kings.

(Yoruba)

LEKOLWANE, THE BOY INITIATE

Lenapa, father of the black cockade
Father of the cockade extending to the
    shoulders.
Lefata, wander on and go down
To go and see how huts stand
To go and see dark-complexioned girls.
A dark-complexioned young man, I, Lefata
A young man with a beautiful voice
A young man to be called a chief
A young man to be given a shield.
Girls love him without knowing him
They go about breaking themselves into small
    pieces.

Of throwing the *kotjane* stick:
When I throw it at partridges, it becomes too
    light

And goes and falls in a hot place
Where sit a lion and a rhinoceros.

The multicolored bird, the blue crane
The bluish-gray one, with an unaging head.

(CHORUS)   *O a lla, o a lla moholodi*

It cries, it cries, the blue crane.

(CHORUS)   *O a lla, o a lla moholodi*

Father, mother, O my uncle
Our cattle are numerous as the stars
Our cattle are numerous as that grass!

(CHORUS)   *O a lla, o a lla moholodi*

Keep quiet, I am castrating a cat
Shrieks of applause are not made for a cat.
They performed this operation once at
     Mathebe
The cat jumped unexpectedly
And an old man tramped
On a woman recovering from childbirth!

An uncircumcised boy smells like a he-goat
An unexcised girl smells like a pig with a litter.

Book-reader, reader of nonsense
Uncircumcised, says in his fear
"Don't you see I am holy
Purified by the school atmosphere?"
An unexcised girl in her fear
Chops off her hair and remains with a shining
     head
Folding her blanket clumsily.

I have no sister and swear by a stone
Stone, I swear by an iron one.

My brother and I: He captures the white one,
    I the black
That they may match their colors in the cattle
    pen.

I am a short strong man, a grysbuck, a red
    hare
I am an eland, a buffalo, a bully!

Dark-complexioned Letsila
Brother to famous warriors, Sebine and
    Mpanne!

(Sotho)

FREDDJE PETJE, SCHOOLBOY

Axee! We greet you, Sotho of the north
Feather of lightning that flies far
Flies far as Ledimanyana in Pietersburg district
Country of black-fruited *hlakola* trees
Where I arrived, as far north as Mphasa
And crossed and bent my knees
I, slender son of Bakxaxa people
The slender one, active and smart.

Axee! On my way back home
On my way northward I saw white men
With flat straw hats like old mealie baskets
Shouting to the youths
Who sleep in a group at the cattle post.
Smoke from a stick of wood:
Puff puff, live coals in a little cave;
Whitie sneezes and capers about.

Axee! When I arrived at my home in the north
They said, "Go home, you wretched Rhodesian!
When we punished you, we said you were a man
Thinking, you'll stay and pick vegetables for us
Thinking, you'll stay and protect us from Fierce-as-lion
Warriors, children of Nowhere-in-the-distance
Children of the laughters."

Axee! It's the hardships of Sebilo all over again:
Those up in Mphasa call me "Jackal of Sebilo"
Yet I am the agile one
I, the little black weasel
I'm going home to "Don't give me, I'm satisfied"
There they smear me with white clay and I shine
'Til I blind the moon, the white maiden
I, child of "Brave as a lion."

Eeeee-uuuuu! Come and see the Sotho of Bothsa
Child of the one who cries without stopping.
His mother has gone to Ledimanyana in Pietersburg district
That's the country of black-fruited *hlakola* trees
To which I took foot, but the foot failed
To which I took hand, but the hand failed
Don't look at my hand, being short like this.
I crossed the rivers of Semphekekhotse.

I am not a mere black one; I am white-trimmed
I am the red and white one of Lekope
I am the weaverbird that cries in the rivers
Whistling sounds far across the mountain passes
Passes of the wild animals
As far as the place called Moxodi
Where the cattle are milked, croaking like frogs
Taught by the black one, slayer of the pig.

Axee! You, Ntsce my child
Go back home to the north,
Go fetch the weed that causes pleasure

From Motsatsi of the rivers;
She will give it to Father-of-the-darkness
At the river no one crosses alive;
At Mphasa there's a weaver of anklets, bracelets
If you go there you'll not be heard of again.

Axee! Come and see a swarm of people
They smear me with fat and I shine
And I shine too bright for the northern sisters.
I, child of the chameleon, have no color
If you want me, don't pick up the phone
But cast the bones of the dead.

(Sotho)

AKPALU, POET

There is a song, we shall sing it
Let the poor forget their sorrows
Akpalu plays a drum, the drum of joy
The sons of Anlo mob him
Clear your voices and sing *Agoha*
There is song, we'll sing it
Let the poor forget their sorrows
Let us play it, our debtor-drum
Come, let us play it . . .

Alas, my children turned out to be my songs
That is how things have gone with me.
Let everyone know them, those who say:
"Die, that I bury you" . . .

I was made by a great God
I was made together with other poets.
You call yourself a poet,
Can you sing with Akpalu's voice?
Who deceived you?
I was made by a great God

I was made together with other singers.
The song of the drum
I do not sing it meagerly—
It was from old men I heard it.
A child who thinks he understands so much
Cannot understand *Agoha.*
Agoha cannot die.
You may understand the surface
But not the deep words . . .

I am on the world's extreme corner
I am not sitting in the row with the eminent
Those who are lucky sit in the middle
Sitting and leaning against a wall
They say I came to search
I, Akpalu, can only go beyond and forget.

(Ewe)

COMMENTARY

Although the institution of praising a person may be found every-where, the conventional forms these praises take vary from language group to language group. Generally, in its most condensed form, a personal praise is a "strong-name," attributive of characteristic power, which is only partly idiosyncratic, the rest being genealogically de-rived. However, in some groups, as we shall see, a praise-name may be acquired by means other than inheritance plus ceremonious des-ignation. An extended personal praise may be composed, in some cul-tures, by a poet attached to one's household, in other cultures by oneself. In general, a distinction should be made between a fixed praise, whether spoken or drummed or both, and improvised songs of homage (or unabashed flattery), some of which may be remembered (even unto succeeding generations), others not. If a professional praiser praises you, he would be expected to work some of your fixed verbal features into his spontaneous song-likeness. For the rest, the praiser might make your latest accomplishment, escapade, or mishap into a little cautionary story; he might expatiate on your physical or social endowments, including deeds of your ancestors; and at some point he is certain to extol your generosity!

AMBARA. The Dogon *tige* of an individual person works both horizontally and vertically to weave him into social place and mythic time. A *tige* thus secures each man in a context inherited from the paternal ancestor reincarnated in him. The ancestor's position in the world and his life-force are both reincarnated verbally in the *tige*. To pronounce it reminds a man who he is and serves to put that identity into motion.

In this case, "abundant cloud" will remind Ambara that he is a Dogon. Such, according to popular belief, was the greeting given to the primal smith when he arrived on earth with the possibility of rain. On another level of sophistication, the word here translated as "abundant cloud" means "occult knowledge" or "mystery," that which only a Dogon initiate may know. "Hollow bamboo" is the succinct praise-name of the Dyon branch of the Dogon people and recalls their arrival in the region known as the cliffs of Bandiagara. Following the ancestral snake, the Dyon journeyed underground and emerged again into the air through a narrow uterine canal. "Fatigue" sinks Ambara into the neighborhood of Sanga, where his forefathers wore themselves out carrying soil from the bottoms of evaporating ponds up onto rocky terraces—the beginning of agriculture in that inhospitable environment. Again, more esoterically, for "fatigue" read "separation," both denominations having to do with man's existential status, the curse of the human condition. Ambara belongs to a branch of the Dyon family that was for a mythic seven years expelled from the double villages of Ogol; hence the family name "Banished brothers." "Mud" (indication of water source) refers to the quarter in Ogol where his immediate family lives. The final epithet designates Ambara's own personality type, but it is not unique to him; he inherited his interpretive facility from a paternal forebear, whose life he will relive under different worldly circumstances. The source of this *tige* is Solange de Ganay, *Les Devises des Dogons* (Paris: Institut d'Ethnologie, 1941), p. 149.

ABATAN. As noted in the introduction, "praise" in Yoruba means a salutation to the head, container of the various components of soul-force that make one what one is. A person's *oríkì* will include a series of epithets evoking prominent members of his or her lineage and denoting its common place of origin. These epithets, called *oríkì orílẹ̀,* are appended to the individual's first names, known as *oruko.* The first name may indicate parental response to one's birth, as does "Child whom we favor." Or it may recall circumstances prevailing at the time, as suggested in the introduction, or record the intercession of a divinity. Or a Yoruba's first name may be "brought from heaven," by which is meant a name necessitated by certain noteworthy features of the neonate. Perhaps direct observation, ratified by divination, will happily confirm the reappearance of a grandfather's traits, in which case the child will be named Babatunde (father comes again).[2] The entire praise-name, including the *oruko,* the *oríkì orílẹ̀,* and the personal *oríkì* that may over the years accrue, is rather like a verbal coat of arms.

Abatan's praise-name was collected by Robert Farris Thompson and originally published in a collection of essays called *Tradition and Creativity in Tribal Art,* edited by Daniel Biebuyck (Berkeley: University of California Press, 1969), pp. 153–154. When Thompson met her, Abatan was an old woman in her eighties, a master sculptor, renowned potter and poet, and priestess of the cult of Oshun and Eyinle. Both these are river divinities, associated with fertility and medicine. Eyinle is also a legendary hunter, one of whose praise-names, Abatan (meaning "I-wish-we-might-spread-far"), was conferred upon a child who was destined to fashion cult objects for the god by parents who believed the divinity had graced their lives with a baby. Those names beginning "Child of" recall Abatan's ancestry. Unlike many alienated artists of the Western world, says Thompson, Abatan lived a life of prestige, her creative accomplishments keeping pace with the distinction of her pedigree. She lived, that is, to bear out her name.

When a group of singers and drummers arrive to praise a distinguished person like Abatan, their praises—to please an old woman by teasing her into reminiscence—might refer to the days when she was known to be the most graceful dancer in the region. This also would be known as *oríkì.* And when, at least once a year, her ancestors were

[2] The principles operating in the selection of Yoruba first names may be found in many African cultures.

officially feasted, chanted *oríkì orílè* would consist not only of the lineage strong-names recorded here, but also of the miniature narratives of which they are a mnemonic summary. Whether true or for the most part apocryphal, these anecdotes linked to Abatan would bespeak character and the personal vitality admired by all Yoruba.

ZAILA. This little praise-song (*taki*) is a drummer's improvisation that stuck, not only to the girl herself but in the memory of an old woman recalling the days when she and the popular butcher's daughter were special girl friends (*kawa*) in Zarewa, northern Nigeria.

At social gatherings of young Hausa, girl-praising is a highly competitive game. Young men vie for the favor of a young woman by attempting to outdo each other in donations to the drummer on her behalf. So long as she is drummed for, she dances. But others are dancing, too. Outbidding others for the drummer's attention silences praises of her rivals until Zaila alone is left to elicit praiseworthy extravagance from her determined admirers. It is the drummer who pockets the cowries, not Zaila.

The source of this *taki* is *Baba of Karo* by Mary Smith (London: Faber and Faber, 1954), p. 57. Unlike Zaila, Hausa VIPs have lengthy set praises as well as occasional improvised ones. For a description of various forms praising may take among the Hausa, see M. G. Smith, "The Social Functions and Meaning of Hausa Praise-Singing," *Africa* 27 (1957) and A. J. N. Tremearne, *Hausa Superstitions and Customs* (1913; reprint ed. London: Frank Cass, 1970).

ONGIYA. This little praise-shout is called a *mwoc*. How does a person acquire one? Often as the result of a funny incident, says Okot p'Bitek, in *Horn of My Love* (London: Heinemann, 1974), pp. 168–169.

A friend and I went to woo a girl. We met her on the way going to fetch water; she took us into her mother's hut, and asked us to wait for her. There were some beans cooking on the stove, and very bitter smoke from the end of the firewood. So my friend tried to stop the smoke by pushing the piece of firewood into the stove, and in so doing knocked the pot over. We were all covered with ash. When the girl returned, we did not stay long, because of the shame. Who ever disturbed a cooking pot in his mother-in-law's house?

The situations calling for the invocation of *mwoc*-power are adrenal. If provoked, one shouts it and at once begins to fight. A palpable hit in the course of a bout elicits the *mwoc* in a triumphal mode, as does the accomplishment of a kill in hunting. When dancing, one shouts one's *mwoc* at the peak of ecstasy (like the disco gesture of raising one's fists to the strobe-lit sky). When age-mates meet, they may exchange *mwoc* phrases: I give you the first line of yours, you give me the first line of mine, and so on until the two poems, intertwined, have been completed.

GIRL FRIENDS OF KEMPUMBYA. Heroic recitations, called *ebyevugo*, are a form of praise-poem characteristic of the cattle aristocracy of the Ankore region (Uganda). Among the Hima people, custom required a noble youth to display his excellence by composing and reciting seminarrative declamations having to do with his own heroism, that of his comrades, and with the beauty of his cattle. Among the women of Ankore, a parallel literary form, also called *ebyevugo*, gives accomplished friends the opportunity to praise each other in an informal, leisurely way. Hima men declaim their praises at top speed. Hima women sing them, accompanying themselves on the *enanga* harp.

Here, one after the other, Kempumbya praises various members of her age group and expects the praised ones to join in the chorus. She calls them "goddesses of the drum" because they are progenitors of a nation whose power resides in, or is symbolized by, the chief's sacred drum. Since to the Hima nothing is more beautiful than a beautiful cow, Kempumbya bestows upon her friends bovine epithets like "spotted one," "deep purple one," "big-eyed" one. Aristocratic women in this culture are supposed to be active, powerful, well-fleshed-out, and fashionably dressed—or so one gathers from Kempumbya's praise-descriptions. This aesthetic, as well as their solidarity as women, is not limited to the Hima, nor to the eastern part of the continent.

Source: H. F. Morris, "The Praise Poems of Bahima Women," *African Language Studies* 6 (1965), pp. 54–55. Morris recorded this song in 1955. With his permission and with the help of his notes I have tried to move his preliminary translation a little closer to the poetry of the original.

GEORGE AMAKIRI. This is a *kule,* or drum-praise, collected by E. J. Alagoa, hospitable and always helpful historian of Ijọ oral traditions. It was recorded at Abonnema, Rivers State, Nigeria, and published in "Ijọ Drumlore," *African Notes* VI, 2 (1971), pp. 68–70. Ijọ *kule* are composed for drum alone, and the sign of a Kalabari Ijọ's high cultivation is his ability nonchalantly to recognize, while dancing in a masquerade, the *kule* of any prominent person of the past or present, of any deity, of any neighboring town. (Robin Horton has called the ceremony in which this expertise is tested "an ordeal for aristocrats.")

Of course, a master drummer must know all regional *kule.* Not every individual is entitled to one; they are earned only by persons of great distinction (wealth, valor, political influence), like the man who composed this praise in his own behalf over a hundred years ago. George Amakiri was a self-made aristocrat. Born a slave, he became the adopted son of King Kariobo, who apprenticed him to a British supercargo. Eventually he established his own warring and trading canoe-house and then expanded its operations, like an Onassis. By the last quarter of the nineteenth century, this "crocodile with the cavernous mouth" had become the dominant chief in the entire Kalabari region and was far more powerful than its titular king, his foster brother.

Kali kulukulu kalika is the drum ideogram for Kalabari. The people of Bonny, Okrika, and Ogoloma were rivals of the Elem-Kalabari people in the palm-oil trade, by which George Amakiri amassed his fortune.

FAKOLI KOROMA. This young man, whose praise-utterance (*fasa*) is deceptively plain, plays an important part in the Malian national epic, *Sunjata.* He is the nephew of Sumaworo, a magician-king who is the protagonist's most formidable enemy. When Sumaworo willfully appropriates Fakoli's wife, known for her excellent cooking, the young man in a rage defects, taking his army of vassals with him. Together Sunjata and his new right-hand man, Fakoli, defeat their common antagonist at the battle of Krina.

Sunjata's title of honor is *simbon,* meaning hunter. Historically, it would seem, the future unifier of Mali was able to gain adherents from a host of rival clans by securing the support of the pan-tribal hunters' association. Similarly, Fakoli not only supplied his chief with military reinforcements and expertise but also, as a powerful priest of the Komo secret society, contributed the magical strength and political influence of that organization, founded by the special caste of blacksmiths and dominated by the Kamara and Doumbiya families. As scion of smiths (chief of the Doumbiya), Fakoli assured Sunjata, scion of hunters, invincibility.

This praise is excerpted from a version of the epic recited by the late Wa Kamissoko of Krina to his friend Youssouf Tata Cissé, a Malian scholar. Wa's recitation is transcribed and translated by Cissé in *L'Empire du Mali, un récit de Wa Kamissoko* (Paris: SCOA, 1975; the *fasa* is given on pp. 390–391). In Wa's version the *fasa* is dramatically uttered by Fakoli as he introduces himself to Sundiata for the first time. "Who are you?" asks the hunter-king, impressed by the vivacity of this very small (just under five feet) young man. "I am Fakoli, come to aid you in combat," says the hero of the Doumbiya, and proceeds to recite his credentials.

These, in praise form, are saturated with recondite references to the Komo society, which concerns itself with knowledge of man in the world. (Self-knowledge and ontology are considered by such African initiation societies to be complementary disciplines.) The two lakes symbolize the universal element in which the initiate "fishes" for cognition. The "five freed chiefs" make up an important social category to which the Doumbiya and the Kamara belong, as does the reciter Wa's own family of Kamissoko traditionalists. These families go back to pre-Malian Wagadu (ancient Ghana), where they were exempt from captive status[3] and from paying feudal dues because of their competence in the dangerous practices of transformation (ore to metal, deed to fame, intention to incantation) and thaumaturgic ritual. The "tree" Fakoli refers to is perennially green, like knowledge, and is a fixture of the Komo sanctuary. "Backbone and magic" again indicate his hieratic role in Komo. Articulation of the spinal column suggests the dialectical power of logos in traditional Malian philoso-

[3] Proper to all craftsmen in the traditional stratified societies of the western Sudan.

phy. Magic in this context is an aristocratic virtue, a shamanistic aptitude in those days and in that place being a necessary constituent of the fullest manhood.

MAYGARI, TRUCK DRIVER. Garoua is located on the banks of the upper Benue River in the republic of Cameroon. There Maygari drives for the Compagnie Française des Textiles. The praise-poet, Bouba Malam Jarida, works in the (Adamawa) Fulani tradition of literate flattery. Praises (*mantooje*) are composed for clients, who listen to the sung version and then may keep the poem to read and reread at leisure. But Bouba Malam Jarida is not, strictly speaking, a Fulani; he is, rather, acculturated to the Adamawa region. His father was from Bornu and his mother a Hausa woman from the Benue. Nor is he completely literate. He can write but does so with difficulty and in a rather indecipherable hand. However, his lively imagination secures him a living. The source of this *mantooje is Poésie Peule de l'Adamawa*, Pierre Francis, ed., Classiques Africains (Bruges: Julliard, 1965), vol. I, pp. 364–369. Out of thirty-two verses, only seventeen have been given here, namely those showing that the driver's prestige resides in his powerful machine, and those making clear the economics of professional praise-singing. The other verses, for the most part, consist of standard Islamic homilies.

MNKABAYI. This exceptional woman channeled the course of Zulu history. She began her political career as regent for her younger brother Senzangakhona. Later, as head of a military kraal (and a tremendous power behind the scenes), she first encouraged the ambitions of her nephew Shaka, who became king in 1816, and then fomented the conspiracy that led to his assassination in 1828. Thereupon she supported the claims of one of Shaka's brothers, Dingane, which meant acquiescence in the murder of the rival claimant, Mhlangana.

The Zulu word for praise-poem, *izibongo*, is a plural noun derived from the singular form, *isibongo*, meaning "clan name." An ordinary person may acquire several praise-names (also called *izibongo*) during his life. These are shouted by his supporters and by himself as he demonstrates his skill in combat or in the dances of self-display (called *giya*) that were traditionally performed by Zulu warriors. A man who achieves rank hires a professional (*imbongi*) to work his separate praises up into a unified *izibongo* and perform it in a suitable manner. The praise-poem of a chief not only presents him to himself and others as someone worthy of admiration but often includes a note of admonition as well, for the *imbongi* represents the otherwise constrained voice of the people. Out of the tension created between the necessity to extol and license to characterize truthfully is created a heroic poetry of great literary distinction.

For example, Mnkabayi is greeted in the male gender, "Father of guile," a characterization appropriate to the devastations reported in stanza one. These are signs of her political power. In stanza two her preference for politics over marriage and a "normal" woman's life is handled with acumen and a certain satirical forbearance. The old women criticize Mnkabayi, but is it not true that her sympathetic accessibility to petitioners (through "main gates" and "narrow") was her way of being responsively feminine? Further, in a motherly way she protects her people from the ire ("venom") of the chief. Malandela is the grandfather of the Zulu clan for whose descendants she, by her intrigues, cleared the path to conquest.

The source of this eulogy is *Izibongo, Zulu Praise Poems,* edited by Trevor Cope (Oxford: Oxford University Press, 1968), p. 172. The stanza break indicates a pause by the performer for breath.

MCAYI, THE DAUGHTER OF VUMA. The source of this *izibongo* is an article by B. W. Vilakazi: "The Conception and Development of Poetry in Zulu," *Bantu Studies* XII (1938), p. 114. Vilakazi, whose prime concern in his analysis of this poem is with its musical and rhythmic patterns in Zulu, does not say who Mcayi is or was, nor does he provide an exegesis. But as a poet himself, he has something very illuminating to say about artistic intention in such compositions:

> You will notice when you follow the subject-matter that there does not seem to be a systematic treatment of the main theme so as to form one complete and analysable vista. . . . The poet seems to ramble without control over his subject-matter. But [looked at] objectively, the whole poem is laconic and staccato, the gaps between different [subjects] demand mental experience of the whole poem before the analysing of its contents. . . .

When I read [such a] poem and come on a gap, there I discover the end of my stanza. . . . Stanzas in [oral] Zulu poetry are like lights shed on a sculptured work from different angles. These lights operate independently of one another, yet bring into relief the whole picture which the artist presents in carving. . . . The [oral] poet in tackling his theme acts like an exhibitor of sculpture in the arrangement of lights. The piece of sculpture and the lights are one configuration indivisible as a mental setting which induces an aesthetic sense. Analysis can only be reached when one knows where every light [outlining the sculpture] has been placed.

"She is of a roundness"—Vilakazi's translation reads, "She is like a ball."

"Fights between the striped and the plain white"—I imagine Mcayi is given to wearing a striped skirt and a white top, and I also imagine this image has something to do with the cattle offered for her bride price.

"Can mealies be boiled on rocks"—Here, I think, the hearthstones supporting the pot are meant. The wild tinder is her nature, a metaphorical fierceness tempered, in the Zulu language, by the use of smooth nasals (*m*s and *n*s), which suggest the continuous hum of connubial love.

SHAKA. The number and order of praise-units depends upon the occasion and upon the artistic will of the performer; but the format of these units depends upon the time of their composition. During the reign of Shaka (1816–28), as the Zulu, defeating neighboring clans, developed into a nation, the *izibongo* began to develop a stanzaic form of expression. The linked couplets of the pre-Shakian praise expanded into groups of lines arranged with a certain rhetorical direction and emphasis. The typical Shakian praise consists of a statement, followed by some kind of an extension and/or development of the theme, which in turn leads to a conclusion. In Cope's book, Shaka's praises run to 450 lines, from which I have selected fifteen (in addition to the opening salutation): a sampling of three stanzas. The first of these, beginning "The joke of the women," is notable for its twist-of-fate conclusion in seeming contradiction of what has gone before. The second, "Fire of the long dry grass," depicts with increasing intensity the havoc wreaked by Shaka; as a fire behaves, so did the Zulu chief, and so does the stanza itself. The final stanza focuses on the human results of a typical Shakian rampage. We know the name of the poet who composed Shaka's praises. It was Magolwane. Source: Cope, *Izibongo*, pp. 90–92.

SUNJATA. The formal praises of the first stanza affiliate the Malian national hero to the four male mythological ancestors of the Mande people. With this formal invocation the traditionalist of Krina begins to share yet another narrative with his friend and scholarly "patron." Source: Youssouf Tata Cissé and Wa Kamissoko, *La grande geste du Mali*, Vol. 1 (Paris: Karthala-ARSAN, 1988), p. 43. The second stanza is a composite. Sunjata is associated with the lion. Since it was Youssouf Cissé who gave the folk etymology of the phrase "Lion born of the cat" to John William Johnson, I have appropriated and retranslated it here. [John William Johnson, *The Epic of Son-Jara*, text by Fa-Digi Sisòkò (Bloomington: Indiana University Press, 1986), pp. 101, N 32, 185.] Similarly, the praise-phrase "To remain where the Hunter's altar is placed" occurs with a different wording on p. 100 of Johnson's text, accompanied by a literal (exoteric) explanation of *dankun*, which, thanks to Wa-Cissé, it is possible to amplify here. Dankun is a very dangerous because very mystical place of transformation: a liminal (Cissé calls it a "ritual") triangle delineated by three paths—two separating and heading to the uncultivated bush and to the farm-plots, respectively, and one cutting across the angle formed by them. The apex of the triangle touches the road to and from the village. Indeed, all three paths may be thought to be coming back as well as going (different names are given to them, depending on how they are conceived); thus they represent origin and descent genealogically and religiously. Besides Hunters' sacrifices, all important rites (including those held by Nyagwa, the women's secret society) are held here. Source: *La grande geste du Mali*, Vol. 2 (Paris: Karthala-ARSAN, 1991), pp. 217–219, and fieldwork with the *donsonton* and *nyagwa* in Mali.

I suspect that Sunjata's resting place is being at least symbolically alluded to by this phrase. Where else on earth to "locate" the remains of the hunter-hero? The source for the final lines of this composite set of praises: *La grande geste*, Vol. 1, p. 163. They are sung to Sunjata, who has just succeeded in crossing the river and returning (on a bridge of linked Somono canoes), by a welcoming group of women, who proverbially appeal to the hero to exercise the virtue of speaking clearly, without guile; self-reflexively, so also may the bard!

THE KING OF OYO. The sacred kings of the Yoruba, like their divinities (orisha), are praised with an attitude toward cosmic power (of which they are conduits) that always reminds me of Rilke's evocation of angels: They embody the plenitude that, with us, must always remain an aspiration; they infuse us with their strength and yet they could, with no effort at all, destroy us. These *oríkì* of the king of Oyo are a series of metaphorical statements, charged with tenderness, violence, proverbial wisdom (the measured view of the Greek chorus), and a catachrestic humor, all of which reflect the metaphysical wit of Yoruba spoken culture. This is a praise of the personage, not of any individual. Source: Ulli Beier, *Yoruba Poetry* (Cambridge: Cambridge University Press, 1970), pp. 37–38.

LEKOLWANE. This is the generic name for boy-initiate, and the text is a composite praise formed of excerpts given by S. M. Guma in *The Form, Content and Technique of Traditional Literature in Southern Sotho* (Pretoria: J. L. van Schaik, 1967), pp. 136–145. Unfortunately —because this is not his purpose—Guma does not give a full text as composed and recited on coming-out-day by any individual initiate; but since it is important here to establish the genre, not only for its own delights but as a precedent for Freddje's self-portrait, I have combined some of Guma's illustrative passages into a piece that I hope will have a certain flow to it. Nothing like the flow of an original, however, recited, while grasping a *kotjane* stick in one's hand, as a test of unflappable memory and composure before a clamoring audience!

There are four special areas of Sotho praise-work. *Lithoko* (plural) are professionally composed for chiefs and notable warriors. Diviners compose them for their bones (see Chapter IX). Laymen, especially hunters, compose them for animals, herdsmen for their cows. And upon circumcision and its attendant ritual instruction, young men were expected to compose their own—the less imaginative with a little help from the bush instructor.

Each *lekolwane* begins by exposing to the public for the first time his new name (begining with an *l*), which may or may not during the years to come replace the one given by his family. Here Lenata is one such circumcision-name; Lefata is another; and the Letsila of the concluding stanza is a third. The name is then extended, as Lefata's here is, by flattering self-description. Throughout the praise the boy attributes wonders of deed and aspect to himself, associating his qualities now and again with those of animals, which involve the spontaneous composition of brief animal-*lithoko*. As warriors are praise-linked to ferocious animals, so the initiate also links himself to prominent warriors. At a certain stage the praise may include a little song (*lengae*), whose chorus is taken up by his age-mates. When the song is concluded, he goes on, perhaps with a bit of narrative in which one of his exploits (real or imaginary) is told, perhaps with succinct comment on the meaning of circumcision as a rite of passage. I was particularly struck by the sequence about the castration of the cat as an expression of what everyone who undergoes the initiatory operation must fear; and also by the fact that at the time when at least one of these verses was composed, the traditionalists seem to have been stronger than those under missionary influence ("Book-reader . . ."). Or perhaps again this is an anxiety being shouted down. Form and matter coincide as male fellowship is transferred to the cattle-pen. The couplet is the essential unit of traditional Sotho praising, a unit well defined by linking the word at the end of the first line to the word that begins the second line. This is difficult to reproduce in English, where sound and sense simply can't chime the way they do in the original and where to reproduce Sotho grammatical constructions would make for distracting "quaintness"—fakely folkloric. However, the couplet about the initiate's integrity (swearing on ironstone) should give an idea of this consonance.

FREDDJE PETJE. This *dithoko* (singular) was composed at the Lemana teacher-training institution (in the Transvaal) and published not long thereafter by H. J. Van Zyl in a collection called "Praises in Northern Sotho" (*Bantu Studies* XV, 2 [1941], pp. 148–153). A missionary teacher asked his pupils to write, in Sotho, praises of anything, of anywhere or anybody, in traditional *lithoko* style. Some wrote of animals; one eulogized the Swiss mission school as "the little fountain that quenches thirst." Freddje Petje wrote about himself in the heroic format of a young warrior's boast, and in so doing revealed an identity crisis (which it was always the latent purpose of such *lithoko* to shout down) exacerbated by the South African racial situation. Official insistence on "nativism" (Bantu-ism) must put the consciousness of someone like Freddje in a double bind. From an equation of traditional magniloquence with black humiliation there is no escape—except into fantasy.

Freddje is a displaced person, at home nowhere. The lines about "foot failed . . . hand failed" refer to the fact that he could not negotiate a marriage contract with any family in his mother's country. He imagines going to a place where he does finally belong, where he will be rubbed with the white clay of the initiate until in his beauty he outshines the moon and attracts by such medicine all women, even whites. But he is rejected. There is no such place; and his zigzag flight leads him to defiant lethean territories (the "river" and the "weed"). Could his composition teacher by any stretch of his own imagination have seen the suicide in Freddje? Did this remarkable poem give that thought relief?

AKPALU. "The poet must never lose despair," said a Russian colleague to Denise Levertov. Sitting "on the world's extreme corner," the (traditional) Ewe dirge-singer had this to say to Kofi Awoonor, the (contemporary) Ghanaian poet:

> I came into the world with song. No one can sing with my voice. But I have nothing. Neither children nor wealth. My reward is beyond and here in the words I leave with you, the youth. My songs are gifts from the creator himself.

Looking in on Akpalu alone, destitute, with shaky jaws, at the age of ninety-two still brooding upon the savageness of life, who could surmise his astonishing reputation? His name has become synonymous with the slow dirge performed (according to his models) by Ewe women mourners. Like Magolwane in Zululand, Akpalu revolutionized a traditional genre. And yet, in traditional Africa (as elsewhere), the master potter may be honored and integrated but the poet, no matter how much he is admired, remains a marginal figure. Being word-struck, he is dangerous, to be regarded with suspicion, even feared. This strangeness, of course, forces him in upon himself, deepens his awareness, embitters him as it extends his perspective.

It is not unusual for a professional bard to interject self-referential verses into the flow of his compositions. Often he will take apostrophic time-out to comment on his fatigue, his hunger, his inimitable wisdom, powers of observation, style, or magic. Thus self-pity and the exhilaration of word-mastery are common by-products of the poetic process, no matter what the culture. So it was Akpalu's genius to discover that in lamenting the dead, one in effect praises one's own drowning deeper than the occasion warrants. If "in effect," why not right out there on the dark song's surface? Akpalu accomplished this, became famous, and withal even more bitter, isolated, sorrowful. Source: Kofi Awoonor, *Guardians of the Sacred Word* (New York: NOK, 1974), pp. 36, 37, 42, 19 (excerpts only).

III: *Clan Praises*

DIARA

Diara, Lion
Big bone-cruncher
Roaring in the thickest of thickets.
Stranger in the morning
Village chief by evening
You have curved the world like a sickle
You have straightened it out again into a road.
Cavity catching bullock's blood in Bamana country
He may not revive the corpse,
Yet sends young men to death before their time.
Forbid the clawed stranger to trample the millet:
The huge animal will trample it despite what you say.
Cudgel shaking fruit from baobab trees of the Bambara;
Going—harvests dry fruits
Returning—exacts obedience from the green.
Staff of authority centered
Between Minianka and Bamana.
I say Diara: Lion and Cudgel.

(Bambara)

MPANGU

Ancient of days in Kongo
First to follow the king: entirely a man

I, Mpangu, yield to none
Descendant of Nkumbu-Nkumbu, our grandmother.
When we set forth from Kongo
There were nine caravans
Nine staffs held by chiefs
One basket of ancestral bones.
We brought these to consecrate our chiefs
Grass rings also.
The roads were safe
The villages where we put up, peaceful.
We arrived at Nsimba ford
There we stayed together
We did not separate.
We crossed many rivers
Waters of every kind.
One woman stayed behind
Mother of her clan
At Mfidi ford.

(Kongo)

OLUFE

Passing through, we Oyo never used to linger
To greet people of Ife, ruled by the Oni
Passing through, we Oyo never used to linger
To greet those ruled by the king of the spirits
Nor were we accustomed to prostrate ourselves
     before you reptilian people;
But I have ventured to greet the Oni's people
But I have waited, standing, to greet subjects of a spirit king
But I have gladly prostrated myself before reptilians
And creepers like the centipede
And creepers like the earthworm.
Children of wagtail bird by the city gate
And of the one whose root across the path could not be extirpated
And of the one who exhibited cowards' corpses
And of the slave who doesn't eat *ogunshere* soup:

Come to my house and eat silk-cotton-leaf soup
Children of the exhibitor of corpses!
Traveler bound for Benin, but discovered on the road to Oyo
I wash only my head with soap, not my whole body
I wash only my neck with a sponge, not my whole body.
In the backyard of Crown-is-sacred-vessel
      a stream takes its source;
Your crowns are numberless
Massive the king's crowns
Oruru's crown: somebody grabbed it and became the Alafin!
Oruru, child of those who ate saltless food insipidly
Owner of Ile-Ife, also called the Oni
A personage dreaded everywhere in our land
Crown-of-divination
Handsome as a carved image
Crown-of-divination, child of sorcerous-bird, who beats out
      praise-names of Our Mother, also dances
         to Obatala's praise-drum far as the sacred grove.
Popular Oruru, from inside I heard the *igbin* drum
From out-of-doors I heard it
So I went to see the display
But out-of-doors I found no drummers
Nor were there dancers.
An albino saw me
The albino beat me
A cripple stretched his long arm
And slapped me on the mouth
So I quickly turned back to our house.
When I got there I found eight visitors.
I offered them food
They said they would not eat
I offered them drinks
They said they would not drink
So I went to market to look for a palm oil seller
But I found no palm oil
I went to market to look for a bean cake seller
I found no appropriate bean cakes
For those I found in the market

Were black as if fried in palm-kernel oil.
The whole house was filled with prophetic voices.
Old man, blessed with profit-making luck,
    carry on with your palm-kernel-oil business
And I'll carry on with mine!
Who, trading in palm-kernel oil, would not keep fit?
Child of the slave woman Adikun, gift from Ilawe.
So much for this lineage
These, the praises of the owners-of-Ife.

                                        (Yoruba)

BERETUO

THE AWAKENING

Kon kon kon kon
kun kun kun kun
Spirit of Cedar tree
Wood of the drum
Spirit of Cedar tree:
The divine drummer announces:
Withdrawn in sleep
Presently returning
Cockcrow at break of day
Cock signals awakening
Very early, very early
As we instruct
So you will understand
As we are calling
So may we succeed.

Spirit of Earth, condolences
Sorrow is yours
Earth covered with dust;
Spirit of sky, wide, wide,
Earth, dying
Upon you I rely
Earth, living
Upon you I rely.

The divine drummer announces. . . .
Spirit of elephant
Foremost quarreler
You and the drummers go forth
You and the drummers return home
[With a drum-head, listen:]
You of the bulk, fiery one
Swamps swallow you up, elephant
Breaker of axes
The divine drummer announces. . . .

Spirit of fiber, Ampasakyi
Drum-string fiber
Tautener, where are you?
If you have been away
Come back, I'm calling you
I, learning
May I be successful.

Spirit of drum-pegs,
Ofema wood drum-pegs
Knock nobs, where are you?
If you have been away
Come back, I'm calling you
I, learning
May I be successful.

Clock-bird, Kokokyinaka
How do we answer you?
This is your greeting: Anyado!
We call you "drummer's child"
Drummer's child sleeps,
Awakens with the dawn
I, calling,
May I be successful!
Honored witch, spare me
Do not slay me, elder
The divine drummer announces. . . .

CALLING THE
ANCESTRAL ROLL

Spirit of Asiama Guahyia, of Adanse
Long-table-has-placed-authority
Queen mother who came from the Sky
The divine drummer announces:
Withdrawn in sleep
Presently returning
Cockcrow at break of day
Cock signals awakening
Very early, very early
As we instruct
So you will understand
As we are calling
So may we succeed.

Kwaakye Panyin,
Kwaakye, the tall one
Where did you come from?
From Mampong where rock
Wears down the ax
Destroyer of towns
Condolences, condolences.

Friend of the shield
We gave you sword and shield
So terrible that in three days
It devoured backbones.
Baafo Atiadu
Atiadu, the short one
Condolences, condolences.

Shield, coated with dust
Caused by tramping feet
Maniampong,
Dust of whose battle caused
Little rodent to fall from its tree
Where did you come from?
From Mampong
Where rock wears down the ax.

Boahin Anantuo
Where did you come from?
From Mampong
Where the Creator made things
Boahin, with an eye like flint
Whose strong-name is Ampafrako.

The shadows were falling cool
Cool for me at Sekyire
Who is chief of Sekyire?
It is Boaten Akumoa
Whom we grow weary of thanking for gifts
Akumoa, you were of royal blood
Since long ago, from Mampong
Of the worn ax.

Declaring war, he does not turn back:
Atakora Panyin
Where do you come from?
From Mampong of the worn ax
Condolences, condolences.

Odomankoma
Created the thing
The generous hewer-out
What did he create?
He created the herald
He created the drummer
He created "touch and die"
The executioner
And they all claim
To have come from one pod.
Come, herald, and receive
Your Colobus-monkey-skin cap!
And what was your heritage?
Yours was a good master.
And what was your heritage?
Yours the death-dance.

Asumgyina, son of the herald
Condolences, condolences.

Osafo, the tall one
Osafo the red
Brother of Osei Tutu
Where did you come from?
From Kumasi
Residence of kings.
Stream crosses path
Path crosses stream
Which, then, is elder?
Did we not cut path
To meet stream?
Stream had its origin
Long ago in Odomankoma
Who created the thing.
Osafo Kautanka,
Condolences, condolences. . . .

(Twi)

TSHIMINI

INVOCATION
AND PRAISE OF
THE CLAN
FOUNDER

Eagle out of the light
Plunge down with your drum
To empower your head
To summon your councilmen
Tshiabanza
Eagle out of the light
Eagle of the strong word
Of the hard-wood lineage.

I am the rat
That breaks hard ground
Ordinary termite mounds—too soft
I hunt only the toughly housed.

Mulamba
Weeping at the sight of a dead goat
The weeper readies the cooking pot
Mulamba
Acrid beer spoils the brew
Black oil discolors the red
Vileness seeks men
Men abhor vilification
Mulamba
Takes a goat
Buys a cleaver
Takes another
Buys a long shield
To protect us from uprisings
Mulamba
Heeds not the dying
Reckons only the dead
Mulamba
Head-pad, minding no burden
Imposes its own weight
Mulamba
Hatchet never minds thorns
Hoe never minds muck
Bowl never minds scald of porridge
Mulamba
Road, unacquainted with sighs
Relegates sighing to what must
Cede to its rise
Mulamba
To whom was presented the leopard
To whom the defeated presented their own:
Bea-Nkwadi and Muamba-Tshima
Mulamba
From an iron-hearted people
Open-handed: Tshiongo's household
Tight-fisted: Mulamba's household
Elder brother is brought food, not called
But Tshiongo was summoned

To drink beer at Mulamba's
Mulamba
Defender of all the white eagles
May we be called by their name!
Mulamba
Kin to the dwellers on Ntambwe hill . . .
Tschibale men are your kin
And the Bowa people on Kayumba hill
Tschinene hill
Ntumba hill . . .
And on Kamonayi hill
Home of Ngandu.
In Kabwe village once
Stood a palm-stem
Wrapped in antelope skin
Once in our land all men were valiant
Nowadays one sees old women
Ranks and files of graves where lived
Kavuadia and Kazambu
Mutengele and Munzenze . . .
All valiant men.
Thatch-perching insect
Pops into the wakeful eye:
Mulamba wouldn't sleep in a common hut:
Millet seeds loosen
Drop sleepy winkers
Mulamba was like the son
Of famous Tshiaba.

THE SINGER GIVES
HIS CREDENTIALS

I am of the Mbobo
And of the Kabondo people
My father is Kabongo
My mother, Mulolo.

PRAISES OF THE
CURRENT CHIEF'S
FRIENDS, HIS
NEIGHBORS, HIS
KIN

Ngandu
Burning heat which never harmed the house
Makes bush inflammable . . .
Chicken broken out of the shell at dawn
Mid-morning already a bird of prey

Nkumbikumbi, vulture:
Misses what's in front of the house
Grips what's behind
Misses the chicken
Grabs the grazer beside.
In our land lived valiant companions of
    Mulamba
Muscles glistening with oil
Here rang praises for Ntumba
Tall man, sounded depth of the river
Tall man, killed at the start of battle
Short men, what shall befall us?
Nearby live the Mbonda people:
Like Ilunga
Couldn't tell one woman from another,
The one he grabbed: "That's mine."
In our land lived Kashile of the proud stride
And Kabulu, brother of stingy Kamuania
Who used to tilt her cooking pot
[So you could see it was nearly empty].
Kabulu
Hard tree's knot
Exasperates hatchet
He let them drag away their dead
And followed after to fight on their own
    ground
Kabulu.

THE BATTLE
SONG OF THE
TSHIMINI IN
HONOR OF
KABULU, THE
CHIEF'S
FATHER

Fear not, here they come
Worthy to fight with you!
Fear not their lances—
Each blade forged at home
Fear not their arrows—
Fashioned of palm-ribs, sharpened.
Onward! Out of powder
They're on the verge of fleeing
Now they're burning second wife's house
Don't let them into first wife's yard

Now they're burning the furnace
Don't let them touch the forge!
All you bold men
They're burning our houses!
So? We'll move on
And wherever we go
Build new houses.
Kabulu, he thinks:
The one to strike them dead, that's I
They are coming to bear me in triumph
But no, they're hauling me away with the
   wounded!
Now is the day brave men are dying:
Ravaged the fields
Destroyed all the seed for planting.

RETURN TO   In our land lived Balubuila
THE REPERTOIRE   Nephew to Mulamba,
OF PRAISES   Torch-source for sorcerers, Mulamba.
In our town lived a red-complexioned man
Would eat no termites, lest he vomit
In our town lived a dark-complexioned man
Would eat no greens for fear of bad breath.
Our valley is so deep:
I saw something moving
Was it man or spirit?
Here comes the Executioner
To polish off the Victim
Who murdered the Defender
Who plotted fratricide.
Do not with bared knife provoke the leopard,
He won't object to a lance,
He won't object to a cudgel.
Our people are great pathing traders
Like Tshibangu, brother of Kamuania
Who used to tilt her cooking pot
[So guests could see how little was in it].
Attack the lion, attack the leopard

Thunder's unassailable.
In our land, hoe works out of its handle:
Nkembia's brothers, tireless farmers.
"Forceful," gameless brother of Kapinga
You'll wait in vain for her cooking.
"Fine-mouth," firstborn to first wife
Eats bananas, eats soft *kakonde* fruit.
Forest: all underbrush burned
Only tall trees standing
Mulamba.

THE SINGER
INTERJECTS
ON HIS OWN
BEHALF

Who gives me no food
Who gives me no drink
How about a little tobacco?
The singer of the land
Knows everything, knows secrets
A dolt requires explanations.

THE SINGER
CONTINUES
HIS
PRAISE-WORK

From Nyonga hill by Nkengibwa river
We are; from Kananga hill
Near Tshikuyi tree we are
From Tshiombi hill; from claybanks
Whence we used to fetch clay for potting.
Friend Ntumba, black complexioned—
Were this a malady, or like a wound
You could apply a remedy.
Kabulu Muzenga, husband of many women
Husband of Ntumba, Mukendi's sister
Ntumba, lovely *nkanselelenge* fish
Resembling *musangi* fish, but more luminous.
Grasshoppers, taken from a chicken
And given to a child, oblige: Tshibadi.
Others standing prompt to help brothers:
Mulamba and Tshiongo;
Tshiongo's surrounded by beautiful men
Mulamba's surrounded by ugly.
Month of the tall grass
Hoes rest together in the shed

Month of the tall grass
Speak evil of no man:
Words heard behind tall grass
Can lead to fighting.
Mbakula Tshibangu, did you find a cock
Bound to a stake in Milembe's yard?
Foolish Tshidimba of the Mukendi people
Why did you test Mulumba?
Kapulu fruit may lie forever in the stomach:
Mulumba swallowed and survived.
Crossroads, source of quarrels
Travelers' feet, always on the go
Farmers' hands, return to cut grass on home
    soil:
Farmfolk, all of us, with full granaries.
Ntombolo monkey
Won't sleep near Mbele monkey
For fear of losing tufts of hair.
Kampunga-Malenji, birds of beautiful plumage:
Sleek tail-feathers
Smooth, glossy down.
Rich man eats only bush meat
Hunts without protective charms.
Tornado, rips off raffia skirt
Wind, bends palm branches down
Cold, staves in the door
What? A door gapped by cold?
Leopard, born on a certain day
No-matter-when are born innocuous animals.
Among us grows a palm, with a hairy chest
Among us grows a strange tree, coiffed like a
    statue
Among us lived Kalume and Kabooka:
Kabooka killed a leopard; Kalume, antelope.
One basket on a competent head stays erect
A second basket sits askew, apt to tumble
Stupid, the jackal abandons its young
On the bush path of the hunger.

Spirit-wanderer, torch in hand
Kills children of his own kind
Mother survives, crying.
Friendly Mukwanga people, friendly
    Nsumpi . . .
Friendly Bowa people, near Dilunga rocks
Friendly Ndoba people, near Nyemvu
    mountain!
Over the strong prevail the strongest
Burdens press upon the strong
Upon the frenetic, meager-waisted mason
    wasp.
You, Kabulu:
"From the strong I take their vaunted
    overmuch
To the weak permit increase of riches."
Brother-in-law, take me at once to the
    marriage broker;
May the marriage broker return me to my
    relatives!
That nonentity hit me
That nincomppop
Whose beard barely makes it to other men's
    knees!
That superfluity
Thrown in with the goat as dowry
He'll never catch up with his age-mates!
Two sorcerers, Bilombo and Mbambakana—
Bilombo jinxed Mbambakana
Mbambakana fixed Bilombo!
Does not the forest
Provide itself with wild beasts?
Does not the village
Provide itself with a headman to defend it?

THE SINGER
REMINDS US HE
IS HUNGRY

Singer lacks a wife
Who can console?
Who can console with cooking?

| WIFE'S
COMPLAINT:
REPRISE | Can heart, embittered by indulgent love
Keep lavishing affection upon a toad?
A toad with warts, with slime on its feet? |

WIFE'S
COMPLAINT:
REPRISE

Can heart, embittered by indulgent love
Keep lavishing affection upon a toad?
A toad with warts, with slime on its feet?

SONG OF
MULAMBA:
REPRISE

Mpimpi deer, with well-formed limbs
Hard as Kapanga-Nzevu wood
Tough as dried meat
Mulamba
Chicken without a burial plot
Chicken died in action
Gravely boiled in the pot
Tendril, unknotted its entire length
Mulamba

BATTLE SONG
OF THE
TSHIMINI:
REPRISE

The day bold men are struck down
Is now; to battle!
Flee not the enemy
Rather, fall with them!
Let each choose his adversary!
Kabulu, you yours
Mulamba, you yours
Tshimbombo, you yours!
Brave men of Kabulu
How is it you behave like *mandonda* rats
Defeated, scampered
Crammed into another pack?

THE SINGER
HAS HAD
ENOUGH

I am the little cricket
Continues singing in his hole
Until sung out;
I sit transfixed in my song;
Whop the drumsticks into the drum!
Were I to go on I might croak
Like a broken frog!

(Luba)

COMMENTARY

Traditional African poetry, as it reflects notions of African personality, is a poetry of belonging. The isolation of the individual, whether attributed to man's "fallen" state or to the prison of a cogitating ego or to estrangement inherent in the human condition, from an African perspective seems like madness. Psychological separateness like ours could only be regarded as tantamount to annihilation by someone whose vital force is in continuous relation with that of a family composed of living as well as dead persons.[1]

One's land is not one's own in Africa but belongs in usufruct to the family members who till it; no more is one's soul, a significant component of which is an emanation of someone who has gone through life before. Plurality of souls mirrors a complex system of social and ritual obligations. Clan praises speak of such affiliations, thus—for each member who hears them—affirming a dual sense of belonging and of social differentiation.

Where, before the inevitable migrations and dispersals, do we hail from? With what landmarks—mountains, hills, rivers, ponds—with what species of trees do our people continue in memory to be identified? What animal or bird is legendarily our protector? What deeds or eccentricities characterize our common progenitor? What specialized occupation runs in the family? These are the sort of questions clan praises in various ways may be said to answer.

A Kamara, be he from Guinée or Mali, belongs to a line of smiths, a Kouyaté to praise-singers. A Kamara is affiliated with baobab trees and dog-faced baboons. Ologbin and Onigbori are so-called "Nupe" lineages from across the river, resident among the Yoruba, whose specialities are praise-singing and masquerading. The Ologbin are asso-

---

[1] What then of the "marginal" status and, often, bitter melancholy of the professional poet as discussed in the commentary on Akpalu (p. 37)? It is not his job to expatiate upon his own discomfort; the community for whom he composes and recites would not tolerate more than a modicum of this sort of thing, a few injections of despair directly into the text—no more. But he has other ways of indirectly expressing his "madness"—by conveying a sense of the transience of human enterprise, for example, or by wry humor. However, the professional poet thinks of himself as having inherited his voice from a predecessor or as having received it from some divinity. In this sense even he is "affiliated."

ciated with rain, the Onigbori with red monkeys. The Tshimini of
Eastern Zaire praise the eagle. Such affiliations, grounded in apocry-
phal stories and certainly at one time in ritual behavior, are imaginal
constituents of character, often stated in a proverbial mode, as are
fragments of the partly historical, partly as-if stories of successive clan
members, including those within actual memory.

Short forms of clan praises are routinely recited out of deference
to heads of family. Formally elaborated, their effect is empowering
and restorative. When one is faced with a serious undertaking, a rec-
itation of one's full clan praise is tantamount to a summoning of an-
cestral assistance. To be reminded at a funeral of such corporate
continuity is a relief. Yet insofar as historical calamities have not only
dispersed but decimated the clan, the recital of its common apo-
thegms and vitae elicits a common nostalgia, a woeful perspective on
generations of men. To sit at a Seder, to dance an Adae celebration
(in Ghana) are similarly cathartic, commemorative experiences.

DIARA. Among the Bambara, so Dominique Zehan tells us, the ge-
neric term for clan name, *dyamu,* itself a sort of résumé of a clan
personality more extensively expressed in praise-poems, subsumes the
word for spiritual double. Thus a *dyamu,* such as Diara, depicts the
dya of any person answering to that family apellation; and by *dya* is
meant the externalizable aspect of a person, an aura at once active
and conscious, including both that person's comportment and the
moral qualities revealed thereby. The Bambara etymology for praise-
poem of the type illustrated here, *burudyu,* is "trumpet-fundamental"
(*buru-dyu*), meaning that which is at the base of a person's brilliance,
the clarion call of his celebrity.

A life that fails to make an impact is forgotten. A man with a
strong, lengthy name pays not only his own passage along the river
of life but those of his descendants as well. Thus N'Golo Diara, who
reigned as Bambara king at Ségou from 1766 to 1790, lent his fame
to succeeding generations of the lion-hearted. The Diara are a very
old family whose antecedents precede the establishment of Sunjata's
empire. From his mother Sunjata himself acquired the lion praise-
name. But it is N'Golo's representative power that is being vaunted
here.

According to Louis Tauxier's *Histoire des Bambara* (Paris: Geuthner, 1942), which presents a winnowing of oral and written sources, N'Golo Diara began his career as a slave given by his uncle to Mamari Koulibali, founder of the kingdom of Ségou, as a substitute for a payment of millet-tribute owed to the king. (By "slave" is here meant one who was forced into permanent military service in the king's guard.) N'Golo's familiy fortunes had reached their nadir, but once in Ségou he swiftly began to revive them. Two military coups followed upon the death of Mamari. His first successor was assassinated because of his cruelty, and the kindly assassin was killed in turn for propagating Islam. In the wake of this second uprising, the entire Koulibali family was exterminated—with the exception of a pair of royal princesses whom N'Golo Diara managed to whisk off to safety. One of these he married. He also activated certain animist divinities in his behalf. (Hence the line about blood-sacrifice, a sign of his traditional piety.) This "stranger" of the morning was quick to impose order upon chaos by evening and sent the green youth off to complete the conquests begun by his renowned predecessor, Mamari. Thus he bent to his authority the inhabitants of Macina, of Djenné, of far-off Tombuctu and made of the Minianka a buffer state against the Mossi, who ultimately defeated him. For all power has its limits: You can order a young man to battle, but you cannot bring a casualty back to life again.

The source of this *burudyu* is Dominique Zahan's *La Dialectique du verbe chez les Bambara* (Paris-La Haye: Mouton, 1963), pp. 137–138.

MPANGU. The source of this *ndumbululu* is J. Van Wing, *Etudes Bakongo* Vol. I, Bibliothèque Congo No. 3 (Brussels: 1921), pp. 47–48.

When the Portuguese arrived at the mouth of the Zaire river in 1482 they found a kingdom, ruled by the Manikongo, that consisted of six principal provinces. One of them was called Mpangu, and this is the history of its eponymous ruling clan. It tells of a migration northeast from the place (Mbanza-Kongo in Mpemba province) where the capital of the kindom was situated. From a "hill of partition" near the site of Mbanza-Kongo, a company of chiefs were sent forth, each to claim his own parcel of territory and rule it on behalf of the Manikongo, who had led them in conquest. Which is to say that those who ruled the famous kingdom were strangers, in the beginning. No one knows whence these chiefs came, nor is it sure when the series of migrations to the provinces began. Father Van Wing says that of the Mpangu must have taken place at the end of the fourteenth century.

Convinced of the importance of clan praise-poems as historical evidence, Father Van Wing asked an old chief, renowned for his wisdom, to recite that of the Mpangu:

> For a long time he resisted, inventing a thousand pretexts, expressed in the form of proverbs. Finally, battle-fatigued, he threw off his leopard skin, seized his lance and executed a chiefly dance with stupefying suppleness and vigor. After which, he stood himself before me, fixed fiery eyes upon me and recited his *ndumbululu*.

What Van Wing learned was that the migration proceeded in stages. Having crossed the Inkisi river (which they called Nsimba: "hold-together"), where the paramount chief established a village, the clan broke up into factions and fanned out. The chief and his party went on to found the provincial capital, so Van Wing learned from other sources, on the banks of the Ngufu, affluent of the Inkisi. Was the woman who stayed behind ancestress of the reciting chief? Father Van Wing here does not elucidate.

OLUFE. Yoruba clan praises are called *oríkì orílè*, which salute group origins, mores, and distinguished founders of lineage. *Oríkì orílè* may be chanted by the wives of the household or by professionals. Among the bards who perform them are the Ijala singers, who gather to entertain assembled hunters, devotees of the God of Iron, at the annual festival of their common patron, primarily at funerals but upon other social occasions as well. Their repertoire includes lineage praises, praises of animals, of distinguished hunters, and of Ogun, the God of Iron, himself. This praise of the Olufe (royal) lineage of Ife, as performed by Adigun Alogunlofun, a master Ijala artist from Ibadan, was transcribed, translated, and annotated by S. A. Babalola in *The Content and Form of Yoruba Ijala* (Oxford, England: Oxford University Press, 1966), 118–122. What is especially interesting about this praise is its outsider's point of view. This is an exaggerated account of how the Ife people would strike a non-Ife person. They are "other"; in some respects they seem odd; and here and there the artist dramatizes oddness as downright weird. Thus the socially differentiating aspect of clan praises, rather than the belonging aspect, is placed in the foreground, though of some of his own contrasting ethnic habits Adigun makes cheerful mention. Using the Yoruba text and Babalola's notes, I have taken modest liberties with the English version in the interest of clarity, for the Ijala artist prides himself on the use of theatrical innuendo to characterize lineage notables, and it is difficult to appreciate this technique if references remain obscure to the point of mystification.

"Passing through"—The singer, an Oyo Yoruba, would not normally take time out to praise the people of Ife. In olden days it would have been downright dangerous to stop, because the people of Ife reputedly sacrificed human beings to their divinity and one might find oneself seized as victim. But to please them here he will metaphorically stretch himself full length.

"Reptilians"—The crocodile is a sacred animal in Life, as are earth-crawlers.

"Wagtail"—Babalola says this probably refers to a lookout at the city gate who was nicknamed "the wagtail bird."

"Exhibited cowards' corpses"—In wartime, all able-bodied men were conscripted; deserters, regarded as cowards, were publicly executed and their corpses exhibited.

"Ogunshere soup"—Leaves of the *ògúnshèrè* tree are commonly used in soup. The Olufe people, worshipers of Obatala, would prefer leaves from that divinity's sacred tree. "Slave" refers to the fact that the second ruler of Ife was a domestic servant, Adimu, whom the reigning king appointed regent during his absence. The epithet "slave" is applied to all sons and daughters of the royal family.

"I wash only my head with soap"—The royal familiy reputedly used medicinal charms in water during a once-and-for-all-time prophylactic ablution instead of taking a daily bath with treated soap and sponge. The singer treats only his head.

"In the backyard . . . source"—This is a contraction of two bits of lore: (a) One of the Olufe was named "The crown is sacred; it has a sacred water vessel like that placed in a divinity's shrine," and (b) The members of this family were the only ones permitted to use water from a pond formed by a stream that flowed behind the palace.

"Oruru's crown"—When the first king of Ile-Ife died, the diviners said that the eldest son (praise-named Oruru) should inherit all the crowns of his father and the second son (Oranyan) all the lands. Playfully, the second son snatched a crown from Oruru's head, saying, "You have enough, I'll take this away." Which he did, and became the Alafin of Oyo. All the crowned kings of the Yoruba traditionally derive their right to wear regalia from the first Olufe and recognize Ile-Ife as source of their civilization.

"Crown-of-divination"—*Ifa-ade* is a member of the Olufe lineage. The following line is a praise of his beauty.

"Igbin"—This drum is played by Obatala, highest-ranking divinity after the creator himself. Since Obatala shaped man, all persons having physical defects, like the "albino" and the "cripple," are sacred to him. Here we are at the shrine of Obatala; trespassers, we are not allowed in.

"Palm oil . . . bean cakes"—The singer effects a witty transition from Obatala worship to the cult of witchcraft (anticipated by "sorcerous-bird") as practiced by the Olufes. Obatala's sacrificial food must decidedly not be cooked with palm oil, but witches and wizards drink it, and they eat bean cakes.

"Prophetic voices"—Is it their witchcraft which enables the Olufe to make predictions, or rather their association with the cult of Ifa, oracle of the Yoruba, whose center is located in Ile-Ife? Apparently the latter, as the singer jovially compliments them on their success in the palm-kernel-oil trade. Palm nuts are the sacred counters of Ifa divination.

BERETUO. Among the Ashanti, the spirits of past clan chiefs are honored at Adae ceremonies, which occur twice during each of the forty-day cycles by which time is traditionally measured. On such occasions these distinguished ancestors, whose blackened thrones are sacrificed to, also receive tribute from the reigning chief's exclusive talking drums. The drummers begin by awakening the spirits dwelling in the various components of the instrument: cedar tree from which the shell is fashioned, elephant whose ear provides skin for the head, the wood of the pegs and the fiber of the strings that fastened down the tightly stretched head. They also awaken the spirits of earth and sky, aspects of creation which made these materials available and lesser divinities like witches who might interfere with the praise-task if not properly placated.

The *atumpan* drummer rightly considers himself to occupy an extremely important position in the world. He is the only human being permitted to drum these sacred praise-histories, *yampeaa*. His counterpart in the planetary world is the moon and in the animal kingdom, Kokoyinaka, a beautiful dark blue bird, whose drumlike call originally provided an idiophonic model for *yampeaa*. Of the three primal beings created, the drummer takes the mid-position between herald and executioner. He represents experience, a mean between the extremes of being and becoming, or knowledge mediating between order (logos) and process (nature).[2] Which is why, metaphorically associating his vigilant consciousness with creation's dawning, he speaks of himself as the "divine drummer."

R. S. Rattray, one of the first field anthropologists in Africa, recorded the *yampeaa* of the Beretuo clan on an old-fashioned cylinder apparatus in 1921; his text was published in *Ashanti* (Oxford, England: Oxford University Press, 1923), pp. 266–285. The eminent Ghanaian musicologist J. H. Nketia reports having checked on the accuracy of Rattray's text and found it fairly good, so I have used it as the start of my English version, which also relies on "awakening" material printed in Nketia's *Drumming in Akan Communities* (London: Nelson and Sons, 1963), ch. 2, passim, and upon a fairly recent clan history collected in Mapong by Eva Meyerowitz and published in *The Early*

[2] See J. B. Danquah, *The Akan Doctrine of God* (1944; reprinted. London: Krank Cass, 1968), ch. III.

History of the Akan States of Ghana (London: Red Candle Press, 1974).
The spelling of the names of the nine ancestors praised here is that
given by Meyerowitz and to her I am also indebted for their vitae.

Asiama Guahyia is the ancestress of the branch of the Beretuo clan
that founded the principality of Mampong—eventually a part of the
Ashanti confederacy, established by the famous Osei Tutu, who
reigned as first Ashantehene from 1701 to 1730. She in turn is the
descendant of Asiama Nyame, the mother of the entire clan, who
came down from the sky. Where? According to clan tradition, which
merges the two Asiamas, the village of Ahensan in Adanse was the
rocky origin-site. However, recent research suggests that the neolithic
dwelling place of the Beretuo was the cliffs of Bandiagara, now in-
habited by the Dogon. In the langauge of the *yampeaa,* stone-ax
means old (immemorial) environment, and is therefore attributed to
the founded city, locus of clan power, Mampong.

Kwaakye Panyin and Baafo Atiadu were Asiama's first and second
sons. It was the latter who completed the migration begun by his
mother in the late seventeenth century. His successor, Maniampong,
is praised in warlike imagery because it was he who added territory
to "Old" Mampong by conquering neighboring peoples. His successor,
Boahin Anantuo, as commander of Osei Tutu's army, defeated the
Denkyira, thus ensuring his clan an important position in the Ashanti
confederacy. Under the sixth ruler, Mampong's location was trans-
ferred to what appeared initially to be a safer location. Sekyire, men-
tioned in this sixth praise—of Boaten Akumoa—is the name of the
region surrounding Mampong. The eighth clan chief, Asumgyina, was
the son of a herald, a fact that occasions the recital of the creation of
the three primal men. The herald's ritual cap is made of Colobus
monkey skin and adorned with a solar disk of gold. The drummer's
heritage is "a good master" to teach him well that he may not falter
in his task. The "death-dance" (*atopre*), with its energetic movements,
is performed by the chief as he accomplishes the ceremonial shooting
in honor of his ancestors at the triennial Odwira festival of purifica-
tion. It was also performed, under constraint, by someone accused of
treason, moments before his state execution. The ninth praise-history,
and the last given here, includes a sacred song ("Stream crosses
path . . ."), proverbial in its application to man's spiritual dependency,
often used to evoke the water-principle in man and nature.

"Condolences, condolences" is the drummer's refrain directed to the surviving head-of-clan, in whom a *yampeaa* recital arouses a solemn sorrow, reflections upon sovereign transience akin to those expressed by Shakespeare's Richard II.

TSHIMINI. *Baluba badi ne miaku misheme:* "The Luba have fine words."

Common pride of language enables visitors of other, even hostile, lineages to appreciate a well-sung *kasàlà*, lengthy praise-song of the Luba people of Kasai and Katanga in eastern Zaire. Well-sung also implies well-constructed, exploiting with utmost refinement the sonorous possibilities of the CiLuba langauge. What one might call the potential *kasàlà* belonging to each male lineage is a cryptic record of people associated with virtues, with events, and with one another, as remembered through many generations. The singer rearranges parts at his discretion, interlarding them with social comment and personal reflections, stated most often in proverbial or anecdotal form. The genealogical and to some extent the moral perspective of any performance will always be that of the reigning chief, who keeps the sacred objects that hold the kinsmen together.

Kasàlà bards (unlike their counterparts elsewhere) are not members of a closed fraternity, to whom a stiff fee must be paid. The rigors of their profession, not the least of which is the expected "method" performance, have always been considered sufficient sacrifice to the shades of their predecessors. The art is learned through informal apprenticeship, and the artist is dependent for his living upon the goodwill of his audience.

In earlier times the *kasàlà* was sung in battle by a noncombatant to inspire lineage leaders and their warriors, particularly when things were going badly, and was also performed at funerals of chiefs. The genre was revived during the prelude to Zairian independence, when martial praise-songs were broadcast over the radio in secessionist areas. They continue to be sung at funerals, now at those of lesser clansmen as well, upon occasions requiring arduous communal work, and during ceremonies marking personal achievement, thus reflecting prestige on the group, such as the ordination of a priest or the certification of a teacher.

The traditional performance, with its litany of dead heroes, was designed to move the audience through a state of remorseful yearning toward a desire for action. To the initiated elders of the community, however, the *kasàlà* communicated on a different level, consonant with the philosophical detachment achieved through discipline and experience.

This *kasàlà*, collected and published in CiLuba and Flemish by R. van Caeneghem ("De Kasala-zang der Bakwa-Tshimini," *Congo* XVIII, 1 [1937], pp. 107–120), honors the reigning chief of the Tshimini, Kabuta Mpatu, great-great-granson of the lineage hero, Mulamba, whose genealogy can be traced back six more generations to the eponymous founder. The praise begins with a twelve-line invocation of Tshimini, followed by the clan motto, in turn followed by the heroic song of Mulamba, the Tshimini ideal personified. The battle song, here patently complimenting the chief's departed father, is the fourth canonical part of the Tshimini *kasàlà;* the reprise of its martial strain lends unity to the recitation, as does the use of Mulamba's glory as a leitmotif throughout. The balance of the piece consists of scattered memories of past greatness, reminders of human strength and frailty as exemplified by Tshimini behavior and of genealogical, political, and territorial ties—evocative of colonial disruption—interspersed with quodlibets on the part of the bard, whose train of thought can be deduced only through a close reading of sequences and appositions. Features ascribed to particular personages, if seen to apply more generally, follow an undeniable logic of association. The brief textual notes that follow are based on extensive comment appended to the original Flemish version by van Caeneghem.

"Eagle"—The white eagle, from which the lineage founder derived his name, is the protecting and protected spirit of the group.

"To whom was presented the leopard . . . to drink beer at Mulamba's"—Any leopard killed during the hunt was presented to the chief; such trophies were presented to Mulamba even though he had not been elected to that office. His elder brother, Tshiongo, had been successful in *his* candidacy and therefore should have been brought feast food and beer, but Mulamba defied custom and treated Tshiongo like a younger brother.

"Hill . . . hill . . . hill . . . palm-stem wrapped in antelope skin"— Until they were moved by the colonial administration for reasons of military and political convenience, villages used to be built on hills. This recital of the Bowa hill settlements, which must have stirred bitter memories, is augmented by the image of the antelope skin, a sign of power and evocative in this context of former grandeur.

"All valiant men"—Past heroes, headmen, and warriors under Mulamba's command.

"Thatch-perching insect . . . Tshiaba"—Mulamba is described as too heroic in size and too fastidious to live in an ordinary house, with millet stored on the second floor. Tshiaba and his son were fighters from another Luba lineage; the singer implies that Mulamba's importance was not merely parochial.

"Burning heat which never harmed the house"—A riddle, the answer to which is the sun.

"Stingy Kamuania"—The chief's paternal aunt: her gesture is the opposite of the acceptable invitation to share food. This trait seems to run in the family—compare Mulamba's household, above.

"Second wife's house . . . first wife's yard"—This is a warning not to retreat. The chief's medicines and regalia were stored in the first wife's house, his precious iron in the second wife's.

"Executioner . . . fratricide"—The men involved in the incident recalled here are mentioned by title rather than by name. Kazela, official Defender of the clan, was a reckless person, responsible for the death of two of his brothers. This verse, like those before and after it, hints at dark disorders.

" 'Forceful' . . . cooking"—Why should she cook for him? He brought her no meat from his hunting expedition.

"Hill . . . hill . . . potting"—Places where the Tshimini used to live before the whites made them resettle along the highway.

"Husband . . . Ntumba"—These women recall interlineage affiliations through marriage.

"Grasshoppers"—This is an example of helpful behavior. Both chickens and people like to eat grasshoppers.

"Cock bound to a stake . . . swallowed and survived"—The singer here refers to two incidents involving Mulumba, one of the heroic Mulamba's sons: first, a quarrel between Tshibangu and Mulumba, who eventually won out; and second, Mulumba's surviving of a "poison trial," which involved swallowing a *kapulu* fruit.

"Hunts without protective charms"—The Tshimini are successful hunters, who disdain the flesh of domesticated animals. The strong hunter, by village custom, is forbidden supernatural hunting aids.

"A door gapped by cold?"—Only if the door is improperly constructed, with chinks in it.

"Killed a leopard . . . antelope"—A heroic formula, a slot into which any two distinguished names can be set. In this case they are headmen in the time of Katekelayi, the hero Mulamba's great-great-grandfather. Have their particulars been forgotten?

"Basket . . . spirit wanderer"—Extremes of Tshimini behavior. They avoid unnecessary quarrels and yet are capable of the most evil sorcery.

"Brother-in-law"—A bitchy woman complains about her husband. The singer thinks this theme so amusing that he goes on with it a few lines later.

———

"Crammed into another pack"—A reference to the time the Mpatu, defeated by the Kaanunfu (both branches of the Tshimini clan), took refuge with the Kaninda people. Later, having made peace, the Mpatu returned to their homeland.

IV: *Lamentations of Women*

SU-DOM: AKAN FUNERAL DIRGES

ADUANA CLAN
Karikari Poti of Asumgeya
When I am on my way, do not let me meet
Believe-me, the terror
It is Karikari Poti, the Terror
Who spells death to those who meet him.
Pampam Yiadom Boakey Akum-ntem
Grandchild of Karikari Poti from the town
Across the river, near our sacred grove
Where the leopard roars, comes to town for its prey.
O Mother
What about us?
O Mother
Your children and I will feed on the spider
Now even the mouse is too big a game.

(Twi)

BERETUO CLAN
Grandam Gyaamma Kani of Sekyire
The slim but strong woman
She must concentrate on one thing
She would start a new farm
Then stop to keep the old one going
She would find material for trapping
Then stop to tackle cloth-weaving.

Grandchild of Gyaamma Kani comes from
Kontonkyi in Sekyire
Where the stone wears down the ax.

(Twi)

ABOADEE NTORO
Ofosuaa Nyanee, precious bead that strings others
The woman who grinds millet in her ritual vessels
Offspring of Nwanwanyane Aduanwoma Mmubuo.

When on my way to Seewaa's house
I tread on skulls
Returning from Seewaa's house
I tread on jaws.
It is she, Seewaa Kotoropabi
Whose shade trees are bearing tears and teeth
Offspring of Nwanwanyane Aduanwoma Mmubuo.

(Twi)

AFUA FOFIE GRIEVES FOR HER MOTHER
Grandchild of Kwaagyei of Hwedeemu, who drinks
    water from the sacred lake at Abono
Daughter of a spokesman, herself an orator
Mother, it may appear that all is well with me
    but I am struggling.
Nyaako of Anteade, grandchild of Agyeman, the priest
O Mother, I am struggling, all is not right as it appears!
Mother, if you would send me something, I would like
    a parcel and a big cooking pot, generous to strangers.

The god of the sea has failed; the medicine gourd
    has vanquished
O Mother, there is no branch above me to grasp.
Mother, if you would send me something, I would like
    parched corn
So I could eat it raw, were there no fire for cooking.

Mother, the parrot will catch a skin disease from the
     fowls and die!
Grandchild of Kwaagyei of Hwedeemu, who drinks
     water from the sacred lake at Obono
Mighty cooking pot, savior of strangers
Mother, it may appear that all is well with me
     but I am struggling.
Mother who sends gifts, send me something when someone
     is coming this way.

Mother, there is no fire in the deserted dwelling
From which I could take a brand to light my own.
Helpful wicker basket, coming to my aid with lumps of salt
O Mother, I would weep blood for you, if only this were
     allowed Otire's child.

Grandparent, crab that knows the hiding place of
     alluvial gold
What is the matter, child of the spokesman?
Mother has allowed this death to take me by surprise.
O Mother, I am struggling, all is not right as it appears.

                                                          (Twi)

AMBA ETSIWABA GRIEVES FOR HER MOTHER
Ee Mama, Mama! Aba Ya *ee!*
You know how things are.

Mama *ee ee ee* Mama *ee!*
Mama, you know all, come over.
Mama *ee ee ee* Mama *ee!*
Ee yea ye we're in sorrow.

Mama *ee* you know how things are here
You know there's no one with your wisdom
Mama *ee*
Mama *ee,* so long away from
Your children. O woe!

Mama *ee*
You know how things are: separated.
"Far-off place" is nowhere
So, when someone's coming our way
Send us something in our need.
Mama Aba
Aba Yaa *ee*
You know how things are—still the same, the same;
Mama, store of our being *ee*
We, the household of Abokyi
We're doing all we can, in vain.

Ee
"Far off place" means nowhere to go, Aba Yaa *ee*
Left alone in an empty house, we are abandoned children
Abandoned little ones, Mama Aba Yaa.

Ee
Who would return, bring breath to us?
Who but Father Adom: may he then come!
Ee ayee ayee ayee, often, I say, we have to struggle—O.

May our people stop by now and again: we're running
    out of credit;
In time of war, needy heads confer together, Mama Mama *ee*
Store of our being, come bring back breath *ee*
You know how things are here:
Abandoned little ones among ruins to rebuild Mama, Aba Ya;
We, the household of Abokyi
We're doing all we can, in vain:
Please send someone, now and again, our way
When someone is coming by here, do send help, help
    sought in vain.

Mama *ee* who will accompany us when we're going?
Will Ansa? Ah, no one's remaining.
When we're troubled, we don't know—no place to turn.
If only Father Adom, would he come!

O help help help us!
When someone is coming along
Send help!

Our people left long ago—O
From our ancestral home comes child of Parrot-eats-palm-nuts,
Amba: I can find nowhere to go—
My grandfather: the one who weighed gold
And the scales broke;
I, Amba Adoma
Member of grandfather Kese's household;
We don't know where to go! May they come
Our people, we are very low
So when someone's passing this way
Send us something
Yes
I'm grandchild of Parrot-eats-palm-nuts.

(Fante)

NDAAYÀ'S *KASÀLÀ*
A *Dirge for Ntumba, Her Nephew*

(1)   O *yo i wee yoo o yee*
                  yo yee e yoo!
        Ntumba, son of the Kalombaayi
                  from Mwamba Kabooka's territory
        While I am begging, why do you injure me?
                  You, son of the Ngandu from Chief Makanda's
                      village?
        While I am praising you, son of the Ntanda
                  of the Kalomba, whose bodies gleam from
                      stream-bathing?
        He! Ntumba, son of the Ngandu
        While I'm calling you, son of the Muuka from our farthest
            frontier
                  Me, tidy *nyunyu* bird, deep skimmer
                  daughter of the Angry, who pocket their spleen

While I supplicate, why do you flee
    O son of the Kalombaayi
    of the terrible house of Mukanya
    of the "councilor" people, Ciloole?
You, breaker of roads
    like our lineage litigants who leave
    everything razed to the ground when they flee.

(2)   *O yo yo i wee yo e yee!*
Child born after graves accumulate—turmoil's termite
    heaps
You've ruined my homecoming for me
    daughter of the talkative Mushiilaayi
    of Nkongolo, our founder with the glazed face of
        pottery
    of Ntanda, incisive-tongued
    of Nkongolo—none dared interrupt while he was
        speaking
    of the talkative Mushiilaayi
    who wore bush paths into roads with their feet.
Why is this journey destroyed for me?
    Daughter of the Ngandu of Chief Makanda's village
    of the Mutumbo of Mwamba's district
    of Malaba: Broom-reconciles-rubbish
    of Nsaka: "Those people would be better off with
        scrap hoes:
    disarm them!" of the talkative Mushiilaayi.

(3)   I stand at the crossroads
        among those who settled by salt lakes
        "wife" of Ribs-showing and his father, Katende
        me, Ndaaya, from Ribs-showing's son's village.
Ntumba, named for one who dared strike his mother
        yours belongs to the Kaboya serpent: never bites
        a Mbuyamba, a Mupompa, she.
Ntumba, son of Nkongolo, whetstone, sacred rock amid the
    plain

defender of his people
hunchback daring the sword
of heroic dimensions: there is he!
Nkongolo, inheritor of the sun's first rays
So I glorify you through your parents' names.
Ntumba, mother-striker, why such stubborn silence?
Are we fighting? Isn't this a conversation?
Such a war, your male death, recruits men only:
Were it woman's affair, I'd take up my pestle!
 Me, chicken men chase after nightfall
 songbird, daughter of those who never fled enemy
 nor disclaimed their sorcery.

(4) I stand at the crossroads
  (O Mbombo, my darling daughter
  from Fertile Hill—friendly house of crops
  from Repulsive River—muddies calabashes)
Me, Ndaaya, daughter of the frontier
I fall silent, daughter of the Ngandu
 of the "councilor" people;
 restless songbird quit her village
 of the Angry people where Kalonji
 head of the chalk-mining team
 sits down to skin a crocodile
 near the grotto peopled with vampires
 where, nowadays, cattle would come to drink
 for the river turns out to contain riches
 so we scrub ourselves with twenty-franc notes when
  we bathe
 careful to save the hundred-franc notes for
  headscarves!
But tears won't revive the dead—fill a jar first
Why then have I come calling *beebeleebele* across the
 frontier?
Why am I here, I, Ndaaya, "wife" of Kabooka the strong
 of Peaceful-quail: promenades in the bush
 of Miscellaneous-inundation

of Intrepid-goat
of Red-cricket?

(5)   O mother of Ntumba, *beebeleebeele wee yoo*
Why then have I come to these lamentations?
Finding myself in a house filled with people
I will praise you, my own mother, from Mukendi's village
    daughter of the Mbaayi
    of the Lungu, my dear
    of the Mulangaa Kabongo.
Nor would I forget my father
    Nkasa of the numerous friendships
    beele beebeebeleebeele
    son of Grandmother Ndaaya
    Sorcerer's-stare-sees-soul's-double
    Nkongolo Mutombo, generous father
    drew souls to your side as if by sorcery.
Father, since you abandoned me,
I have become a wanderer
    in porridge-fullness time
    in hunger-season
Shelterless against the heat, I carry my household
    including Shade-tree-of-my-mother-in-law
    bundled up in my cloth;
    three days in the village
    four on the road
But who will go call my father
    Nkasa of the numerous friendships
    brother of Cibangu:
    Dry season discloses sociable paths through the
        bush?
Canoe uses up oars: Long, long have I been praising you,
    Father
    powerful son of the ritual wife
    sword-point recoiling upon the thrust;
    provoke the lion
    never the feeble antelope;
    leopard has entered the forest

    black mongoose won't follow;
        bongo antelope has entered the forest
        other peaceful ruminants will follow.
May hate cease to burn what's painfully constructed!
O Father, leopard-defender, long praised with no result!
For I have gone to bed troubled
I have laid me down with a divided heart:
        seeking my father
        seeking my mother
        daughter of Marches-at-the-head-of-the-army
        brother of Assassin-be-careful-of-your-sword!
And you, Mukanga, surnamed Cidiila
How could I neglect my grandfather?
        brother of Assassin-eats-upon-iron-of-his-sword
        Sword-handle, richly embellished, bejeweled, incised:
        kid can't knock down banana tree on his own
        billy goat must butt in!

(6)   At the crossing of the roads I stand
      I, Ndaaya, "wife" of *beebeleebeele*, the inheritor
      The mouth that betrays reopens to praise
      To plead for the one who has given herself away;
      Save me, Ndaaya, helpless "wife" of the strong
      Here at roads' crossing.

      Why then have I come to these lamentations?
      The heart has a home it will enter soon; Ndaaya,
      I come from the village vanity dishonors
            where flattery unleashed false pride.
      Need I expatiate upon *that* Kalonji?
            Arsenal of hopes in the popular mind
            beleebeleebelele, son of the ritual wife
            Canoe devours oars: talking, talking.
            We avert our eyes
            lest he read our minds
            As the knotted tree to the blunt ax, Kalonji
            Cane wand attracting truth to its side
            it's around Kalonji we're all grouped:

the Anga and the Nsumpi lineages
the Ndoba and the Bowa lineages
the Nshimba and the Manda lineages
and Kalonji's own Nsana;
Conquering independence for the lower Kasai
he gave it away to imbeciles
knotty tree-trunk, son of the ritual wife
Such, truly is a man's size!
Leopard, son of those who never fled enemies
Warrior, of the unyielding shield
of those not to be restrained from the charge.

(7)   On to our village now!
I would praise you, Kabonda
O man of the raging heart
offspring of courage contorted like iron
who never counted men of the opposing side
whose own bravery sufficed;
I would praise you, Mulumba, warriors' pride
Dry-season-never-calm
Bird of Yamba plain, of Ngoma forest
offspring of those swept up in the turbulence and
thrown
into Kangu River, which their piled corpses dried;
I would praise you again, Kabonda
offspring of those who've set their butts on the
Cikuuya:
hardened banks won't be budged from the
Cikuuya.
Listen, you would-be politicians
Life on earth there was before man sprouted
Tough weeds there were before hoes met
resistance.

(8)   Where am I? Standing my ground at the crossroads.
Running short, I've pounded past sundown
stray chicken men chase after nightfall.
Can a childless woman ever be wealthy, comrades?

Woman who loves to be on the go, that's Ndaaya
    in porridge-fullness time
    in hunger-season
    exposed to the heat of the sun.
Listen, sister, human things alter:
    young, a woman becomes old
    she-goat turns billy-goat
    another, having given birth
    look, suddenly she's sterile!

Now I want to praise Beeya, strong of body
Thunder! *ee yo yoo i yoo* how could I have forgotten
Beeya, leopard, nephew who conquered my heart
    kinsman of Nkongolo, of Kanyiki, of Kazaadi-the-
        strong
    born to Nsantu Kanyeba:
    pounder of manioc
    grinder of corn
    hard-working woman of the Anga people
    from Conveyor-belt: headquarters of the mining
        corporation
    son of those who consume the inedible
    young man of the cemetery:
    on the way to which, fancy asphalt
    laid down on sandy base buckled.

(9)   Child promised to restore a grieving mother
    I swore never more to set foot in a house of tears
        swore to sing no more lamentations;
        those sung before in my own house
        unearthed heart-springs.
    Glib-to-speak: you're mere children who've seen nothing
    Me, I've already seen what cannot be untied:
        I lay down, fluttering like a falcon
        eye throbbed as heart pounded
        sword smote my kidneys
    Even now, at the thought, *ntung, ntung, ntung*
        so speaks the sick heart of Ndaaya

as when eyes discover a wild animal
as when hand of hungry man, red with oil, advances
    toward porridge
as when bride beholds husband.
Ntumba, wait until I send you a message:
    pass by, remember me to Beeya, the student
    pass by, salute [my mother, the singer]
    and don't forget to visit my father
    brother of Cibangu, leopard.
Beeya, Conciliator, united the family of men
    in "porridge" village, where Katenda herded his
        followers
    my own village, where men browse, gorge themselves
    on applause
    where vanity dishonors. Didn't hired flatterers
    so swell up Katenda's son that he fed on his own kin?
Why then have I come to these lamentations?

(10)   Dear brothers, this death of yours is men's affair
O Ntumba, were it women's affair, I would brandish my
    pestle!
    Daughter of the Kalombaayi
    why I am what I am remains impenetrable:
    Born a man, me they would have handed a sword
    should I not then have become a hero?
    Wouldn't I have known how to fight as they fight—
    at dawn like the Kabwela
    in broad daylight like the Mboobo? . . .
Dear brothers, death came to me like a thief in the night
    as I went to bed with a divided heart
    daughter of "the talkative."
Today the funeral drums are calling me to sing:
    Ah, were voice strong as drum
    already mine would have reached my mother! . . .

(11)   Yes, war has ravaged me today, sister of Cibangu
    but who remains to protect Ndaaya
    daughter of "the talkative"?

I must call my companions, but who will respond?
  who procure for me a Defender?
I stand at the crossroads, mother of "moral force"
  I have trapped bitter crickets
  I have grubbed for ashen cicadas
And I go to bed with a divided heart:
  restless, I have counted beams
  vagabond, I have counted roofs
Daughter of the Kalombaayi, bathing till their bodies gleam
Ah, brothers, misfortunes weigh me down, Ndaaya:
  in one direction orphan
  in the other direction sterile
What can I say that you men might believe me?

(12)   Ah, daughter of the Kalombaayi, human things alter:
    young, a woman becomes old
    she-goat turns billy-goat
    having given birth
    look, suddenly she's sterile.
  Did I not give birth to a child with gums strong as cut
    teeth?
  O daughter, since you went away I've been inconsolable
    my child, of the Muuya people, of the Mulumba
    of the Citenda who live in Mwanza's village.
  O daughter, see how women of my age group prosper:
    third wives moved up to first place
    first wives cast off, or demoted.
  At the crossroads I call Mbombo
  Daughter placed in my womb by ritual
  And then fall silent
  For going along the road I remember
    we passed a "satisfied" man
    who stared her up and down;
    in my own eye I felt the shock [of his evil one]
    then, heart-knock
    sword smote my kidneys

Even now my heart jumps, *ntung, ntung, ntung*
As when eyes uncover a wild animal.

(13)   Stop, my song!
              song of the daughter of Katende-Kabooka village
              where there are no stray goats
         If I sing one more word may I be broken!
         May ghosts, sorcerers steal me away in the night!
         Sister of Cibangu [the hunter]!

(Luba)

EKÚN ÌYÀWÓ; THE BRIDE'S LAMENT

VARIOUS WOMEN OF ÒYÓ
My father, thank you for indulging me

My mother, thank you for making me comfortable
and for clothing me with the best: with wisdom.
Children I shall bear will tend to you with fondness.

The *eda* rat is always attentive
My father, Akande, "Seeing is greeting honor"
Wood turned into ceiling beams remains motionless
Rat—always responsive to its offspring's cries
Father, hearing my voice, arise.

The house in which a child is nursed without dying
The house in which a child is nursed without falling sick
Bidding farewell, one would not look at such a house reprovingly.

How to keep from disgracing oneself,
Child of 'Lalonpe?
Once arrived at one's husband's house,
how to avoid making clumsy mistakes?

Asked to perform a task requiring maturity of mind,
how to ensure adult behavior?
how to keep from behaving like a child?

Sour water has been ill-treated.
Misuse is often the lot of buckets of rain.
One could be insulted in another person's house
Ejide, simply for being someone else's offspring.

When I feel lonely
I'll return to our family house
Something painful—one needs to share it
But I have no one to confide in now,
Child of esteemed Kuluku.
My friend, you and I have sat eating pounded yam
while raking foolish people over the coals
We have eaten ọkà together, gossiping mercilessly
My friend, our miniskirts those days prevented us
from bending down to roll the mortar out of the way
But when it comes to pounding and embracing
Ibironke, "Two have arrived," I'm on my own.

A certain river, a certain river
that flows through the bush
Those who walk in front dare not drink
Those who walk behind dare not bathe
But I, Ayoka, reaching that hidden river, wash my face
and all at once become an elegant woman.
My waist is strung with lovely beads
Count them, beloved age-mates
If any are missing, strip me naked.

Everybody's been taking lovers
I chose a lover and couldn't prevent pregnancy
I tried to abort myself, abort myself
but that medicine he deceitfully recommended
that love-medicine was no remedy, at all!

If bad luck dogs a hunter, lack of bushmeat seems endless.
And farmers, a few withering years
and ensuing harvests seem out of the question.
When misfortune haunts a woman, barrenness seems inevitable.
But wait, your *ori* [head: intimate spirit] is only being capricious.
You will become pregnant
and, God willing, give birth to plenty of children.

CHORUS: Dry up, river, that she may pass
                           Dry up, river, that she may pass
                           The bride's sandals never step on soggy
                               ground
                           Dry up, that she may pass [without incident].

Commiseration, members of the household
Commiseration, travelers on your various journeys
The pounded-yam seller of Oke-Apo felt so sorry for me
    though her yam was well-cooked and ready to peel,
    she misplaced her knife, when I appeared.

                                                    (Yoruba)

SUSANNAH FARAMADE OF ÒKUKÙ (RÁRÀ ÌYÀWÓ)
Clear the way and make room
Make way, and go gently
And let me see my mother
May good luck attend me today.

I'm going to my new home now
I'm going to my home to have money
I'm going to my new home now
I'm going to my home to bear children
If you say your good luck will escort me
It will escort me right to my room
May good luck attend me today.

I would have liked to be a hunter, but I have no quiver
I would have liked to be a blacksmith, but I have no bellows

When I would have liked to go on living in my father's house
I, Abike Omotanbaje
Child of the Okin people, I did not turn into a man
May good luck attend me today.

"Speak on, speak on," that's the way of the pestle
"Keep talking, keep talking," that's the way of the stirring-stick
If you want me to speak, I could speak until tomorrow
It's my work, it's my trade
I never weary of it
I don't get bored with it
Laying your head on your arms doesn't end your trouble
Complaining to everyone doesn't pay your debts
Even the people who work have no money [*i.e., how much less the
      lazy man!*]
Sweet potato grows abundant leaves
Children will inherit from all of us
I lived by the sea, I know the sea
I lived by the lagoon too, I know the lagoon
And this is my return from the sea
The day will never dawn when the cat doesn't go hunting
May good luck attend me today.

White cowries bear witness to wealth
White beads bear witness to a worshiper
Whatever child I may bear
I, Abike, "The child put an end to disgrace,"
I say, indeed, he will bear witness for me.

I've left the stage of "Come in the evening"
I've left the stage of "Drop in on your way back"
I've joined the club of mothers of newborn babies
Mother of a newborn baby that is a boy
May good luck attend me today.

They're making arrangements about the ram
The ram is grazing in the yard
When I was not in the house
"Laughing-teeth," they made arrangements about me

They plotted and planned
Plotted and planned till they got the date-fixing fee
Got the date-fixing fee, but the rest is left to me alone
May good luck attend me today.

I am not yet tired of young girls' games
A towering head-tie is not big enough for me to wear to market
Cloth of a pound a yard is not enough to wind round my head
But now I've left that time behind
"Laughing teeth," thanks to my father's standing
May good luck attend me today.

The family enjoys the privileges of the family
Someone born among us enjoys the privileges of being one of us
The farm-hut enjoys its own privileges in the farm
The *gongo* worm enjoys his in the dung-hill
The forge enjoys the privileges of the pliers
And I enjoy the privileges of my mother
May good luck attend me today.

When I was coming to earth
My mother, I brought 14,000 cowries' worth of kola
When I was coming to earth
My mother, I brought 12,000 cowries's worth of kola
Not because of death, not because of disease
But because of the co-wives of the world
The kind that are your enemies from birth
Whatever co-wife I may have
Child of the Òkín people, may she behave like a mother to me
May good luck attend me today.

My mother did me proud, to my satisfaction
She didn't let me beg for clothes from the abusive
She didn't let me beg for clothes from the scurrilous
I wear cloth that is my delight
She didn't let me wear shoddy cloth through the town
May good luck attend me today.

(Yoruba)

COMMENTARY
For Nini

. . . Sister, I'll play her part;
You heard what Creon said,
"Pass then, to the world of the dead,
And if you needs must love, love them;
While I live no woman shall rule me."

Banished, banished again.
Once we contained it all
Now, condensed to our cooking pots,
Banished
To the dark half, to the bitter end;
Doorways of houses we once were,
Apertures standing at the brink
Or east or west,
And life slips easily through our practiced hands.

We have carried our stools to the House of Lamentations
There sit we down and sing out over the end,
Calling loss back from oblivion,
Clothing the lineaments of the dead,
Recalling not one but all, all . . .

Women across the continents and centuries have everything to learn
from one another. Once, deeply discouraged by the course my own
life seemed to be taking, I declaimed a poem called "Impersonating
Antigone," in which the voice of Ndaaya from the Kasai slips into the
consciousness of Sophocles' heroine in order to comment on the cul-
tural definition of women. Midwives and mourners—in these capac-
ities the powers that be have always conceded our competence!

Clan praises in the mode of lamentation are performed by women
experts across the continent of Africa from Ghana to eastern Zaire.

SU-DOM: FUNERAL DIRGES OF THE AKAN. Many are the musical
and verbal expressions mobilized to make an Akan funeral as exciting
and important as custom demands. There are drums and bands with

trained vocalists, and there may be pipes, horns; but there must be dirge-singing—the prerogative as it is the obligation of ordinary women. Traditionally, mothers taught daughters a full repertoire of clan dirges; and as they grew older, some women began to excel in their interpretations of the various fixed forms of the genre. An Akan woman need not confine herself to a single dirge format; in the course of a funeral celebration she may, if she has the skill and knowledge, express herself continuously in various types, from the most classical to the most improvisatory.

J. H. Nketia says that the formal differences between the "dirge" and the "lament," also sung at funerals, are attributable to their diverse purposes. The lament is a generalized statement about the brevity of human life; the dirge bears down upon the immediate occasion, addresses the deceased as a member of a family, and expresses individual grief. Akan dirges are begun when preliminary and private rites for the corpse are completed; they announce the start of public mourning and continue throughout the funeral, even in the midst of other musical tributes paid for by the bereaved family.

The women of the household begin to wail, and as the singing mounts in intensity, friends and neighbors rush in to greet the bereaved and contribute their dirges *ad libitum*; for one death recalls another, and not all dirges are sung for the dead person the funeral is specifically honoring. The singers of dirges, Nketia says, rarely sit down. They pace back and forth, accompanying their songs with graceful motions of the body and head. "The arms may be seen clasped across the breast or in front of the body or held at the sides or at the back or supported on the head—all to convey the anguish of the singer to the gathering." Occasionally a flick of the head or hand punctuates a statement. These are kinetic patterns we associate with the blues. Dirges are not, strictly speaking, for dancing. This comes later, with the band's arrival.

A striking poetic feature of all dirges is the use of imagery of oral dependence: bereavement expressed as nutritive deprivation: "great breast run dry." This is balanced by the attribution, as if in angry frustration, of aggressive male energies to the ancestor, male or female, to whom the mourned person is metaphorically as well as genealogically connected. As these counterpointed emotions find expression, the singer at the same time reaffirms the links binding all individuals to the persistent community. This process is intended to strengthen the recently dead person's soul in its transition from one state of being to another and concurrently to remind that soul of its future obligations to the living.

The poems given here are from J. H. Nketia's collection, *Funeral Dirges of the Akan People* (1955; reprint ed. New York: Negro Universities Press, 1969). Page references for each selection will be given below. All but the last dirge are in the Twi dialect of the Akan language. Amba Etsiwaba expresses herself in Fante. I have, in the interest of clarity, edited Nketia's English versions; if, in so doing, I have in any way perverted the meaning, may he forgive me! With the final dirge I have hazarded a phonetic experiment. For this poem, "Amba Etsiwaba Grieves . . . ," Nketia, in an appendix, gives a musical transcription and a Fante text that includes the ejaculations of sorrow (*ee*, etc.) missing from the dirges printed as poems. Working with the suspensions, the measured rhythms, and the phrasing of the musical version, I have tried to come up with an English rendering that would give some sense of live performance.

Aduana Clan. Each Akan belongs to one of seven principal matrilineal clans, each of which has its own dirge-language. But the format of dirges follows pan-Akan literary tradition. Nketia has isolated four standard dirge types (but I have given only three). The first, exemplified here, is sung for an individual-as-clan-member. This one is a tribute appropriate to any Aduana—that is, the references and expressions are typical of Aduana dirge-singing and the name of a particular deceased (here italicized) is simply added at the correct place in the poem.

The format of type one is fairly rigorous. The first sentence gives the name of a lineage ancestor and is followed by an extension of that name, a phrase revealing character. In this case, "Believe-me" is a strong-name equivalent to "the Terror": Karikari was a man to be believed; whatever his announced target, he was an unfailing marksman and therefore someone to be feared. After the praise-extension, the name of the deceased is inserted and linked to the ancestor ("Grandchild of"). At this point a hallowed place of ancestral origin is mentioned, a reference meant to draw assembled clan mourners toward their common source, beyond any particular ancestor one could mention. The "sacred grove" here is that of Santemanso, whose shrines are tended by the Aduana clan. There are ruins there of a town that historians believe was founded about 1600. When this town was destroyed, the Aduana moved across the river and founded Asumgeya. The final section indicates the effect of the death of this particular person on the singer. The metaphor she chooses to express her sorrow is drawn from a traditional store of deprivation imagery. (Nketia, *Dirges*, pp. 57–58)

Beretuo Clan. Here is a clan dirge from the Beretuo repertoire given in its generalized form—that is, no specific name precedes the phrase *"Grandchild of,"* and the poem contains no valedictory image of grief. It was selected because of the lively characterization of the ancestor, Gyaamma Kani, a woman whose vigor led her to take up male pursuits like trapping and weaving! The reference to place of origin should be familiar to readers of the Beretuo drum praises in the preceding section. (Nketia, *Dirges*, p. 157)

Aboadee Ntoro. In addition to matrilineal clans, the Akan have a second system of social affiliation called *ntoro.* There are twelve principal *ntoro* groups, which commemorate the male contribution to personality. With each of these groups is associated a body of water, still or flowing, and a resident water-spirit. The Aboadee *ntoro* is a subgroup of the Bosompra, whose members "drink" the waters of the Pra river and whose characters are distinguished by the epithet "tough ones." If a mourner chooses to situate the deceased in the paternal (nonblood) line, she must employ a format different from that used in clan praises. The *ntoro* dirges consist of a succession of short stanzas, like this one, each illustrative of ancestral character. The use of decapitation images as metaphors of power is standard practice in Akan dirges of all types; but here the conceit is fancifully drawn out, as it could not be within the confines of the clan-praise format. Not only were enemies' skulls tokens of chiefly strength, but in the old days there were human sacrifices at important funerals. (Nketia, *Dirges*, pp. 172–173)

Afua Fofie Grives . . . This is an example of yet a third type of dirge, which focuses on the singer's response to the death. The expressions of deprivation are eloquent and at the same time conventional. This relatively free form must include some features of the more restricted types: references to a clan ancestor (here, Otire of the Aduana), to an ancient domicile (here, Hwedeemu and Anteade are lineage-locations), and to a water-source, implying the *ntoro* group spirit. (Nketia, *Dirges*, p. 196)

Amba Etsiwaba Grieves . . . This further example of the free-form dirge shows the possibilities of a flowing, uninterrupted performance (a sequence of stanzas). Nketia praises this dirge for its straightforward, spontaneous expression as well as for the singer's sense of lyric composition: "She keeps up the central thought of the opening stanza and develops it, building it up gradually to a climax by means of reflections, repetitions and the usual references that one would expect to find in an Anana [clan] dirge [of any type]." (Nketia, *Dirges*, pp. 204–207; musical transcription pp. 261–285)

NDAAYÀ'S *KASÀLÀ*. The *kasàlà*, as we have seen, is the most prized literary genre of the Luba people of Kasai. Traditionally, this form of clan eulogy was always sung at critical moments of communal life— on the eve of battle, upon the death of a dignitary—by male bards. However, Luba society provides an opportunity for certain women to become specialists in the genre.

Daughters accompany their mothers to funerals, where women gather to give utterance to grief in an informal mode known as *mwadi* (lamentation). Of these girls, a very few will begin to refine and organize their verbal expression; eventually, as the vicissitudes of life sharpen and deepen their painful talent for introspection, and as the empathetic responses of those around them confirm a growing power of communication, such women will be sought after as artists of the funeral occasions, and their expressive products will be known no longer as mere *mwadi* but as proper *kasàlà*. How do the women's *kasàlà* differ from the men's? By their lyricism; that is, women's *kasàlà* seem to belong to the singers themselves, as reflective individuals, rather than to the lineage groups from which they spring and to which the contours of their songs pay tribute of remembrance. Further, because of the social context in which the women's artistry developed and to which by custom it is confined, the tone of their *kasàlà* tends to be grief-stricken. Or, more precisely, it is this "blues" tendency of the genre itself that women, who need pay no deference to martial enthusiasm, develop in elaborate and personal ways.

"Tendency of the genre itself": Here one must take note of the uncertainty principle at work. Who knows how, originally, the *kasàlà* sounded? Times change, and with them the modes of art. When van Caeneghem began to record *kasàlà* performances in the thirties, the institutions upon which the genre historically depended, and its verbal integrity as protected by the elders, were already in the process of disintegration as a result of colonial rule. But litanies of dead heroes will always elicit solemn consideration of the brevity of life; and we saw how historical change exacerbated the anguish of the Tshimini bard who mentioned hills inhabited no longer, by colonial fiat. In a *kasàlà* for the Bakwanga lineage, recorded about the same time, the bard deplores the joint deterioration of mores and language in a poignant single stanza that evokes in this far-off listener thoughts of George Orwell, who fought a similar battle about this time:

Now they act in their own interest:
Authority's in the hands of young men;
No longer do the bearded take precedence.
White men have fallen upon us like an affliction.
Our children they call, in their ignorance, "antelope's kids";
Please examine: no stripes on the backs of our grown men.
Sun, our own people now call *ntanku* instead of *diba*
Strap, they call *mfimbu* instead of *mukaba*
Cord used to bind goats: changed from *monji* to *nshinga*
Moon, no longer *nsungi* but *ngondo*.[1]

A result of this bitter situation is the heightening of the singer's sense of self; thus, a Luba dirge for a dead clansman becomes in effect a threnody for a dying ethos, a personal lamentation on the instability

---

[1] R. van Caeneghem, "De Kasala-zang van de Bakwangastam," *Congo* II, 5 (1936), pp. 695–696. The new words are either Swahili or imports from dialects spoken in the Zaire lake district.

of the human condition which is at the same time a swan song of culture capitulating to anarchy.

A generation later Patrice Mufuta recorded, among others, the lamentations of *Ndaayà*, a woman of the *Citèkù* lineage (*Le Chant kasàlà des Luba* [Bruges: Julliard, 1963], pp. 128–153). Her *kasàlà* is throughout a most personal testimony, an outraged avowal of her disintegration in the context of a thoroughly disintegrated society. She sees its heroes in retrospect as already corrupted and corrupting, and she deplores the violence, lodged by some fatal inertia in men's hearts, that has been tearing her people asunder. With this vision of history, Ndaaya ironically attempts, in the traditional manner, to link the prominent members of her own and her client's lineages: setting word traps to catch their ghostly power. Another woman *kasàlà* singer interviewed by Mufuta described the power of her song as deriving from the expressiveness of a sobbing voice; but Ndaaya disagreed. Beauty, she insisted, stems from truth; each idea evoked in the process of praising the deceased must be linked to another, and the language used to convey these logical leaps must be agile—witty, that is, a tough and sinewy language of alienation that makes the listener aware of what's going on. In this respect Ndaaya is working in the consciousness-raising tradition of the men's *kasàlà*.

Thirty-five years old at the time of the performance here recorded, Ndaaya, whose child is dead, whose husband is no longer in the picture, considers herself a "wanderer." Hence, Ndaaya is an anomaly in a transitional society where women are expected to lead established conventional lives even though their men go off to earn wages in another country. Having learned her art from her mother and elder sister, also professionals, Ndaaya is clearly in control of her medium, if not of her unhappy life. The dead child she is called to mourn, a nephew, provides her with a traditionally sanctioned yet crucial occasion for complaint. At the same time, the genre that gave her the chance to train her wits in defense of her sanity and of her erratic existence leaves Ndaaya free to develop her own counternostalgic approach to modern times. Her control legitimates originality. Thus, she elevates our common womanly strain of bitching about things into searching social commentary. Humanity itself, one feels, is on trial as Ndaaya puts a series of nagging questions to the unresponsive otherworld of dead men.

This performance ran to 495 lines in its CiLuba transcription and literal French translation. From these, 167 lines have been cut. A still shorter version was contributed to *The Penguin Book of Women Poets*, edited by Carol Cosman, Joan Keefe, and Kathleen Weaver (New York: Penguin, 1978). The original bilingual text was not printed in stanzas; but since the human mind craves divisions, I have tried to follow Ndaaya's train of thought and punctuate accordingly. The textual notes below are based on Mufuta's thorough commentary.

(1) "Ntumba"—The child she has come to mourn bears the name of a spirit who should have protected him during infancy. Thus, in invoking the male-child, she in a sense invokes the wayward spirit. The deceased is mentioned four times early in the *kasàlà*; after that Ndaaya begins to invoke other ghosts.

"Kalombaayi"—"Mwamba Kabooka" was the founder of a line of ruling chiefs, called Katende, after his son. An itinerant merchant at the time of the coming of the white man, Mwamba was sent by the then chief as his emissary to the Congo's territorial agent. Upon his return, Mwamba refused to surrender the agent's ceremonial gift and comported himself as chief in his own right. The ensuing conflict continued for generations.

"Ngandu," "Ntanda," and "Kalomba" are sublineages; the "Muuka" live at the frontier of the lineage; that is, beyond Muuka territory another lineage begins. Ndaaya and Ntumba both belong to the lineage founded by Mwamba Kabooka, whose surname or strong-name, Kalonji, means "angry." The "Angry" pocket their spleen—that is, they know how to control it and keep it ready to use against enemies. Ndaaya, assuming this praise-title, depicts herself as one who stands her ground, ready to fight. The dead boy, Ntumba, by contrast, reacted to injury by fleeing this world.

"*Nyunyu* bird"—*Kasàlà* singers are so called because the nyunyu fly low across the countryside and therefore know what's going on; the word also means to have profound knowledge. Like the *nyunyu*, Ndaaya has considerable physical charm, of whch she is well aware.

———

"Breaker-of-roads"—Kaboya Nkongolo, founder of the sublineage to which both Ndaaya and Ntumba belong, was reputed to have reacted to contention by fleeing and destroying. The Nkongolo people are said to maintain the tradition; before they decamp they burn their houses and uproot their sacred trees. Breaking roads here refers to the above, to Ntumba's departure from this life, and more broadly to mass migrations of recent Luba history. The Luba people who migrated to Katanga, only to be forced by civil wars at the time of secession to return to their homes, regretted having burned their bridges behind them.

(2) "This journey"—Ndaaya had returned from the provincial capital to her village of Katende-Kabooka to rest. Learning of her little nephew's death, she was required by custom to enter the house of lamentations. All her misfortunes descend upon her head as she sings. The praise-phrases in this stanza contrast images of sociability with those of aggression.

(3) "Crossroads"—Here one hesitates where to turn. Here one also meets misfortune. It is tempting fate to stand where people have deposited the illnesses and evils of which they have been cleansed, where witches come looking for food, where vagabond ghosts malinger.

"Wife"—Like "daughter" or "sister," "wife" throughout implies a willing, fond attachment. Ndaaya never mentions her real (former) husband's name. Here she links herself with Mwamba's son, Katende and with his grandson, surnamed "Ribs-showing."

"Mother-striker"—When a male dies, the men accuse the women of sorcery; a man's relatives actually strike his widow. Women react similarly, but more mildly, to deaths of females in the family. Ndaaya exaggerates this custom into an elaborate conceit in which she imagines herself a woman-warrior.

(4) "Mbombo"—The death of her daughter is the source of Ndaaya's deepest grief.

"Kalonji"—The "angry one" has several identities in this *kasàlà*. As the aggressive founder of a group comprising several lineages, the Kalonji who drove other clans out of the plains in which his people were settled sets the political tone of the piece. In recent times, Albert Kalonji founded the secessionist state of South Kasai, promising wealth and progress for the Luba-Kasai and a revival of ancient traditions. Ndaaya apparently sees this attempt at political self-determination, which failed, as a vindication of her own strivings for independence, which so far have brought only disdain and poverty. The Kalonji who was head of the chalk-mining team exemplifies an enviable strength, coupled with insouciance. The rest of the stanza telescopes events (to achieve the condensation expected of the *kasàlà* artist) with the wild verve that is Ndaaya's trademark. Here are the facts: Near the place where Kalonji skinned the crocodile, on the Lubi river banks, is a grotto where an entrepreneur wanted to set up a bar. First it had to be cleared of vampire bats. Meanwhile, several kilometers upstream, at the confluence of the Lubi and Cinyama rivers, the state of South Kasai had established a model cattle farm. The local population had begun to exploit the diamond-bearing Cinyama; hence the singer's banknote fantasy. Ironically, the future patrons of the bar are seen as cattle from the model farm. The entire area is being commercially transformed!

(5) "Beebeleebeele"—This is a word used like a signal drum to communicate across distances. The sounds spell out the name intended. Thus, by means of a sonorous conceit, Ndaaya signals to the world of the dead.

"Shade-tree-of-my-mother-in-law"—This is an ironic reference both to her homelessness and to her broken marriage. The spirit of one's husband's mother resides in a consecrated tree planted by the son and tended by the first wife.

"Brother of Cibangu"—Her father had no such brother, nor does Ndaaya, although she frequently refers to herself as "sister of Cibangu." She is probably referring to a great hunter of the village, so popular that all the girls called him their brother. This fictive association might be regarded as something like an *animus* projection on her part.

"Leopard," "black mongoose"—Here the leopard stands for the envious person, the sorcerer, and the black mongoose for the herbal doctor, whose medicines won't work if the evildoer gets there first. In the following lines, the situation is reversed. The antelope symbolizes a person who seeks tranquility, like her father.

(6) "The heart has a home"—The home of the heart is in the spiritual world. Occasionally Ndaaya suffers from a seemingly suicidal despair. "The village vanity dishonors"—The vanity that dishonored her village, in Ndaaya's opinion, was that of a young prince named Mwamba, who surrounded himself with a coterie of nonlineage (perhaps also non-Luba) flatterers and refused to obey his father, chief Katende Mande. In the ensuing fratricidal war, Mwamba literally lost his head.

(8) "Pounded past sundown"—Chores are supposed to be finished by nightfall, for this is the time spirits begin to walk among men. Only the very poor are exempted from this regulation. She here declares her poverty; also, defiantly, she is asking for trouble!

"Beeya"—This was a grown nephew of whom Ndaaya was very proud. She does not tell us how he died, but in an image reporting a fact—that the asphalt road laid to the cemetery cracked in the rainy season—she tells us how she feels as she travels this road in her memory.

(9) "I lay down, fluttering like a falcon"—Apparently Ndaaya suffered a cardiac arrest at the time of her little daughter's death.

(12) "Placed in my womb by ritual"—That is, a spirit was contacted, served by ritual—libation, a sacrifice, praises—and in return did its best to ensure a successful pregnancy for Ndaaya.

———

"A 'satisfied' man"—This is a euphemism for sorcerer, a man who is the opposite of satisfied, that is, envious. Here Ndaaya recalls having met such a man, who gave her daughter the evil eye.

EKÚN ÌYÀWÓ. Source for the first group by Women of Oyo (Oyo state, Nigeria): Dejo Faniyi, "Edun Iyawo: A Yoruba Traditional Nuptial Chant," *Yoruba Oral Tradition*, edited by Wande Abimbola, Department of African Languages and Literatures, University of Ife, printed by offset lithography (Ibadan: Ibadan University Press, 1975), pp. 677–699. English texts revised, with reference to the Yoruba, by Judith Gleason. Source of the second group by Susannah Faramade, wife of Joseph Ajeiigbe Faramade of *ilé* Arogun, recorded in February 1976: Karin Barber, *I Could Speak Until Tomorrow: Oriki, Women and the Past in a Yoruba Town* (Washington, D.C.: Smithsonian Institution Press, 1991). First published by Edinburgh University Press: Volume 7, International African Library, pp. 78–79, 110–113, 263, 282–283. Additional stanzas ("Clear the way . . . ," "When I was coming to earth . . . ," "My mother did me proud . . .") and additional lines to complete " 'Speak on, speak on' . . ." kindly supplied by Karin Barber from unpublished manuscript. In its complete version Susannah Faramade's performance consists of twenty-seven stanzas. The eleven excerpted here are arranged sequentially and correspond to stanzas 1, 4, 6, 14, 17, 18, 20, 21, 22, 25, and 27 of the original text.

In Okuku, slightly west of Oyo, this genre of expression is locally called *Rárà Ìyàwó*. *Rárà* usually refers to the royal bards' oríkì chant. Praising herself, the bride is "queen for a day." Here the standard Yoruba term, *Ekún*, "lament," a derivative of "weeping," is generically applied to both sets—the composite from Oyo as well as the individual performance from Okuku. In the course of such a celebratory lament, situational pride vies with regret and apprehension. As the bride moves in song from the house in which she has grown up to another, located in her husband-to-be's family compound, the performative genre accomplishes a womanly rite of passage. From "in" to "in" is her trajectory; yet for the moment she is out and about, accompanied by a sisterly chorus.

Faniyi collected these stanzas from various women in Oyo and arranged them according to conventional themes of the genre: (a) asking for parental blessing, (b) anticipating trouble from in-laws (and co-wives), (c) regret at leaving girlfriends combined with worry about not being ready to take on adult responsibilities, (d) disingenuous praise of her own beauty, and (e) expectation of children.

[*Notes: Oyo women*]   "The *eda* rat"—this singer, having lost her father, address him at his grave site within the compound.

"Lovely beads" and bad "love medicine"—The bride is expected to be a virgin; but the singer who took a lover does not conceal the results. Would this be the case in Okuku?

"Bad luck dogs a hunter"—The singer here stops to address a woman concerned about barrenness, thus projecting her own fears and assuaging them.

"Dry up river"—One of three chants, recorded by Faniyi, which musically handle the possibility of meeting another bridal party along the way and engaging in an impromptu (and rather scary, for most) competition.

[*Notes: Susannah Faramade*]   "I would have liked to be a hunter"—Compare Ndaaya's warrior-woman stance in section (10) of her Kasala. This stanza follows a tribute to her elder brother.

"White cowries" are a traditional symbol of wealth; the beads of a devotee are the identifying sign of her allegiance to a particular divinity and membership in its cult; the singer's future child will validate her womanhood.

"They're making arrangements"—Susannah has no more say about the marriage contract, transferring her to her husband's lineage, than a sheep. And it is she who will have to experience the resulting consequences, presumably with the wry humor here evinced.

"The family enjoys"—Karin Barber uses this stanza to comment upon the paratactic structure of *oríkì* generally, which by generating a series of structurally parallel assertions (usually in a fanciful proverbial mode) creates a "rhetorical climate in which the real claim can be excepted as incontrovertible." Susannah's privilege is her relationship with her mother.

In sum, the bride's performance displays her beauty, intelligence, and skill in absorbing and improvising upon the various set themes of the genre, her filial gratitude, and her understandable, even befitting reserve as far as her new status is concerned. But it also affords, within its own limits, an initial opportunity to speak her mind. Thus in time may she become what Laide Soyinka is fond of calling "a no-nonsense Yoruba woman."

V: *Pride of Hunters*

We had spent the better part of two days tracking a Kob antelope, off season, through sharp-edged grasses so high that Baru, the hunter, had to climb up on an anthill occasionally to see what was what. As he stood poised on one leg, with his other foot in its ragged canvas shoe resting on the calf muscles of the supporting leg, the smoke from his pipe said which way the wind was carrying our scent. But our truest compass was time, which showed us, through the degrees of yellowing, sometimes verging into brownish, on the ragged tip of a grass blade, how long ago a set of teeth had grazed there. Perhaps, if we were lucky, the depth of a molar-shaped hoofprint would confirm that the Kob had passed by in the early morning dampness. At mid-day, to clear our vision and cool our heads, the hunter found an open space and, begging permission of a certain small plant, he began to strip one stem of its leaves, extolling their properties. Subsequently we chafed the leaves between our hands, sloshed with canteen water. Yet, cool, bright-eyed, and oriented though we thus were, we never caught up with the antelope. Not that this mattered. It was the engrossing artistry. . . .

Now we were back in his compound listening to the rain beat on the tin roof over our heads. There was to be a party. Baru had sent word to all the hunters in the neighborhood, including his special crony, Sedou Camara. One by one the guests stomped in, dressed in their formal leather boots. Sedou Camara was there already. When the room began to fill, he exchanged his slouch hat for the ceremonial peaked cap—dog-eared, studded with cowries—of his trade. Soon the harp and its accompaniment drowned out the sound of the rain.

> O Baru, killer of lions
> O Baru, he is a sorcerer
> Who turns into a vulture
> Flying high above the forest
> Spotting game, O Baru, Baru
> Master of hunting . . .

And with a knowing grin, wielding his antique rifle like a baton, in his ceremonial headgear—a crown of lion claws with a leather fringe—Baru danced to his praises. High stepping, suddenly crouching, pirouetting to take aim at a distant phantasmal creature, Baru acted out past and future expeditions. Then everyone shot off blanks to the resounding tin roof. The room filled with smoke. Most of us fled to the porch, choking. But the bard kept on playing; staring intently, he kept on singing, "O master of hunting, O Baru, vanquisher of lions . . ."

HAUSA HUNTERS

It is not for the meat
But for sake of the game
That we hunt.
If you think meat's our aim
We will go back!
Meat's to be found at home
Or at the butcher's.

BAMBARA HUNTERS

Breakers of big skulls, crackers of fierce jaws!
He who's never finished fighting predators
    slips off to catch forty winks.
This doesn't mean you, hunter
    who feeds on ripe figs
This doesn't mean you, hunter

who drinks deep from the springs
You who kill only a little piece of game, yearly
Have made over your powder and balls to your sweetheart, truly!
Nobody brings down game from the bedstead
Especially when one's right hand is placed
      upon a waist looped with fine beads
Especially when one's trigger finger
      is poised on one's penis sheath.
Vile, vaunting hunter
      don't think you're the one I'm praising!
But rather you, who brought down mother-of-elephants' children
But rather you, who are responsible for the rarity
      of mother-giraffe's children.
Because of you the massive buffalo
      son of Nansou of the bloated umbilical
      shows himself no more in the bush!
Braver than the brave
      Now you, too, have finally disappeared forever!

YORUBA HUNTERS

Eee! Eee!
I danced to loud music of our *agogo* band
On the day the high priest of diviners passed away;
When the chief of farmers died, I knocked on his grave
      with my hoe-shaft, ceremonially;
When the father-of-singers-for-Ogun died, I assembled
      all my Ogun paraphernalia, wore them on my person
Alone I danced to our loud, loud hunter's drums . . .
Hunter's ceremonial hoe-haft
This is it, isn't it?
Assembled hunters, do wake up, you performers! . . .
Hunter's beads, green and yellow
These are they, aren't they?
Assembled hunters, do wake up, you performers! . . .
I will chant a salute to my father, chief of hunters;
As you know, no meager boy can kill a bushbuck

Bushbuck bearing sharp horns on its head
Which the younger hunter, killing, thereupon believes
    he has cut from his own neck the knot of misery;
Yes, when a young hunter kills the bushbuck
    he casts away misery.
Animal whose sides are lined with white streaks
Dàùndàùnbìrì, with eyes close to its forehead
    like those of *àwọnyè* fly
Hunter's ceremonial skin
This is it, isn't it?
Assembled hunters, do wake up, you performers. . . .
The hunter suffers hardships out there in the open
Dried forest leaves his only fuel;
I cheerfully endured everything, save the rip in my trousers
Here are the hunter's trousers, do you wake up
    assembled hunters, performers. . . .
Our drumhead is made of leopard skin
    and skin from the ear of an elephant
When we play on earth, its sound attains the nether regions
    whose inhabitants prick up their ears
    like the rats in my father's house. . . .
Ogundiji, who like rain thrashes the lazy man
If your ears are ringing with the sound of your name
    please utter no curses,
It's we, your cult colleagues, calling. . . .
Eeee!
The day the hunter's smock is dropped into the basket
Its destination is way beyond the savanna;
Ogundiji's now goes into the basket, bound for a distant country;
    And the squirrel
    And the chipmunk
Animals perform due rites for their fellow creatures;
    And the green fruit-pigeon
    And the heavyweight cane-rat
Animals perform due rites for their fellow creatures;
    And the green fruit-pigeon
    And the red-eyed turtle dove
Birds perform due rites for their feathered brothers;

Take up your load
Take up your load
Big head, take it up quickly, and go your ways!

NYANGA HUNTERS

You, Hangi of the drum
And you spirits, Nyamurairi, Kabira, and Nkhuba
And you, Meshemutwa, Muhima, and Kahombo
May you be already out there, for I'm on my way
Help me, that I may kill much game
Give me the benediction which endures
That I may return from the hunt successfully.
You, my fathers, help these dogs
That they may put up and hold at bay
So I need not return with an empty bag.
You, my fathers, help us out there in the bush
May the hunters not be wounded by thorns and brambles
May the spear look past the dog to the game.
You, my fathers, may we be light-footed in pursuit
May we not stumble on roots
May snakes get out of the way of dogs and hunters.
You spirits, watch over us out there on the hunting grounds
May we meet eyes glowing in the confines of the forest
May this game wound neither dogs nor hunters!

AMBO HUNTERS

(1)   Light up my eyes [O guardian spirit]
      That I may see well where I am going!

(2)   I had a father
      The wailing is great.
      Father, it is dawn.
      I remember the great hunter

They are bursting into tears
Let me take, let me cry
I, who had been dividing the meat.

(3)   How fine is my gun
How fine is my gun
Ah, when my father was alive . . .
I mourn for Siliyolomona
But I must see the tracks.

(4)   It is fine in the bush
I, the hunter's son
I have slept on leaves
And chewed, along with the meat, the hide.

(5)   Let us make offerings, hunters
The spirits, may they roam in the evening!
You, angry spirit of my father
Cutter of trophy tails from vanishing animals!
My father has fed the bush!
(Alas, I was hoping to feed the village.)

(6)   A little child has cried:
"I'll go with you, father, to cover the game-pits!"

"Stay at home, my namesake
This time we plan to see all the streams!"

(7)   Hurry, there went the game!
Hurry, there went the game:
The grass is trodden.

(8)   I shall taste the mark of the game
When I find them where they lie!
Abundant the spoor
But the game have slipped away
They are gone!

(9)   The big gun got stuck;
         When it saw the game
         It rotted on the spot!

(10)   My feather is lost in the bush
         May it change into game!

(11)   That giant elephant
         Whom will he knock to the ground?
         Whom will he knock to the ground?
         He carried away the tusks
         He who pulls out *mwenge* trees by the roots!

(12)   You follow the wild pig
         Me, I'll follow the hartebeest;
         You follow the wild pig
         Me, I'll follow the hartebeest
         The big game with horns!

(13)   "Hunter, you are pierced!
         "I, the roamer whom you love."
         "Wait, let me take out the thorn!"
         "I, the roamer whom you love."

(14)   My wife, grind meal
         Tomorrow I shall journey
         To reach the game herds
         I shall not return until I tire
         Sing cheerfully
         For I am a wild dog!

(15)   My mother-in-law talks of meat;
         Wait, I must finish what I'm doing
         What's relish without porridge?

(16)   The child cries for the liver;
         I, your old father, am vanishing
         I, dog of the game

When I was an able hunter
I used to play with the animals
Now even flick of their tails eludes me!

(17)   Make haste, make haste
By this stream he slept
Simwenda slept in the evening. . . .
You youngsters
You left your comrade in the bush
He slept alone
Bewitcher of animals!

(18)   Where we were yesterday
There lies our accomplishment:
See the vulture, see the vulture!

(19)   You slave, beggar of meat
You slave, beggar of meat
Come see how it hurt me
How it drove me up onto an anthill
How it broke for me the leaves, that meat!

(20)   We are tired of this bush
There are no shadows in it
No shadows, I tell you
There are no shadows of game!

(21)   *Munyanya* bird, that *munyanya*
[crying with contentment]
He has buried the beer!

AKAN HUNTERS

PRINCIPAL   (1)   The hunter will go: he will bring meat
RHYTHMS OF THE   The hunter walks alone: but he is brave
HUNTER'S DRUM   The heel of the elephant is strong
                        Strong is the heel of the hunter.

THE HUNTER HAS KILLED AN ANIMAL WITH A POWERFUL SPIRIT	(2)	The hunter has killed And tears are very near his eyes O Suadomo The entangling creepers lie upon you Lie upon you, are you going to remove them?

THE HUNTER
IMAGINES THOSE
AT HOME MADE
ANXIOUS BY HIS
LONG ABSENCE
	(3)	Vagrant child of the eagle
		    goes about performing brave deeds
		The rousing servant of the community
		    who kills big game
		May father please tell me
		    when he expects to return
		That I might ready some food for him.

HUNTING SKILL DEVOLVES FROM FATHER TO SON	(4)	The great gun, my soul: Father's long gun is my soul Great gun is my soul, my soul Long-barreled gun is my soul.

THE HUNTER'S
IMPORTANCE AS
EXPLORER AND
PROVIDER OF
CHIEFLY REGALIA
PERMITS HIM
THUS TO BOAST
	(5)	Is the chief greater than the hunter?
		Arrogance! Hunter? Arrogance!
		That pair of beautiful things on your feet
		The sandals you wear
		It is the hunter who killed the duiker
		The sandals are made of duiker-hide
		Does the chief say he's greater than the
		    hunter?
		Arrogance! Than the hunter? Arrogance!
		That noisy entourage of yours
		The drums preceding you—
		Hunter killed the elephant
		Elephant provided ear for your
		    drumhead
		Does the chief say he's greater than the
		    hunter
		Arrogance! Than the hunter? Arrogance!

COMMENTARY

Like a poet, the African hunter is a mediator between the unknown and the familiar. His recondite paths lead him away from the cultivated world to a spirit-saturated natural environment whose alert participants he and his fellows have schooled themselves to be.

The world of the forest requires purity and proposes danger. From the petty tensions of village life, from boring agricultural rhythms, and from the subordinating claims of political authority, the hunter mercifully removes himself to an intense alternative existence where chance and skill interpenetrate.

The village is a world of talk; the forest is a place of listening. The village is comfortable; the forest exacts austerities. In the village women produce children; from the bush huntsmen return with game. The inedible trophies of the hunt—horns, tusks, tail-whisks, claws, and skins—serve as symbols of patriarchal power and spiritual authority back in the world of culture, about which the hunter's heart always remains ambivalent if not out-and-out adversative.

The forest also provides play for the imagination. Strange encounters and transformations occur in its remote, overgrown precincts. The masquerades which appear in the village square bring this occult wildness briefly into the ordinary world of civilization, materialize it in costumes consisting of plant fibers, noisy pods, shells, animal skins, horns and claws, and carved simulacra of composite beasts of the imagination. And the tall tales the hunter tells are incipient dramas, epics.

The mystique of the hunter is cross-cultural and fraternal. Whether his venatic community hunts in a group or prepares him to go off alone, the African hunter transcends ethnic boundaries. All hunters, whatever language they speak, are brothers whose activity in agricultural societies is primarily of ritual rather than economic importance.

The meat he provides is a treat, not a staple. After all, even the relish in a sauce is usually furnished by scraps of fish or poultry, more exceptionally by the flesh of a domesticated animal. Hunting is a heroic activity, to be approached well doctored with medicinal charms, with a disciplined body, with a clear eye to penetrate obscurities and detect traces, and with a power of speech enabling the hunter to

charm animals and then to placate the angry spirits of those he suc-
ceeds in finishing off. Hunting is a courtship without connubial com-
plications, a love-game in which a well-praised and well-stalked animal
must yield.[1]

HAUSA HUNTERS. The philosophy expressed in this praise is like
that articulated in Imamu Amiri Baraka's famous essay "Hunting Is
Not Those Heads On The Wall." All who regard with revulsion our
rage for consuming and collecting turn their minds and hearts with
relief to cultural situations in which an activity is valued for its own
sake. This poem, in a slightly different English form, was published
by Willard Trask in *The Unwritten Song* (New York: Macmillan, 1966),
vol. I, p. 42. The original source is Roger Rosfelder, *Chants Haoussa*
(Paris: Seghers, 1952), pp. 22–23.

BAMBARA HUNTERS. This praise is sung at funerals of Bambara
hunters whose lives have embodied the ideals of the hunting frater-
nity (*donson*). According to Youssouf Cissé, about two percent of the
Bambara of Mali are hunters. They enter the association voluntarily
as novices, and their seniority depends upon their years of initiated
participation in the *dōsō* rather than upon chronological age or social
status. Thus, hunters defy the gerontocracy of clan organization and
the rigidities of the caste system. They also, by their reliance upon
traditional (animist) philosophical beliefs and values, present an un-
remitting challenge to Islam. In hunters' societies, says Cissé, despite
centuries of Moslem proselytizing, the ancient myths and moral stan-
dards of the Niger bend region are kept intact.

Central to the beliefs of the Malian hunters are the mother and
son of the bush, Sanin and Kontron. Whoever worships these divine
forces knows no race or clan and leads a life of ritual purity. The man
who enters the bush to hunt must be chaste; and even when residing
in the village he must avoid promiscuity. Hence the satirical depiction
in this praise-poem of the distracted womanizer, that self-indulgent

[1] We are speaking of traditional African hunters here, not of those corrupted by Eu-
ropean "big game" intruders into the forest, nor of poachers corrupted by the inter-
national market for ivory.

betrayer of the huntsman's austere principles. These principles are linked to the acquisition of sufficient magical power to overcome the unleashed spiritual ferocity of wounded or killed animals. Furthermore, according to the Bambara, character is the basis of luck, without which the hunter is himself a prey to unforeseen disasters.

Source: Youssouf Cissé, "Notes sur les sociétés des chasseurs Malinké," *Journal de la Société des Africanistes* XXXIV, 2 (1964), pp. 210–211.

YORUBA HUNTERS. Eulogies chanted at Hunters' funerals are known as *Ìrèmòjé*. The Iremoje performance begins at about ten P.M. and lasts until dawn. At the center of the gathering—which includes members of the hunting fraternity and their drummers, family members, and a general audience of townsfolk—on a forked stick are placed the deceased's hunting outfit and his paraphernalia, thus creating a temporary effigy to whom the body of the chants is directed. Tributes are sung to each item of the hunter's equipment, after which it is placed in a basket and at dawn ceremonially carried into the bush and abandoned. The singer of these lines is a professional Ijala chanter who specializes in Iromoje events. The phase of assembling and praising the dead hunter's things is called *Ìkópà*. When this has been done, the artist joyously lets himself go to extol the life of the hunter. As this bush life requires close observation of animal behavior and knowledge of praise-epithets with which to flatter the prey into range, the singer includes a tribute to the bushbuck as part of his eulogy to the deceased. The "load" at the end of the chant refers to the basket whose entering contents have been previously itemized with respect and humor. Ogundiji, the name of the deceased, means "Ogun thrashes the lazy man as does rain." All those who use metal tools, implements, or drive vehicles are considered to be worshipers of Ogun, god of iron and special patron of hunters. Source of the verses: S. A. Babalola, *The Content and Form of Yoruba Ijala* (Oxford, England: Oxford University Press, 1966), pp. 260–299. (The original text runs to 488 lines.) Additional information: 'Bade Ajuwon, "Ogun's Iremoje: A Philosophy of Living and Dying," *Africa's Ogun*, Sandra T. Barnes, ed. (Bloomington: Indiana University Press, 1989), pp. 173–198.

NYANGA HUNTERS. The Nyanga hunt in the equatorial forest of eastern Zaire. Once they lived in the high lands of the East African lake region. As intruders, they regard the forest as a dangerous place and envy the ease with which their Pygmy neighbors move within its wondrous entanglements; nevertheless, to leave the village and take up residence in a temporary hunting camp offers a Nyanga banana planter a chance, in the words of Daniel Biebuyck, to be himself, to find plenitude, privacy, happiness.

A fruitful hunting expedition is the result of divine favor mediated through the mystical personality of the hunting dog, companion equally of man and spirits. Both hunter and dog must undergo elaborate rituals (ablutions, magical treatments, empowering benedictions) to put themselves in right relation to the cosmic forces responsible for the circulation of life and death in the rain forest. Such rituals also make possible the acquisition of practical skills.

Most of these divinities are said to live in a subterranean world associated with the volcanoes situated beyond the present Nyanga territory to the east, where the boundaries of Uganda, Rwanda, and Zaire converge. Feeling from far off tremors of the volcanoes they can no longer see, the Nyanga imagine ancestral souls in an angry state of mind, for their spirits never left the old habitat. Nyamurairi, fire, is the ruler of this volcanic underworld. Hangi-the-drum sounds there. But Nkhuba, Nyamurairi's son, lives in the ubiquitous sky as lightning. Kabira materializes in the equatorial forest as a leopard divinity. Muhima is a fertility god. Meshemutwa is a Pygmy spirit incorporated into the Nyanga pantheon. The hunter in the ritual poem presented here invokes these divinities as he leaves the village for the forest. Source: Daniel Biebuyck, "De Hond bij de Nyanga: Ritueel en Sociologie," *Academie Royale des Sciences Coloniales, Mémoires*, n.s. VIII, 3 (1956), p. 132.

AMBO HUNTERS. The source of this sequence of poems is B. Stefaniszyn, S. J., "The Hunting Songs of the Ambo," *African Studies* X, 1 (1951), pp. 1–12. The Ambo live in the Lukuashi River valley (Zambia). They are a matrilineal society; and from the content of the thirty-two songs published by Stefaniszyn and his very brief annotations one may deduce a ritual conception of the hunt allied to that discussed in great detail (but without songs) by Victor Turner in his work on the neighboring Ndembu.[2] Like the Ndembu, the Ambo hunter establishes a shrine, in the form of a three-forked branch driven into the ground, which serves as a path of communication between himself and the spirit-guardian who supervises his expeditions into the bush. It is from this spirit (the shade of a close male relative) that he inherits his vocation, his "huntsmanship," a power symbolized among the Ambo by an inherited weapon. Libations of beer are poured upon the base of the shrine,[3] and upon the prongs, horned trophies of the hunt are hung. If the guardian is angry, he will curse the enterprise by putting the animals to flight, jamming the gun, beclouding the hunter's vision. Then the cause of the ghostly hunter's disquiet must be determined by divination and proper atonement made. Often this cause turns out to be a festering grudge in the mind of one of the hunter's female relatives, perhaps his mother-in-law. For the hunt to be successful, not only must the hunter be in a state of ritual purity but the social community to which he belongs must be in a cooperative state of equilibrium. Hidden anger in the village keeps the game under cover. In the forest, spoor lead to moral discernment and metaphysical truth, as well as to more obvious game.

These songs of the Ambo hunters are "traditional"; nobody remembers who composed them. They may be sung whenever mood and occasion warrant and sung over and over again at beer-drinking celebrations. The order followed here is not that given by Stefaniszyn.

(1) The hunter sets out.

(2) and (3) The hunter remembers his father. Although a man is legally descended from his maternal uncle, his emotional tie to his father is stronger. It was his father who instructed him in the hunt. Here the spoor of the animal he pursues are identified with the traces his father once followed into the bush and hence, I think, with the footsteps or moral imprint of the man himself.

---

[2] See especially "Themes in the Symbolism of Ndembu Hunting Ritual," in *The Forest of Symbols* (Ithaca, N.Y.: Cornell University Press, 1967).

[3] Among the Ndembu this base is made of a piece of termite mound. Just as the termitary teems with life, so does woman's womb, and so does the forest with game.

(4) Like father, like son: The hunter boasts of the austerities of bush life. Bush meat in the temporary hunting camp is butchered without preliminary flaying.

(5) The scene is a prehunt libation at the forked-stick shrine. May the guardian spirits come to drink, for the previous hunt was spoiled by a father-ghost who dispersed the wounded animals. Their carcasses fed the hyena and vulture, while the old man disappeared with the tail-whisks that would have enhanced the hunter's reputation.

(11) This praise of the elephant who got away is sung with nostalgic irony these days. Elephants are scarce and hunting them is outlawed.

(12) This is a song of hunters' rivalry.

(15) Despite pressure from his mother-in-law, the hunter will see to his millet fields before going off into the bush.

(16) An old man's hunting days are over.

(17) The hunters are scouting for their more accomplished companion, who went off alone.

(19) A hunter sardonically addresses his friends and tells them about being attacked by a buffalo or by a sable antelope. I think the broken leaves refer to a magical "tying of the bush" that the hunter had performed at the edge of the trail in order to keep the game he was pursuing within the confines of his competence.

(21) When the *munyanya* bird cries, it is a sign he is satiated. So are the hunters. They have finished the last pot of beer.

AKAN HUNTERS. The Ambo hunters at drinking parties may accompany their songs with the beat of hoe blade upon stone. For the Akan hunters drums are provided by musicians from the community in which they live, and the gong part of these impromptu orchestras is, interestingly enough, provided by struck hoe blades. (See also the ceremonial hoe mentioned in the Yoruba song, p. 102.) Traditionally, the occasions for praising the hunter's profession in song and dance were two: the funeral of a great hunter and the funeral of an elephant. The latter practice, ubiquitous in Africa, will be discussed in the animal-praise section. Suffice it here to say that Akan hunters were ranked according to the number of elephants they had killed, and that a kill always meant a triumphal entry by the hunter into the village and the detonation of a chain of songs like those given above. Now, however, elephants have become rare and so have master hunters, not only because of the death of game but also because modern marketing of crops for cash has made farming attractive to individualistic temperaments who once would have disdained it.

Song (2) is a lament over a carcass. A killing must be regarded with ambivalence. To the joy of accomplishment is joined genuine sorrow because of the hunter's identification with the strong, beautiful animals he pursues, and this grief is tempered with dread lest the released spirit of the victim attack its murderer. It is in order to neutralize this retributive force that the Akan hunter, like the Bambara, becomes expert in magic, medicine, and purificatory ritual.

The source of these texts is J. H. Nketia, *Drumming in Akan Communities of Ghana* (London: Nelson and Sons, 1963), pp. 75–89. Marginal notes are not by Nketia but are based on his commentary.

VI: *Animal Praises*

In memoriam:
Emil P. Dolensek,
formerly chief veterinarian
of the New York
Zoological Society

BUTTERFLY

O Glistening one
O Book of God
O Learned one
Open your book!

(Hausa)

SPIDER (1)

Spider of the south
Hairy one
Mother of fierceness
Your bite does not leave one unscathed—
He will run mad, sleep in the veld.
Spider of the south
Mother of blackness of the murky loam
Your bite, an evil omen.

(Sotho)

SPIDER (2)

Who gave word? Who gave word? Who gave word?
Who gave word to Hearing
For Hearing to have told Ananse

For Ananse to have told the Creator
For Creator to have made the Thing?

(Twi)

SPIDER (3)

Spider, your threads are well stretched
Wily hunter, your nets are well woven
Spider, you are assured of abundant food
Forest, be propitious
May my hunt be joyous as spider's!

(Pygmy)

CUCKOO

Dup dup dup
Rain may it rain may it rain!

(Ewondo-Bulu)

BLACKBIRD

Tyi tyerrr, tyi tyerrr
More than one day, more than one day!
Tyirrr tyarrr, tyirrr tyarrr
Weeds tougher the longer they stay
Weed tougher the longer they stay!

(Bambara)

MAGPIE

Sonè sonè!
Dig in, dig in!
So you won't hoe? So you won't hoe?
Tough luck, tough luck!

Kel esiè o, kel esiè o!
Stir your stumps, stir your stumps!
If you hear them say
Ngon mot, "daughter-of-humanity"
It's thanks to hard work;
If you hear them say
Ngon mot, "daughter-of-humanity"
It's thanks to hard work.

Earth would be generous
Don't beg;
Earth would be generous
Don't beg!

(Ewondo-Beti)

SPARROW

Year we worked
My mother got sick
Year we ate
My mother, cured!
This year, mother is sick
That year, mother is cured!

Shall we eat, or shall we save the seeds?
Shall we eat, or shall we save the seeds?

(Ewondo-Beti)

NIGHTJAR

Mwezi uwale uwale
Moon shine, moon shine
That I may eat tadpoles!
I sit alone on a stone
All my bones rattling
Were it not for my big mouth

All the girls would be calling me!
Mwezi uwale uwale

(Nyanja)

THE LUGUBRIOUS *DUGU*

Disinterred corpses
Of fathers, of mothers
Dug I dug I dug dug!

May it rain *letub tub tub!*

(Ewondo-Beti)

WAGTAIL

Wagtail of the waters, crossed to the opposite bank
Kodu k'o tetena made deep sounds in his throat
Throat reverberated *k'o utlwahala hole* far, far away.

(Sotho)

HONEY GUIDE (1)

Soughs wind in the forest, so swarm the bees
About their hole in the honey-tree:
Similar murmur
Similar humming
Mfounga mfoumfoung
Mfoumfoung mfounga

(Fang)

HONEY GUIDE (2)

Bird of thorn-apple trees
Kinder-hearted than a chief

Don't lead me high
I've no ax to chop a tree;
Tswedi tswerre
Please lead me low
I've a digging stick made of sickle-bush wood
Which is perfect for prodding an antheap.
If you give me, I'll give you—
No need for asking—
A honeycomb with larvae in it.
Tswedi tswerre
Whistling bird of the bees.

(Hurutshe)

CROWNED CRANE

(1)   Crowned crane
       Powerful crowned crane
       Bird of the word
       Beautiful crowned crane
       You took part in creation
       Voice is your gift, *n'guma*
       Speaking the word, you inflect it
       You the drum and the stick that beats it.
       What you speak is spoken clearly
       Ancestor of praise-singers, even the tree
       Upon which you perch is worthy of commendation.
       Speaking of birds, you make the list complete
       Some have big heads and small beaks
       Others have big beaks and small heads
       But you have self-knowledge, *n'guma*
       It is the Creator who personally adorned you.

(2)   People of this place,
       Look, the crowned crane is dancing!
       Crowned crane, praise-singing woman
       During the day the shameless one weaves,
       Astonishing!

(3)   The beginning of beginning rhythm
        Is speech of the crowned crane;
        The crowned crane says, "I speak."
        The word is beauty.

(Bambara)

WEAVERBIRDS

Tswi-tswiri! I, the person, I suspect.
What have you heard that makes you suspicious?
I heard spoken: rumors of weaverbirds
They ate corn in Lesiba's field and finished it.

And when they left they sounded *hummmm*;
They said, "Listen to the numerous weaverbirds
Sons of the Mosima family
Children of the horse that ate the courtyards and the times."

Numerous, the weaverbirds
The gray ones that go about in swarms
Children with the little red beaks
Children making a noise in the mimosa trees.

Tupu tupu! The smoke comes out while dew still glitters
Howaa sweaa! is heard in the early morning.
They're finishing off the corn, numerous weaverbirds
Children with the little red beaks.

At home it's *Yo yo!*
The children are crying
Their mothers have gone to the fields to fight
It is the Zulus who have entered the country!
Take axes and finish off the branches of the trees!
Yo! This year we shall eat fire
We shall lack even a blue-tongued goat;
It is the numerous weaverbirds
The gray ones that go about in swarms!

(Sotho)

BLUE CUCKOO, RED-BELLIED COUCAL

The blue cuckoo
Lays white eggs in the bush.
When war captures the town
The blue cuckoo cries:
Kukuku ogún
Kill twenty, kill twenty!
The red-bellied coucal cries:
Kukuku ogbòn
Kill thirty, kill thirty!
Then death will not fail to come
Then death will not fail to come.
When men begin war
The blue cuckoo cries:
Fools, fools!
The red-bellied coucal cries:
The world is spoiled
The world is spoiled!
Then death cannot fail to come
Then death cannot fail to come.

(Yoruba)

QUAIL

Little quail, little quail
You are picking up the little grains!
And what if he is?
Those are his eyes
Peepers, peepers.
It broke his leg for him:
Only hunger, only hunger.

(Nyanja)

HAWK

Shake, shake goes the wing
Wearer of gallbladder of grass-warbler!
In the evening he wore snippet of yellow-breasted pipit.
Sherre sherre! feminine white hawk.
Picking my way along the precipice to rob its nest
I stepped on cow dung and fell!
There is the hawk on a path overlooking a treacherous cliff
In the act of ripping open a pigeon.

(Sotho)

FROG

Frog you, frog you
Your friend, your friend;
Frog you, frog you:
He is calling his wife
Jump squat, jump squat
He is calling his wife.

(Nyanja)

CROCODILE (1)

Crocodile, who invokes the waters of rain
The black one of the pool
The black one lying on water-slime;
It is the crocodile of the pool
The biter I go about seeking as prey
Son of the father-of-pools to whom tribute is paid
Tribute to the lords of the rivers
To the lords of the rivers, hippo and crocodile;
Great torrents of rain will come thundering down!
It is the black crocodile of the pool
The crocodile who drags a beast into the depths

It drags the beast into the dark depths—
The crocodile has hurled the beast into a cleft tree—
It has taken the beast into the dark depths
The owners of the beast peer into these deeps
They open out the rushes and willows
They think they are looking right into the pool
The pool into which the beast has disappeared.
It is the black crocodile of Modiane of Tau,
Chief of the Moxopa people, robber of his enemies.
The crocodile stays down in the weeds with the beast
It is still down there in the dark pool with that beast;
It is the one that cannot be drowned
Crocodile that must never be poked with a reed
Though he was born in them
Cruel one, killer while laughing
The enemy with laughing teeth is most treacherous!

(Sotho)

CROCODILE (2)

Clic clac clic clac: day of crocodiles
Clic clac: day of people
Teeth below; above, misery!
Clic clac: honor the crocodile
Clic clac: my heart is grieving:
Eyes, mouths, teeth!

(Fang)

DAY MOUSE, NIGHT MOUSE

DAY MOUSE: *Tsiku icha, tsiku icha icha*
                 Dawn, day; dawn, day day
                 That Tsambe mouse is eating everything!

NIGHT MOUSE: *Tsiku bakala, tsiku bakala*
Stay a little, stay a little
Night, while I feed with you!

(Nyanja)

STRIPED SQUIRREL

Za'tsig ndig? za'tsig ndig? za'tsig ndig?
Who cut the creepers? cut the creepers? cut the creepers?
What sorcerer? Mean magic! What sorcerer? Mean magic!
I can't stand dwarf corn—selvage edge of the forest
I can't stand dwarf corn—selvage edge of the forest!
Zel zel vug, zel zel vug
I eat grains of ground meal
Perched on a limb
Swinging teeter-totter, swinging teeter-totter.

(Ewondo)

HARE

Ga re ya gaa koo! Whoops!
Son of the little dark brown one
Little yellow jumper from the stubble
Yonder, son of the spotted one
Leaper from grass clump to grass clump
Jumper from tree trunks
Leaping up, stretching its tail
It places its ear on its shoulders:
Ga re ya gaa koo! Whoops!

(Hurutshe)

WILD PIG

Wild pig, the goats are ill
Cure them, you who root for tubers;

Some of these roots can make the chief fall;
Your colleague is a wallower; watch out
Lest he hex you full of earth while you snout!
Look-around for what to mouth and store in your cheek.
Another pig is the sting of the Ndebele chief
Wild pig of the wild pumpkin,
Holder of lightning in your mouth!
My ochre for anointing besmears my mouth
I eat my rub, I, wild boar of the champing;
Great pig, always in demand, playing both sides against the middle,
Who says, I use my ochre, mixed with fat, to rub my body
I anoint myself with the fat dripping from my mouth.
In Byatladi, where live the raiders of red cattle
Wild pig is a cannibal!

(Sotho)

DUIKER (1)

Duiker, sweet to eat, pleasant to sell
Sweet to take home
Pleasant to offer to one's intended father-in-law.
Olúpétu, bush-dweller
Ẹtu, shredder-of-the-bush.

Duiker, builds a house on the day of death.
Such meat tastes sweet if eaten alone
No need for mushrooms with flesh!
Olúkòjọ, Fàlàkẹ, owner of a white garment
To spread out and sleep on.

Láàyingbó, whose chest is used for making drums
Duiker, sleeps in the bush, extends his feet along the roads
Duiker, camps in abandoned farms
So the farmer sleeps unworried.
Provided the owner of the fallow farm does not die
Such land will not be allowed to revert to bush!

If Duiker meets Hunter on the fallow plot
He stands face to face with him: challenge!

Duiker, you renewer
Whose tail tidies up vagina for her husband;
Duiker, with your diviner's switch
You blocked access to the vulva
Of the wife of the oracular divinity!
Spindle-shanks, you with the prominent tear ducts
Forming elaborate face-marks, like a mask!

Duiker, the sale-price of whose thighs alone can buy a slave.
The bearer of mere snippets of your meat
Keeps on complaining of his weighty load;
Your skin is wide enough for both chief and his wife to sleep on!

(Yoruba)

DUIKER (2)

Duiker, who collects himself for the leap
Duiker, who recoils backward
Duiker of the divining bone, pulling himself together
Self-shrinker, runner, leaper
Who scares up the hares
Duiker of a man's front loincloth!

(Sotho)

BUSH COW

Cudgel, child who rumbles like rain that won't fall
Cudgel who thunders in soggy places!
The coward is seeking a tree to climb
Black cannon!
Olúmęrí, spirit with a razor-sharp horn!
If you've only last year's medicines in your pouch
Do not pursue the bush cow

This beast will devour you!
It's an animal who doesn't care if you say
I'll flee for refuge to my honored mother!
While some bush-cow meat remains in the soup
A child won't dare touch it, he attends to his pounded yam.
When a bush cow roars in the forest
A child runs to the nearest tree and climbs it!

(Yoruba)

WATERBUCK

Waterbuck, son of the one who secures her child to her back
With rags and enters a dewy place
Even your child makes a track;
Waterbuck, whose death at the hands of a hunter
Is greeted with cheerful laughter.
Waterbuck awakes, pastures, and sets off in the early morning;
Having gone forth yesterday, he'll return by the same path.
Top-heavy old masquerader, mother of riches!

(Yoruba)

LEOPARD (1)

It is the yellow leopard with spots
Yellow leopard of the cliffs
It is the leopard of the broad cheeks
Yellow leopard of the broad face: "I do not fear
The black and white one; I get into a small tree
Bend down and scalp to the eyebrows;
Clawer am I, I dig my claws in the pate
So that the enemies I leave behind say
'This was not one leopard; rather, ten of them!' "
Mr. Claws, scratch yourself!
Even for a big man, it's no disgrace to yell if clawed. . . .
It is full of blood, it has got the liver
Leopard of Bolea.

Yellow leopard of the great Maloba clan . . .
Grand old man
Even when it can no longer bite
It still butts its enemies out of the way with its forehead.

(Sotho)

LEOPARD (2)

Gentle hunter
his tail plays on the ground
while he crushes the skull.
Beautiful death
who puts on a spotted robe
when he goes to his victim.
Playful killer
whose loving embrace
splits the antelope's heart.

(Yoruba)

LION

Tawny one, brother of Mothebele, rise up
Tawny one, fawn-colored king of the wilds.
Why, you don't eat what belongs to men
But eat for your part the sleepers-in-the-veld!
A nephew bereft of uncles
Kills and lays claim to all the booty!

(Sotho)

BABOON (1)

Orí opomun, who teaches the dog to hunt;
Dog mastered the art of hunting
Killed his teacher and ate him up!
Gentleman on the hill

Whose beauty intoxicates, like strong drink.
Protruding lip, pendulous as a pestle
See him with a spoon in his mouth,
Iron vest on his chest!

He pretended to be a simpleton
And ate the farm produce of his father-in-law;
He devoured four hundred corncobs on his outward journey
And two thousand six hundred on his way back to the bush.
He said, "What a pity this is the farm of my wife's father,"
Otherwise, he would have eaten two hundred more.
He left the farm and returned to the bush
Mouth swinging like a full bag.
While he was absent from home
Back-of-heads were allocated by the Creator;
Returning, he said, "The back-of-head allotted to baboons is
    insufficient
I shall compensate by borrowing more mouth!"

He made no use of his arms, but shook his buttocks
That prince of the hills;
His mother looked her fill and burst into tears, saying
Such beauty would be the death of her child
With his bald rump, with his grasping hands
Like Eshu's, O husband of redness
O child with eyeballs attractive to women
He who borrows more eyes for looking
Whose children won't let up on their mother's udders
Tree-branch hanger-on!

(Yoruba)

BABOON (2)

Handsome fellow of the precipice
"My foot soles shine on the mountain."
Ox of a baboon, dies in the milkwood tree
Not of its favorite fruit, but of something rotten.

Son of liquid urine
Greatest medicine for children.
Baboon who huddles up when it rains
So that not a drop touches eyes or stomach.
Son of the black hands .
What is the secret of your penis?
Handsome fellow, shiner on the mountain,
"So long as I'm here in the milkwood tree
And the lions come down from the mountain
To strangle me, let me tumble
So I fall on a bed of my favorite fruits
Me, handsome fellow of the sheer precipice."

(Sotho)

COLOBUS MONKEY

You with a face of lead
You require much gunpowder.
Colobus, hurling himself along
As if slung from a sling.

Colobus, born of Colobus
Touraco bird on the tree!
Twin, you belong to the people of Isokun;
Colobus, son of the man who died in masquerade costume!
Hawk said the vault of heaven is his!
Abuse me, that I may follow you home!
Twin, call me by my praise-name
That I may turn aside from you!
Had I known in advance
I could have accompanied you home
To Isokun, Colobus monkey!

(Yoruba)

ELEPHANT (1)

Through the forest whipped by rain
Father elephant treads heavily, *baou, baou,*
    baou
Diffident, fearless, proud of his strength
Father elephant, whom nothing can subdue
In the forest he shatters at will.
He stops, starts up again, browses, trumpets
Knocks down a tree or two, searches for his
    woman.
Father elephant, a distant hunter hears you.
Elephant hunter, take up your bow

(CHORUS)   *Take up your bow, elephant hunter!*

In the forest where none may pass but you
Take heart, hunter, glide, leap, run!
Meat is before you, enormous, joyous
Meat marching along like a huge hill
Meat that is going to roast on your hearth
Meat for sinking your teeth into
Beautiful red meat, blood to be drunk as it
    fumes;
Elephant hunter, take up your bow

(CHORUS)   *Take up your bow, elephant hunter!*

(Beku Pygmies of Gabon)

ELEPHANT (2)

They march single file, the elephants, the mighty ones
They go to slake their thirst.
Let us go too! They are drinking among the thickets; hurrah!
Listen, smothered roarings in the forest
It is a great sound, this roaring in the forest; hurrah!
The crying of the elephant, the mother;
It is she who calls the hunters to the thickets;
Hurrah! It is she who calls the hunters; ho, hurrah!

Over there is the one with large drooping ears
Hurrah! The big-eared one has just passed us; hurrah!
The comrades are there; the sound of knives being sharpened
There, from the spot where lies the slain elephant
Hurrah! The sound of knives being sharpened; hurrah!

(Thonga)

ELEPHANT (3)

The violent shaker that shakes down living trees as it passes
Father has achieved something, the hunter has done well!

Father has done well, the brave one has done well
I have killed a tree-beater!

Father who beats trees
A male one lies unsheltered from the sun;
I, child of Amankuo, am reponsible:
A male one lies in the scorching sun!

(Twi)

ELEPHANT (4)

Greetings, Death,
Elephant, spirit of the bush
Wearing a pleated gown worth a fortune;
One-armed spirit who shatters trees
Child of forest-destroyer
Offspring of coconut-cracker;
Elephant, you kneel in a huge mass
You with the indestructible tusks
Whose mouth utters a laugh enjoining respect!

Big footprint opening up the thicket into a path
Whose footsteps turn thorny brake into clearing
Who forces his way along;

Death-dealing cudgel
With a back like a drum
Who makes a sound like that of the smith
When he salutes you with his hammer!

Illustrious elephant who hails from the Lagoon
Who looks back reluctantly like a person with a stiff neck
Who carries a head pad, but no load
Elephant balancing the load of his own huge head . . .

If elephant goes by once
The place becomes a road;
If his mother follows
It becomes a wide plain.
Elephant has a head, but is neckless.

Death-stop-following-me:
The hunter who threatens to kill him
Receives this elephantine message:
"If you know what fate befalls goats, leave me alone
But if you don't know, then come along, I'll show you!"

Each eyesocket: a water jar
Throat: narrow as an *orù* pot
If nobody molests you, you molest nobody.
Elephant has but one arm
Yet he can push over a palm tree;
Had he two
He would tear the sky like a rag.
Coverer, who covers his child like darkness!
Elephant goes along angrily
And his body is vast;
A man with a charm dating from last year
Would do well to abandon pursuit
Nor can any charm at all harm him!
Long-tusked progeny of the one who kneels on his head
Elephant who takes four mortars to the farm!

A herd of elephants crowded together
Are like a massive wall;
Huge-tailed animal
It is he who dashes calabashes together and shivers them
It is he whom one sees washing pots and soup caldrons!

(Yoruba)

ELEPHANT (5)

Stripper of trees
Lumbering cow, mother of herdboys
Cow milked in the thorn scrub
Uprooter of thorn trees
Lion cubs must be content with meagerer fare.
Monster of herdboys' country
I hear no thud of your walking
Which is silent, with the help of two canes.
"I split the tree by the river
And when the crocodile seizes my trunk
I extirpate him from his element
And swing him up into the cleft I made
I, fearsome black one of the forests!"

(Sotho)

DOG OF THE NYANGA HUNTER

You, hunter
You, dog of the Pygmy
You, dog of Fire
You, dog of the Drum
You, dog of the Leopard
You, dog of Lightning—
May the animal you are chasing
Not abscond from here.

Spirits, round up the animals
Round them up so they can't flee
So they'll sleep in a bunch.
And you, Fortune, daughter of the Drum
Give your benediction to these your dogs
You, their mistress, may they succeed in killing plenty
And may these animals finally reach your sanctuary!
And you, Death, bless your dogs
That they may kill the animals they pursue;
And you Chief Nyankhuba, and you, Chief Buhini
Help me so that the animals pursued may perish
For when a man hunts, he hunts for his chief
For his family, for the nobles, for the elders
For his nephews and friends;
Help us so this game may be run down once and for all
Not after two or three starts;
Quarry, may you die for shame at the sight of this dog;
May you look at him and decide on a counterattack;
But if so, may my dog defend, defend
Standing his ground, and bite you there!

(Nyanga)

DOG OF THE INFIDEL

O Dog, your breakfast is a club
Your meal a beating;
O Dog, your shadow spoils a prayer;
Cast-off, Hyena's perquisite
Your ribs are like the plaits of a grass mat
Your tail, a roll of tobacco
Your nose is always moist.

(Hausa)

TUNGBE'S DOG, LEKEWOGBE

Drive-the-liar-into-the-bush,
Dog belonging to the Tungbe,
Who gets the head of a giant rat
To eat with his cornmeal porridge;
The dog who knows how to give breast
To his own children;
The dog who understands how to jump
On the grass-cutter's progeny.
The dog who brought the luck of war with him
When he came into this world from heaven;
No day is as sweet as the day
When Lekewogbe followed his master on a mission.
It happened in the presence of Kujenyo
An oracle-priest greater than others;
Ojo Okege was a second witness to the event.
As Tungbe was carrying the sacrifice along
[To be placed near the camp of the enemy]
His dog started to shoot with his mouth: *ha! igi dá!*
The giant rat was so frightened that
It came out of its hole in broad daylight:
Kárakìtà! Kárakìtà!
Tungbe's dog ran after it;
But Tungbe went on without looking back
To see what his dog was doing.
Suddenly Lekewogbe arrived with the rat.
Tungbe said, "It is prohibited. Dog, don't you know
That the children of General Ikoyi are forbidden
To eat giant rat?
Our fathers used this rat to prepare medicine
To scatter the enemy's army."
[So the sacrifice was complete!]
Then Tungbe's dog used the head
Of the giant rat to cure his body!

(Yoruba)

ABRAM MODIPANE'S DOG, THEPUDI

Hunt with the fastest hound
The death of a dog is not distant.
Visitor who works for man
Visitor of small animals.
He says the hares must sleep terrified
Little hearts palpitating in their sides
They hear the dog's breathing.
Dog! Rock-rabbits went to bed hungry.
Hunger, like lightning
No more than the dog can be contained
No more than the snakes
Crying within the belly.
When I passed by the mountain,
The visitor disappeared into a crevice
I heard him barking at the pass
He had brought out an animal!
Thepudi, eater of the uncooked
Breaker of backbones
Slim hound who eats porridge.
Long-mouthed, only dog in the village
The brown one who gathers vegetables
Who goes out hunting early in the morning.
Hunt with the fastest dog
The death of a dog is unknown;
Visitor who provides man with relish
Visitor of small animals!

                                                            (Sotho)

CAMEL SONG
For Abdi Hebe Elmi

If your foot, camel, becomes slow
And you feel you can move it no more
If your gleaming flank, O camel

Becomes like a thorn branch, dry and gray
If your neck, my camel, that you hold so high
Becomes weak and thin like a straw
If your mouth, O camel, becomes dry
And filled with the dust of death
If the heavens, my camel, change color no more
Then the land has dried out.

(Somali)

COMMENTARY

If Praising is perceiving and putting words to the characteristic, then surely birds are the way to begin; for hidden in thickets, trees, grasses, it's their calls that distinguish them. Chirpers, cheepers, sobbers, warblers all have languages of their own to be listened to and repeated in variously inflected human languages, whose prototype by the Bambara is taken to be the crowned crane's mysterious "double call." To alert adult listeners, birds may seem to be repeating brief esoteric statements, like the beginnings of riddles, which the edified can render intelligible by completion. Yet even then, what the bird's interpreter says may be coded in order to ensure gradations of culturally acquired knowledge. For example, the wagtail's deceptively straightforward praise in Sotho contains (in its last line) a peculiar construction, *k'o*, found in secret songs of the circumcision lodge and therefore generative of translation into another, parallel language to which only the initiated would be privy.

Substantial or slight as the creatures that inspire them, animal praises present an intricate combination of affectionate observation and symbolic formulation. Sometimes animals are praised as projections of human values—grace, power, resourceful adaptability; or the reverse, because they display with impunity forbidden qualities—gluttony, irresponsibility, sudden spurts of aggression. Further, and most important, animals are honored as mediators between the spiritual forces of the bush and those investing human communities.

This mediation has been institutionalized and rationalized in various ways—rationalized not only by African sages, but by European analysts who have indulged in various theories of totemism without ever having really listened to what the elders of the village are saying.[1] The most obvious condition of these various sorts of mediation is that in the world of animals-untamed, the individual represents the species, *is* it. Any antelope is *the* antelope. The closest analogy in the human world is the clan, a group comprising all those (living and dead) descended from a legendary progenitor. What myths of original compacts/hereditary alliances between progenitor and animal species representative really mean could be described as "mirrored moral relatedness." If one belongs to a clan for whom the roan antelope is sacred, then upon meeting such a one in the forest, human time-past wrinkles into animal time-present: An individual man finds himself face to face with the epitome of generations.

The dead are commonly identified with snakes, who are continually transforming themselves, going into the earth and reemerging newly vested but ever as sinuous as the rhythms by which we too are governed, could we but shed our constraining opacities. Yet other metamorphoses are possible. A spirit from the world of the dead may materialize in the forest as an animal reminder of something neglected on the conscious surface of life. Or a hunter-sorcerer may become so adept that he can voluntarily shift shape to become the familiar agent of his own will. Among the Yoruba, the ambiguous dark creativity of witchcraft puts on the beautiful feathers of a rapacious female bird; among the Nuer, the mystery of twin births wings its way between earth and sky, luminous, numinous, evasively alighting. The Yoruba, on the other hand, associate twins with Colobus monkeys and the forest. Again, for the Nuer a river goddess is also a certain type of cow called "leopard of the night," and a pied crow as well. Why these identifications? The animal medium is a message. To evoke an animal is both an act of interpretation and an activation of a segment of energy.

Hunters are animal praisers *par excellence*. To recapitulate in a zoological frame the theme already stated in the chapter on hunters: Animal-praising is not only an occupational sideline, the result of

---

[1] Two notable exceptions: Marcel Griaule, *Conversations with Ogotemmeli* (Oxford, England: Oxford University Press, 1965), ch. 19, "The Cult of the Binu"; and E. E. Evans-Pritchard, *Nuer Religion* (Oxford, England: Oxford University Press, 1956), ch. 5, "The Problem of Symbols."

hours spent patiently watching everything that goes on in the bush, but a matter of magical pragmatism, moral hygiene, and male midwifery. Praises flatter the animal prey into proximity, tranquilize it, ensure cooperation in the ritual enterprise. (Birds, be silent! Don't warn the *prey!*) Again, since the climactic embrace is fatal for the wild one, pardon must be begged of its wraith. Thus the funereal aspect of such encomia. But death presupposes rebirth. All animals and their praises being generic rather than individual, praise of an individual animal is more deeply designed to encourage the species to reproduce. The latent burden of the song runs something like: O beautiful antelope, may you (token of the species) perpetuate yourself! Thus, the praise uttered by the compassionate killer is a prayer for the replenishment of life. Short-circuiting existence, the word reinforces that wrinkle in time which occurs when man greets animal in the forest.

Insects and birds are different. Praises to these are not necessarily the province of the hunter. To insects are attributed various symbolic meanings in accordance with their observed behavior. Throughout Africa, ants and termites in their teeming clay wombs are associated with reproduction and reincarnation. Spider may be an avatar of supreme good in one culture, of clandestine evil in another; but always its web-weaving presupposes intelligence. Birds, as suggested earlier, are distinguished from other animals in having consistent speech, a language that, if it can't be reliably interpreted, can be readily imitated. Since African languages are tonal, the inflected calls of birds seem, like drum-talking, to be conveying an urgent message. It is from the play between the warbles of birds and their rhythmic-tonal equivalents in one's own langauge that bird-praises are born, to be the special delight of little children.

To domestic animals man stands in a different relation altogether. Dogs are included here because of their integral relation to the hunting process, and in order to contrast their individuality with the generic personalities of those they help track down. For cattle another verbal grazing ground has been set aside. And a few of the animals from both forest and kraal will reappear in praises for the divining bones (Chapter IX).

BUTTERFLY. Source: A. J. N. Tremearne, *Hausa Superstitions and Customs* (1913; reprint ed. London: Frank Cass, 1970), p. 175. The markings on the wings remind the praiser of Arabic script.

SPIDER (1). Source: S. K. Lekgothoane, "Praises of Animals in Northern Sotho," *Bantu Studies* 12 (1938), p. 213. Whoever is bitten by this ill-omened spider will run mad. I assume, therefore, though no evidence is given by Lekgothoane, that this is a species of tarantula.

SPIDER (2). Souce: J. B. Danquah, *The Akan Doctrine of God* (1944; reprint ed. London: Frank Cass & Co., 1968), p. 44. Here is Ananse-the-spider, avatar of Nyankopon, "the shining" god of the firmament, acting not as a trickster but as the middle term of a three-part creative process. By "hearing," Danquah says, is meant "understanding," a passive realization on the part of the goddess Onyame, the supreme principle of life-flow. Then Ananse-Nyankopon exercised judgment and passed this knowledge on to Odomankoma, the creator. The little poem is actually a conundrum: How did thinking come about?

SPIDER (3). Source: R. P. Trilles, *L'Ame du Pygmée d'Afrique* (Paris: Editions du Cerf, 1945), p. 191. Here we return to the real spider. This praise is uttered by the Pygmy hunter, says Trilles, as he passes by the spider's net on his way hunting. The praise mode turns prayerful.

CUCKOO. Source: Eno Belinga, *Littérature et musique populaire en Afrique noire* (Toulouse: Editions Cujas, 1965), p. 29. The cuckoo, says Belinga, is the symbol of fertility, friend of the farmer because its song makes the rain fall.

BLACKBIRD. Source: Dominque Zahan, *La Dialectique du verbe chez les Bambara* (Paris-La Haye: Mouton, 1963), p. 67. The meaning of the first line is "Do what you are doing thoroughly, because you are working not only for today but for the future." The blackbird's second call warns the farmer to get busy and weed his garden. Bambara babies are encouraged to articulate sounds by imitating bird-calls, each of which is equivalent to a proverb or maxim in their language; therefore the child gets two lessons at once. It was the crowned crane (see below) who taught mankind to speak; therefore it is appropriate that other birds also be preceptors.

MAGPIE. Source: Lucien Anya-Noa and Sylvain Atangana, "La Sagesse Beti dans le chant des oiseaux," *Abbia* 8/9 (1965), pp. 122–125. Among the Beti and Bulu of Cameroon, as among the Bambara of Mali, birdcalls are thought to have an instructive intent; wise sayings are found to fit them. The magpie is imagined as living in a state of perpetual anxiety (like people whose habit it is to repeat the tail end of what their interlocutor is saying?). Thus he sounds the alarm: Get to work! If not, either you'll have to beg or go hungry.

SPARROW. This bird, say Anya-Noa and Atangana, is a conscientious peasant-type who knows the difference between working and goldbricking. His second call shows him attacking the problem of proper economy: How much to eat and how much to put away for planting. Source: ibid., pp. 120–121.

DUGU. Source: ibid., pp. 118–119. The authors don't give the French name for this dismal cynic, so I can't produce an English one. Any guesses?

NIGHTJAR. Source: R. Sutherland Rattray, *Some Folk-lore, Stories and Songs in Chinyanja* (1907; reprint ed. New York: Negro Universities Press, 1969), p. 80 and p. 164. Here is Rattray's note: The song of the night-jar is sung rapidly in a high key, in exact imitation of the bird's cry. Once one knows the words, when one hears the bird itself, it requires little imagination to make it appear to sing them.

WAGTAIL. Source: Daniel P. Kunene, *Heroic Poetry of the Basotho* (Oxford: Oxford University Press, 1971), p. 144. Original source: E. L. Segoete, *Raphepheng* (Morija, Basutoland: Morija book depot, 1915). This bird lays his eggs on river banks.

HONEY GUIDE (1). Source: H. Trilles, "Proverbes, légendes et contes Fang," *Société Neuchâteloise de Géographie, Bulletin* XVI (1905), p. 147. This is how the Fang of Gabon hear the song of the little bird (*Cuculus indicator*) who leads them to hidden honey sources.

HONEY GUIDE (2). Source: D. F. v.d. Merwe, "Hurutshe Poems," *Bantu Studies* XV, 4 (1941), p. 333. The Hurutshe are a branch of the

Sotho people who live at least fifteen hundred miles, as a honey guide flies, from the Fang. Same bird, different langauge.

CROWNED CRANE. This bird (*Balearica pavonina*), according to Bambara myth, taught man to speak by presenting him with the seventy basic phonemes (fourteen consonants and five vowels in various combinations) of their language. Three outstanding characteristics qualify him for his pedagogical role: first, his trumpetlike voice, which he is able to "inflect" so as to produce a cry in two distinct keys; second, the beauty of his plumage; third, the unforgettable dance he does during the mating season. For the Bambara, as for the Dogon, clothing is the word simply manifested ("To be naked is to be speechless"); and dance—palpable rhythm—is the unwinding of the word, its disclosure in action. The tree upon which Crane perches is the silk-cotton tree, a natural symbol of the soul on account of the lightness of its wood and the silky fibers (kapok) it produces. The second praise is sung when the mask representing Crowned Crane comes out. (This is one of the *sogow* animal masks linked to the agricultural cycle of Bambara life.) Weaving is a "verbal" process, which the crane is imagined as engaging in. (Ordinarily, weaving is as far from being woman's work as it is from being bird work!) The third is a praise-motif included in the sacred liturgy of the Koré society (see "Voice of the Karaw," p. 170). The last line is an editorial interpolation based on the explanation given by initiates of the phrase "I speak" in its esoteric Koré context. The inner beauty permitting the crowned crane's miraculous speech is self-knowledge. Source: Dominique Zahan, *La Dialectique du verbe*, pp. 58–60.

WEAVERBIRDS. Source: H. J. van Zyl, "Praises in Northern Sotho," *Bantu Studies* XV, 2 (1941), p. 137. *Howa sweaa* is shouted to scare the birds away from the cornfields. To "lack even a blue-tongued goat" means to be in desperate poverty; the weaverbirds, like an army of Zulu warriors, have laid waste the plantations. Here their destructive potential is unleashed in words; another poet might take up the traditional theme of their sociability. When they arrive in a neighborhood they quickly weave themselves hundreds of little hanging nests in trees. When they leave, these nests remain like golden straw ornaments.

BLUE CUCKOO, RED-BELLIED COUCAL. Source: Ulli Beier, *Yoruba Poetry* (Cambridge: Cambridge University Press, 1970), p. 88. I have changed Beier's title ("Blue Cuckoo") because actually, this is a duet between two birds, both of whom make *ku ku ku* sounds in the forest. The call of the first has a mournful aspect; the second's call is far-carrying; the first is shy, the second a bold bird. The word *iku* means "death" in Yoruba. *Ku ku ku* would mean "death, death, death"—hence the presage.

QUAIL. Source: Rattray, *Chinyanja*, pp. 75, 158. The word *maso* in Chinyanja means both "eyes" and "grain." To keep the pun going across the languages I have interpolated "Peepers, peepers."

HAWK. Source: Kunene, *Heroic Poetry*, p. 145. Wearing a gallbladder on one's wrist is part of a process of purification after having killed a man in battle or dressed a corpse for burial. The gallbladder is that of the animal sacrificed for the occasion. The hawk is in constant need of such cleansing! (The third and eighth lines have been slightly reworded for sonority.)

FROG. Source: Rattray, *Chinyanja*, pp. 80, 164. This song should be "sung in a jumpy, jerky manner, to imitate the movement of a frog," says the ever-empathetic Rattray.

CROCODILE (1). Source: Lekgothoane, "Northern Sotho," pp. 198–201. The beast that the crocodile has dragged into the depths—or thrown up into the fork of a tree—is an elephant! He seized its trunk while the elephant was drinking at the water's edge. Such displays of crocodilian prowess are attributed to the fact that the elephant thinks himself superior and attempts to exact homage of the crocodile; but the crocodile is stronger. He has the power to call down rain. Had Kipling heard this story when he wrote "The Elephant's Child"?

CROCODILE (2). Source: Trilles, "Contes Fang," p. 151.

DAY MOUSE, NIGHT MOUSE. Source: Rattray, *Chinyaja*, pp. 81, 164. The first is the song of the Ndongera mouse, who eats during the day; the second is the song of the Tsambe mouse, who eats only at night.

STRIPED SQUIRREL. Source: Anya-Noa and Atangana, *La Sagesse Beti*, pp. 138-139. This little animal's chatter qualifies him as a sort of honorary bird. His "words," like the cheeps of the mice in the poem above, are the idiophonic frame upon which the praise is built.

HARE. Source: D. F. v.d. Merwe, "Hurutshe Poems," pp. 328-329. *Ga re ya gaa koo* is the cry that human kids make when they see a rabbit jumping from its lair.

WILD PIG. Source: Lekgothoane, "Northern Sotho," pp. 202-203. Because he is always digging for roots, this animal is a symbol for the medicine man (*Ngaka*). Such doctors are reputed to have control over lightning, which is said to be held in the mouth of the thunderbird. Medicine men treat their clients with ointments and rub their bodies with clay; the pig is such a slob: What he eats he slobbers all over himself and calls that a ritual rubbing! Two aspects of the Sotho medical profession are satirized here: the continual rivalry of doctors, and the fact that conflict of interest is of no moral concern to them. The last line suggests that in a more aggressive environment, where men raid cattle, wild pigs are greedy enough to eat their own children. Whether this is a further attacak on witch doctors (bewitching their own kin?) Lekgothoane does not say.

DUIKER (1). Source: R. C. Abraham, *Dictionary of Modern Yoruba* (London: University of London Press, 1958), p. 199. The Yoruba name for the animal praised here is *etu*; his Latin name is *Philantomba Monticolor Maxwellii*. Duiker is the first animal evoked by Ijala singers when they perform a litany of beasts. According to the Yoruba hunters, the creator used duiker to make a charm which would enable earth to be spread upon primordial waters. Duiker's tail is used as a ceremonial whisk by diviners; hence the joke in stanza four.

DUIKER (2). Source: Lekgothoane, "Northern Sotho," pp. 204–205. Curiously enough, the Sotho duiker is also associated with divination. Its metacarpal is part of the diviner's sets of bones (see p. 213).

BUSH COW. Source: Abraham, *Dictionary of Modern Yoruba*, pp. 174–175. *Ẹ̀fòn* (Yoruba); *Syncerus Caffer Beedingtonii* (Latin). Even the cooked meat of this short horned buffalo is so powerful that a child avoids it.

WATERBUCK. Source: ibid., p. 493. *Òtòlò* (Yoruba); *Kobus Defassa Unctuosus* (Latin). Like the animal above, the waterbuck is an avatar of the goddess Oya; of the River Niger; of the tornado, mother of twins; and of the masquerade cult of the returning dead (*Egungun*). The untranslatable praise-epithet with which the hunter greets waterbuck is *Laiyewu!* (*Laiyewu* is a special masquerade owned by the Yoruba hunters.) Then he says, "Son of waterbuck, *ogege* waterbuck." *Ogege* calls to mind something top-heavy with wealth, something that teeters when it walks. Of course this is how the animal walks, humped, recalling a mother with a baby or an *Egungun* dancer with a heavy costume. Making the best of all these associations, I have translated *Laiyewu omon otolo, otolo ogege* as "Top-heavy old masquerader, mother of riches"; but since this is a tentative formulation, I have placed it at the end so that the poem won't appear inappropriately light-headed.

LEOPARD (1). Source: Lekgothoane, "Northern Sotho," pp. 192–195.

LEOPARD (2). Source: Beier, *Yoruba Poetry*, p. 81. Throughout Africa the leopard is associated with chiefly power, with the sacred office of kingship, and therefore with judgment, which can be lethal. In Yoruba culture, Leopard is the avatar of a complex and terrible divinity whose real name is too powerful to mention. Popularly known as Babaluaiye ("king of the world"), this divinity is linked to death, madness, suffering, and deep sorcery. But he is also capable of gentleness, of a merciful *coup de grâce*, of pity. (Yoruba name: *Ẹkùn*.)

LION. Source: Kunene, *Heroic Poetry*, p. 131. This is Kunene's translation of a praise to the lion that appears in Thomas Mofolo's epic-novel about Shaka, the Zulu warrior-king.[2] The lion has raided a cattle kraal. The men, hearing the first roar, flee; but Shaka goes forth, a mere boy, and kills the lion. According to custom, one must turn over the spoils from the hunt to one's maternal uncle, who will keep what he wants and return the rest. Shaka, in fact, sent the lion (unskinned) to his father, who in turn sent it to the great chief Dingiswayo. Later, the father's treacherous behavior toward his son forced Shaka into a loner's role, like that of the lion, whose praise in this context is a foreshadowing of the killer's fate. For another lion praise associated with a hero, see "Diara," p. 39.

BABOON (1). Source: Abraham, *Dictionary of Modern Yoruba*, p. 503. The animal addressed here is the so-called Olive Baboon (*Papio anubis choras*). *Ori* here means "head" and *opomun* is descriptive of the animal's cry. How would you translate this epithet? His lack of an occiput is a descriptive truth; but according to the cosmo-biology of the Yoruba, this means he is without a guardian-spirit/ancestral soul!

BABOON (2). Source: Lekgothoane, "Northern Sotho," pp. 196–197. The urine of baboons, found still liquid on the rocks, is collected as a medicine, Lekgothoane says. From the penis of a baboon an even stronger medicine is concocted: for men only.

COLOBUS MONKEY. Source: Abraham, *Dictionary of Modern Yoruba*, p. 173. As mentioned in the introduction to this section, the Yoruba associate white-thighed Colobus monkeys with twins. Both are said to originate from Isokun, the name given to the sacred grove in which the divinity Shango (see p. 177) hanged himself. They are also associated with the *Egungun* masquerade of the returning dead. According to oracular tradition, the first impersonator of the dead to

---

[2] The original, southern Sotho version of this novel based on oral tradition was published in 1925 by Morija book depot in (then) Basutoland. An English version was first published by Oxford University Press in 1931, a second, abridged, version by Oxford in 1949.

wear a costume carried a child on his back to simulate a hump. The
dead man represented by the masquerade was, in life, a hunchback.
The child was actually the dead man's son, but he was not an ordinary
child nor did his father engender him in human form. Neglected in
the bush, the man's corpse had miraculously transformed itself into
a gorilla, which raped a woman, who produced a half-breed child: part
human, part gorilla—something like a Colobus monkey. The meaning
of these successive incarnations is mysterious; the Colobus monkey,
chattering secrets, swings through the trees. (Yoruba name: *edun*.)

ELEPHANT (1). Source: Trilles, *L'Ame du Pygmée*, pp. 37–38. Given
here are the last two stanzas of an elephant-hunting song. I have not
given the first two because there is no African language text to follow
and, as Trilles's French version stands, I must doubt the authenticity
of the meter in the initial stanzas. What Trilles says about the occa-
sion of the song I have no reason to question, and his documentation
supports a most likely theory: that Pygmy practice set the precedent
for the elephant funeral rites that are held by African hunters every-
where. The song Trilles heard was accompanied by the musical bow.
Singing, the senior hunter responsible for the kill danced out the song.
Then he took some of the fallen animal's blood and offered it to the
four corners of the forest, which is alive with the spirit protecting the
Pygmies, supporting their confident life within its (to them) nourish-
ing confines. The hunters concluded their celebration by dancing atop
the carcass. All of them danced. They sang in Fang. Everywhere Pyg-
mies survive they learn to speak the language of the agricultural peo-
ples who have obtruded upon their forest. And the farmers, who
consider the forest a dangerous if exciting place, think of the Pygmies
as teachers of woodcraft, huntsmanship, dance, and music.

ELEPHANT (2). Source: Henri A. Junod, *The Life of a South African
Tribe* (1912; reprinted. New Hyde Park, N.Y.: University Books, 1962),
vol. II, p. 196. Junod's informant, Zebedea Mbenyana, told him that
the Thonga hunters sang this while dancing on the carcass of the
fallen elephant.

ELEPHANT (3). Source: J. H. Nketia, *Drumming in Akan Communities of Ghana* (London: Nelson and Sons, 1963), pp. 81–82. Funerals of hunters and funerals of elephants are, as we have seen (p. 115), the two occasions warranting the performance of hunters' praise-songs. The celebration of an elephant's funeral begins when the victorious hunter reaches the outskirts of his village. There he fires his gun. To those who come forth to greet him he announces the death of an elephant and describes what happened *recitativo*. The first two songs given here are sung by the hunter dancing upon the carcass after he has concluded preliminary magical rites to placate the animal's spirit. The last song is a standard refrain, punctuating his extemporized account of the adventure.

ELEPHANT (4). Source: Abraham, *Dictionary of Modern Yoruba*, pp. 162–63. (Yoruba name: *erin*.)

ELEPHANT (5). Source: Lekgothoane, "Northern Sotho," pp. 196–199. Here is the elephant's version of his war with the crocodile!

DOG OF THE NYANGA HUNTER. Source: Daniel Biebuyck, "De Hond bij de Nyanga: Ritueel en Sociologie," *Académie Royale des Sciences Coloniales, Mémoires*, n.s. VIII, 3 (1956), pp. 131–132. Here, for easier reading, the names of the various divinities invoked are given as personifications. This praise-encouragement to the hunter's dog is uttered as the dog begins to bay. (For the relation of dog to hunter among the Nyanga, see p. 112.)

DOG OF THE INFIDEL. Source: Tremearne, *Hausa Superstitions*, p. 174. The title given to this praise is meant to reflect Islamic hostility to dogs as unclean, an attitude greatly removed from that of the pagan hunter.

TUNGBE'S DOG. Source: Ulli Beier, "The Yoruba Attitude to Dogs," *Odu* 7–9 (1959–63), pp. 31–32. Lekewogbe, meaning "Drive-the-liar-into-the-bush," is a good name for a brave dog. The dog whose unforgettable exploit is narrated here died almost a hundred years ago! The story goes like this: Tungbe, the owner, was a soldier sent with a sacrifice to be placed near the Fulani camp. What it contained, together with the incantations recited over it, was intended to destroy the enemy. The òkété rat, a traditional ingredient of such magical time bombs, was difficult to procure on the spur of the moment because these rats never come out by day, but Lekewogbe managed to hunt one down. Tungbe told him not to eat it. Didn't the dog know that descendants of the famous general Eso Onikoyi were forbidden to touch òkété rat? Thanks to Lekewogbe, and to Tungbe, the Fulani were defeated the next day in a momentous battle outside the precincts of Oshogbo, where this praise was collected. That this male dog can nurse like a female is a compliment. In various art forms one may observe a symbolic urge on the part of Yoruba (and not only Yoruba) males to acquire female functions, partly because then there would be no need for women. The "grasscutter's progeny" are the little rats his scythe exposes.

ABRAM MODIPANE'S DOG. Source: H. J. van Zyl, "Praises in Northern Sotho," pp. 146–149. This praise was written as a school exercise.

CAMEL SONG. Somalia is a country of nomads. "We are all nomads," said the Minister of Education, who generously helped me visit the hinterland in 1979, which was not easy because of the then war with Ethiopia. For most of his peers, the way of life implied by this poem was but a generation away and I wanted to see it. Traditionally a man with a hundred camels was somebody, a *man*. In 1974–75 a terrible drought struck Somalia. There was indeed the "dust of death" in all mouths. Forty percent of the camels of Somalia died and one third of the population had to be looked after in refugee camps, to which emaciated families from the hinterland were airlifted. Now, almost two decades later, it has been and still is far worse than anyone would have believed. Everyone emaciated. No camels. Guns make the man these days. I look at the old photographs with disbelief. Fishermen casting into surf breaking on the rocks on the outskirts of Mogadishu. Where are the potters of Buur Heybe? Where are the wonderful women of Wehle Weyn: Amina, Hadji Hawa, Sokorey (partisan, head of the women's organization), Fatima (who smoked cigarettes), Fadima (political organizer), and the nomadic women leading camels loaded with slender, curved house posts and smoked wooden gourd-shaped containers containing fresh camel-yogurt? And you, Abdi Hebe Elmi, you with your faith in education, man of my own generation. If you are still alive, your despair must be total. Source of the poem: John Buchholzer (who heard it sung in southern Somalia), *The Horn of Africa* (London: The Adventurers Book Club, 1959), p. 108.

VII: *Regard of Cattle*

OX SONG (1)

You are making me drunk on many colors
O my pied heifer!
I will sing you a song as we go through the gate together.

(Baraguyu)

OX SONG (2)

How to say it? How not to fail in wonderment?
As gray clouds converge in the rainy season:
It was about to storm and lightning flashed—
Ah, the lustrous gray-striped hips of my cattle
Pouring from the narrow mouth of the well at Kitè.

(Baraguyu)

BULL SONG (1)

I have a red bull with twisted horns
So big that men can sit and rest in his shadow;
He invaded farms of the people and ate their beans
And because of him the land trembled.
My father is a proud man: my greatness!

Like a lion am I, my enemies scattered before me.
"Where," says he, "in the world is another like my son?"

(Dinka)

OX SONG (3)

White ox, good is my mother—
And we the people of my sister
The people of Nyariau Bul—
As my black-rumped white ox.
When I go out in search of beauty
I am not a man whom girls refuse;
We court girls by stealth in the night
I and my friend Kwejok,
Whose mother is Nyadeang.
We brought the ox across the river,
I and Kirjoak
And the son of my mother's sister
Buth, ox-named Gutjaak.
Friend, white ox of the spreading horns
Which continually bellows amid the herd
Ox of the son of Bul Maloa.

(Nuer)

COW SONG (1)

Generous wooden bowl of my father
When I have supped from it my heart feels happy
Wooden bowl of my parent
Wooden bowl of the beast whose body produces delicious sauce;
Cattle of our place, Oh, how sad is the lack!
A single one affords pleasure
Absence of any causes dismay.
Dark gray beast with many white spots
Disturber of sleep
The one with the musical tongue.
Powerful instigator of armed attack

Whose body cooks gruel
God with the moist nose.

(Hurutshe)

COW SONG (2)

The lazy pace of the oxen returning fat and sleek
    from their seasonal pasturing
    snatches an admiring "You! You!"
    from the lungs of Fulani women
    as at the sight of warriors from battle.
As for me, their herdsman, who led them to the flood plain
    of the *borgu* grasses, this journey
    draws from my spirit a poem.
Laugh who will! Such mockery could not prevent my saying
    the most charming of my lovers
    she for whom I brave wild animals, terrors of darkness, heat
    she for whom I endure a thousand fatigues
    run a thousand risks, she for whom my heart beats
    is a beautiful cow who adorns herself amid the reeds
    with gold and silver water lilies.
Could he compare himself to me? Could he, the voluptuary
    who slides through the day from one smooth mat to another
    only to sink at night into the arms of a woman
    whose thighs have grown fat and sleek
    thanks to rich milk and butter cows give?
When I see the warthog, proudly pasturing his little ones
    encumbered with unruly teeth, afflicted with ugliness
    how can I not joyously lead her to the watery meadows
    who nourishes her own as well as the child of her proprietor?
My joy is complete, for now I've the ear of these Fulani women
    who listen complacently and clap the beat
    to enflame my poetic ardor; can they be jealous
    when I praise my beloved, they with experience
    of cows as co-wives, but never rivals?
They know, descendants of Ilo Yaladi, that cows who abscond
    with their husbands for days, for months

may reach highest esteem in Fulani hearts
but never crave the same advantages as wives;
So they canot be jealous, these beautiful listeners
    when for a plump cow a young herdsman weaves
    his first song; always courteous to cows
    they must be feeling sisterly tenderness.
If only I could find an accompanist skillful enough
    to modulate my ox-hymn and set the seasonal migration
    of Macina herdsmen to music, and further—
    to imitate the walk of girls who tend cattle
    in the land where black people greet
    each other, *"Lafibe, belafi,"* in Mossi country
    where laws are made the way butchers retail meat.
I brave rain and wind; having no compass does not prevent me
    from unbarring the byre
    and heading straight for the flood plain.
Shriveled over his papers the marabout reads
    sententious words; as for me,
    I draw the theme of my morning prayers
    from the complexity of markings upon cowhide:
    enough lessons there to enlighten the herdsman!
Singing: the respose that I husband in my dream
    suffices to regulate my heart's cadence; these
    carry-over lines are not clumsy accidents; and the
    lowing of my beloved is sufficiently eloquent
    to inspire my final observation:
If the herdsman's occupation were suddenly abolished,
    it wouldn't take many days for people to realize
    that it's an essential vowel among the consonants
    of the other trades!
Who could be so lacking in sense as to say
    to her who furnishes milk, fat, and meat
    that she's a futile expression of existence?
Ohe! Singers and accompanists, say of cows
    that they are animating flowers;
    for when they enter a desolate countryside
    they transform it;
The tufts, the clumps of barren grasses they trample

suddenly appear as multicolored flowers
    with pied buds pivoting from one stem to another!
I am not a professional singer, going from house to house,
    but I wander from flood plains to prairies
    and often, when I sing, it's the king of the bush,
    the one with the frizzy mane, who answers me
    with a roar that silences
    even the little mouse cheeping in the brittle weeds.
My praises to my cow are not exaggerated; for she gives
    everything to man, even her bile, which cures
    earaches, and pains of the heart.
My heart at the death of a cow bleeds; if I didn't fear
    to be misunderstood, whenever a cow died
    I'd wear mourning; and my spirit would liberate
    a solemn music.

                      (Fulani, Macina dialect)

BULL SONG (2)

My bull is white as silvery fish in the river
    white as the egret on the bank
    white as new milk.
His bellowing is as the roar of the Turk's cannon
    from the distant shore.
My bull is dark as raincloud accompanying storm.
He is summer and winter
    half of him dark as thunderhead
    half of him white as sunshine.
His hump shines like the morning star
His forehead is red as the ground hornbill's wattles—
    like a banner,
    seen by the people from afar.
He is like the rainbow.
I shall water him at the river
    and drive my enemies off with my spear.
Let them water their cattle at the well;
    for me and my bull, the river!

Drink, O bull, of the river;
Am I not here with my spear to protect you?

(Dinka)

OX SONG (4)

Friendship has many insides:
There is friendship with girls
There is friendship for food
And friendship where men walk together at night.
I told Dupper, "Take that way,
I, this; we will meet;
There is something we will seize
Under cover of night."
We pulled that calf along
Like people eloping with a girl.
We will swim, Pied One, son of Diing Ajok,
Though the Lol be flooded,
We shall make it to Akortong.
A Nuer jumped out of his byre:
"Dinkas, are you the owners of that *yang?*"
We looked around, thinking Nyang e Yang
Might have followed us;
But it was only the word for "cow" in Nuer language.
Then he asked, "Are you Dinkas of Kwol
That you may go by,
Or are you Dinkas of Ruweng
That we may fight?"
As though men's fighting were like animals'
To begin with no quarrel!

(Dinka)

OX SONG (5)

We, the red and white oxen, wash our hands,
shaking our heads angrily as we walk.

At dawn we will set fire to all the camps.
We will attack them like a woman
who goes at her daughter
for trying to marry with only one heifer.

We didn't sleep last night,
anxious to jump in the dance.

My singing will be heard as far
as the radio, with its breath
like a trapped bee.
I am the full-grown ox with spreading horns,
son of the village,
truly son of Lcak Puoc Wang.

—Sung by John Gatweclul
Attributed to Kuek Taitai
(Nuer)

COW SONG (3)

Which cow has Biel brought—the red and white beauty?
The one with the white back and red flanks?
Go off to the pasture, cow, where Biel Bang's son
is always praising you, where you sniff my tamarind tree.
The one with the spotted head will lead you to the river.
Oh, Spotted Head, with him you will roam to the pasture.
To all that grass, yes, all that grass.
The range goes on and on, all the way to the bush.
Tender shoots can be seen as far as Luol.
Oh, Ding Nhial, you will be fed there.

—Nyaruoth Atem
(Nuer)

QUEEN INKA YA BIRAMBA

Her javelin with a handle of gnarled wood
   cut in the forest beyond Juru:
Having rooted there, grown and produced a dense obscurity
Having covered itself entirely with lichen
Having extended its branches, giving birth to a thicket
A grove, where elephants scratched themselves,
Without making any part of it swing like a branch
Our heroine, queen of the oxen,
Having found it, relentless, seized,
Tore it out by the roots
So it quit the earth with a clap of splintering quartz
Its whole body ardent as coals.

—Ndangamira
(Kinyarwanda)

COMMENTARY

It is not for meat that cattle are kept in the kraal. Indeed, one of the most devastating insults a Dinka herdsman can level at another is "Meat-eater!" For a man to drink cow's milk is as natural as for a child to feed from the breast of his human mother; to eat cattle-flesh is cannibalism.

Among the sparse acacias, seasonal swamps, and high grasses of the East African cattle area—from the upper Nile to the Transvaal— a deep affinity is culturally elaborated between mankind and cattle; and this same bond exists, although expressed with a different aesthetic and metaphysical tonality, all along the West African savanna —from the Senegal River valley to the Benue—between the wandering Fulani (or "Peul") and their lean kine.

Animals that are herded and husbanded are property. They are live-in wealth. They may be exchanged for wives. They reproduce and may be milked. One surrounds them with care, encloses them at night; and they, reciprocally, in a bleak landscape provide surroundings. Cynosures of all eyes, cattle become superstars, constellations of value. Cattle, the herdsman's exclusive preoccupation, are like mirrors reflecting everything else alive.

Among the people who have migrated from the upper Nile (as, indeed, in their own way, among the Fulani), color vocabulary is derived from the variegated tones of hides. The complex markings of the body are a primary perceptual matrix; and all other aspects of veld and sky—flora, fauna, light, and various cloud formations—are metaphorically referred back to the bovine surfaces that microcosmically reflect them. A guinea hen has spots like a certain type of cow; their names, consequently, are interchangeable. Thunderheads, mirrored on the flanks of a mostly black ox, or the gloomy shade of a tall thicket on the shoulders of a gray one, become virtually synonymous with the initially perceived phenomena. Out of such perceptual correspondences has evolved a highly elaborate system of praise-nomenclature.

A Dinka receives an ox-name at birth and another upon initiation to manhood:

> The Dinka frequently pointed out to me those things in nature which had the *marial* color-configuration upon which my own (honorary) metaphorical ox-name was based. The sight of such things calls to mind the ox and the ox calls to mind the courting and other personal display in which it is a necessary companion. In contemplating such things . . . a man is in effect deriving pleasure from contemplating himself—handsome, prosperous and successful with women.[1]

To the name of one's favorite animal one appends phrases of endearment, like these from the kingdom of Ankole: "She who lifts up her horns brown as the Enkuraijo tree" or "He who is not to be dissuaded from fighting." One phrase succeeds another and may be extended by comparison, made moody and therefore lyrical according to the principle of surrogation (the self bovined) to which one has been accustomed since birth.

Such verbal expressiveness is expected of the youthful herdsman, whose culture further encourages him to extend denomination into

---

[1] Godfrey Lienhardt, *Divinity and Experience, The Religion of the Dinka* (Oxford: Oxford University Press, 1961), pp. 19–20.

narrative; and so in his leisure he composes songs in which his self-defining exploits and those of his favorite companions, bovine and human, are intertwined. All names being ultimately referable to cattle, it is impossible for an outsider to tell who is who among the protagonists of these juvenile raids and seductions—an ambiguity that is doubtless part of their subliminal charm for both composer and initiated listener. Although all cattle guardians herd words reflecting the imaginative importance of their charges, some are more skilled at this verbal Transhumance than others. Talent, recognized, may be nudged into a vicarious pastorate. The eloquent shepherd boy may become an official praise-poet and at the cattle-courts of Ankole or Rwanda expatiate upon the apocryphal adventures of bigger-than-life-sized bovine warriors.

OX SONG (1). Source: T. O. Beidelman, "Some Baraguyu Cattle Songs," *Journal of African Languages* IV, 1 (1965), p. 14. The Baraguyu text is only ten words long. Beidelman translates it as follows: "You are making me drunk (with joy) by your many colors, you, my fine heifer! I will sing a song as I pass (with you) through the gate (of my cattle camps)."

OX SONG (2). Source: ibid., p. 6. Here again I have worked with Beidelman's literal prose translation and with his notes. This is a complicated and (ultimately even to Beidelman) obscure image-event. I think I see it; but should I have erred in perception, may I be forgiven by the Baraguyu herdsman who so subtly composed the song!

BULL SONG (1). Source: Captain S. I. Cummins, "Sub-tribes of the Bahr-el-Ghazal Dinkas," *Journal of the Royal Anthropological Society* 34 (1904), p. 162. Lienhardt (*Divinity and Experience*, p. 20) says: "In personal display men are linguistically identified with oxen, which are primarily of aesthetic interest; but in fighting and in relation to their women, they are thought of as bulls, begetters and fighters, each ultimately center, source and leader of his own herd. The bull represents virility for the Dinka."

OX SONG (3). Source: E. E. Evans-Pritchard, *The Nuer* (Oxford, England: Oxford University Press, 1960), p. 47. Line five of Evans-

Pritchard's translation is the touchingly parochial: "When I went to court the winsome lassie." Kwejok, Kirjoak, and Buth are the poet's human age-mates. The "friend" addressed in the last three lines is the white ox who occasioned the poem.

COW SONG (1). Source: D. F. v.d. Merwe, "Hurutshe Poems," *Bantu Studies* XV, 4 (1941), pp. 322–323. This is not an individual composition but, rather, one version of a standard praise that the Hurutshe herdsman would recite as his cattle approach the kraal in the evening.

COW SONG (2). Source: Amadou Hampate Ba, "Poésie Peule de Macina," *Présence Africaine*, Série 1, 8/9 (1950), pp. 175–177. Surely one of the ecological wonders of the world is the inland Niger delta. In the Pleistocene age the Niger was two rivers. What is now the upper Niger rose as it still does, from ancient rounded massifs along the Guinée-Sierra Leone border and flowed into a vast lake, where today there is nothing but desert. What we call the middle Niger then rose in the mountainous plateau known as Adrar-des-Iforas and flowed diagonally southeast into the Atlantic. Then, as the sources of the middle Niger gradually desiccated, dunes encroaching from the desert forced the upper Niger to alter its course. Twisting north and east (away from its lake), this river carved an outlet across the rocky Sill-of-Tosaye into the ready-made bed of the other; and the two streams became one continuous course, more than four thousand kilometers long. But though dunes block the lost lake, another has formed in the depression through which the upper Niger flows north before narrowly verging east to Tosaye. The river floods the plains about this new lake (Debo). The peak rise of twenty-one feet is reached in late November or early December. As the runoff begins to reveal a dazzling new growth of *borgu* grasses, one hundred and sixty-three thousand Fulani nomads, with some million and a half head of cattle, leave their rainy-season encampments and from all directions move into these prime grazing lands that are the old river's seasonal gift to the otherwise struggling savanna. When (hopefully) the rains begin to fall again on this region in late June or early July, the Fulani cattle, having grazed in the wake of the retreating waters to the very shores of Lake Debo, are gently urged homeward by their guardians. They must make their two-hundred-kilometer march with all deliberate speed to avoid getting stuck in the mud; for when it comes, the inundation is authoritative.[2]

The young transhumer who composed this poem has been travel- ing from Lake Debo in a southwesterly direction along a path (*burti*) traditionally prescribed for members of his particular clan. His family's rainy-season camp is in the Macina region on the left bank of the Niger, which he must cross to enter the *borgu* pastures. But at one time he must have traveled to the Seno plateau on the right bank of the Bani branch of the Niger, for he speaks of the Mossi people, whose women tend to their cattle. His attitude toward the luxuriating womanizers he has left back home is comparable to that of the Bam- bara hunter of the funeral song (p. 101 above). A man is a man. For a brief discussion of the traditional religious beliefs of the Fulani, see pp. 190–191. An even briefer personal note: Wading through the *borgu* swamps is rough, even if the water lilies are beautiful. *Borgu* grass cuts and is infested with mosquitoes. I have seen Fulani herds- men walking barefoot up to their armpits in water with their cattle swimming along beside. The poet might well be proud of his youthful accomplishment.

BULL SONG (2). Source: Cummins, "Bahr-el-Ghazal Dinkas," p. 162.

OX SONG (4). Source: Francis Mading Deng, *The Dinka and Their Songs* (Oxford, England: Oxford University Press, 1973), pp. 122–123. This, Deng tells us, is an excerpt from a longish song about the kid- napping of a calf in order to take it into Nuer territory. There the young men planned to barter it for a "personality ox." (Of these a person may have more than one.)

Oxen are pivotal in the aesthetics of cattle and symbolize the opposite qualities of gentleness and submissiveness on the one hand and aggressiveness and physical courage on the other, all of which represent the personality traits of young men, [but] *they* are praised mainly for *their* aggressiveness and courage even as men superficially criticize *them*. That oxen, though castrated,

[2] Statistics are taken from Pascal James Imperato's article, "Nomads of the Niger," *Natural History* LXXXI, 10 (1972), pp. 60–68, 78–79.

occupy such a highly important place among cattle sufficiently symbolizes the position of young men who, though subordinated to their elders, have a very high aesthetic value and gain satisfaction from the recognition of this in songs. (Deng, *The Dinka*, p. 82. Italics added to underscore the marvelous confusion of referents: *"Them"* apparently refers to the young men only, but *"they"* and *"their,"* referring to the cattle, imply the young men as well.)

Ox songs, says Deng, promote both inner and social harmony as experiences that are painful, shameful, or otherwise undesirable (in this case theft) are turned into art, which is not only a personal satisfaction but also a means of achieving social recognition for one's *dheeng*. *Dheeng* is the Dinka equivalent of ancient Greek *arete*. It has to do with outward grace of bearing as well as with honor and inner pride. *Dheeng* is elegant manliness, which in youth, because of one's lack of access to the power structure, is primarily expressed in singing and dancing the virtues of one's personality-cattle.

OX SONG (5). Source: Terese Svoboda, *"Cleaned the Crocodile's Teeth:" Nuer Song* (Greenfield Center, NY: Greenfield Review Press, 1985), p. 13. This excerpt from a much longer *tuare*, or autobiographical improvisation, was originally published under the title "The Radio with Its Breath Like a Trapped Bee" in *Anteus*, Vol. 28, 1978. As Svoboda points out at the conclusion of her book, the difference between singing on the radio and live performance is not as great as from song to written poem. "The Nuer have been particularly loath to adopt wholesale anything Western, choosing instead elements that most suit their land and lifestyle. They search for ways to use modern media to propagate their tradition. . . . (T)hey fill their cassettes with Neur songs and tune to Nuer singers on Radio Khartoum." "Red and white oxen" is the name of an age-group. Svoboda calls them "gangs."

COW SONG (3). Source: Svoboda, p. 14. Nuer women also praise the family cattle. So far as I know, Svoboda is the first fieldworker/collector to have stopped to listen to them do so. A woman's name begins with *Nya*, meaning "daughter of" until their sons receive the six lateral scarification marks on their foreheads that denote full manhood. Thereafter, a woman's name begins with *Man,* meaning "mother of."

QUEEN INKA YA BIRAMBA. The peoples living along the highland corridor of East Africa, slightly inland of the rift valley of lakes, were organized by cattle-rich elites into unified feudal states, whose kings and ruling classes were able to maintain their power by a complicated system of clientship based on cattle indebtedness. In the kingdom of Rwanda, a classical example of the centralized lacustrine state, the Tutsi minority entrusted creation and maintenance of poetic ideology to three specialized types of bard: the dynastic poet, the warrior-poet, and the pastoral poet (*umwisi:* he-who-gives-names). These bards had a built-in audience of connoisseurs among the artistic sons of the king and his wealthier clients. In such conditions the genre of cattle-praise flowered into epic.

Here's how it was done. An elaborate administrative husbandry assigned all cattle owned by clients to the king's army and, in accordance with the mirror principle discussed above, the cows themselves were formed into regiments, which shared commanders with the human units to which they were attached as auxiliaries. Each troop of bovines, newly constituted, consisted of thirty first-rate heifers and fifteen reinforcements. The herdsman in charge selected a pastoral poet to come to their grazing place. About half of the herd, the most promising specimens, were pulled out and presented to the bard, who improvised to each an eclogue, which the attendant herdsmen memorized on the spot. Each of these poems of several dozen lines perforce contained a common term acknowledging the unity of the group. When the first phase of the poet's work was done, he was allowed to select one of the fifteen reinforcements as an honorarium.

When the cows had calved for the second time, they were considered at the acme of their physical development. The height of their horns being relatively stabilized, the best of the lot was easily recognizable. She was entitled Queen (*indatwa*) and became, as a consequence, heroine of the longest and most intricate praise her bard could come up with. Again the poet was invited out to the pasture. To the original eclogue (which he had not forgotten) he now added many songs, all ending with an identical last line—that cow's leitmotif for generations to come. The longest pastoral poem of this nature ever collected runs to 1378 lines, of which a meager 11 are given here.

This epic praise is actually the work of two poets; and its length is the fortuitous result of two deaths, one bovine, one human. Queen Inka ya Biramba of the Izamuji ("the Sveltes") troop of the Akaganda regiment died before the great poet Ndangamira could complete his verbal tribute to her. The king ordered her to be replaced immediately. Then, after 424 lines composed to the new queen, the bard himself fell sick and died, in 1893, of smallpox. But even before Ndangamira breathed his last, the king had called in a substitute bard to finish the job.

Both because of and despite the institution of its origin, Ndangamira's poetry is magnificent. All the excesses of the imagination were at his command. Often in such heroic poetry cows are described as being armed with javelins and fighting against enemy herdsmen—not a surprising conceit given the cow's anatomy, her military affiliation, and the cattle-raiding wars that plague all similar societies. But look at what Ndangamira does with Queen Inka ya Biramba's taking-up of arms!

In another place Ndangamira praises Queen Inka ya Biramba, without Brobdingnagian irony, as one would praise any creature intensely alive: "a vivacity gifted with incomparable speed." So must his own lines sound in Kinyarwanda, when recited pell-mell in the old-fashioned way. Thus must Ndangamira's mind itself have been, out there in the high windy grasses as it raced, against an advancing shadow, to conceive. Source: Alexis Kagame, "La Poésie pastorale au Rwanda," *Zaire* I, 7 (1947), pp. 791–800.

VIII: *Presence of Spirits*

VOICE OF THE DIVINE HERDSMAN

My voice! My voice! Here am I, Koumen.

The sky smiles above my head
The earth quivers beneath my feet
My breath sways branches
Here stand I before my cattle camp
It is the first clearing
    fenced with trellises
      woven of twigs from the marvelous *kelli* tree
      and the virtuous *nelbi*
      covered with rampant *delbi* vines
      whose flowers sing for my oxen
Sing you also for them, birds of the trees!

I am sovereign in breeding
The auspicious white and black hermaphrodite
    lows in the midst of my herd
    whose rare queen she is.

Hurr hurr hurr!
Thrown prone whirr skirr, feathered word!

In the entrails of male and female are contained the seeds
    of future heifers and bull calves
Brilliant foretelling of good fortune!

Go forth, stout oxen and heavy-uddered cows
Jump over the charmed circle
It pleases me to see you go out onto the savanna
    and water at the pond of the seventh sun.
I am Koumen of the many guises:
    whirlwind sucking up the dust
    inundation submerging the scrub.
When, for his own good, I seize hold of a man
I plunge him into that pond where my cattle slake thirst
I whisper into his right ear the true name
    of the black and white one
It is a magic word, which multiplies calves
    and swells udders.

I am Koumen
When my disciple sucks my tongue
My saliva conveys the word
That accomplishes fertility.

The Creator knows me.
Beyond here, he transformed me into an eternal child.
Earth executes my commands
Because I blew down from the sky
    when the waters in ferment
    were about to give birth to her—
    mother of pastures and farms.
I am Koumen the enchanter
I transform withers and humps
    into sleek flanks
And when I am angry, the reverse:
I blow on a herd
    and they turn shaggy and humped
    or disappear into the bush.

Herdsman, would you see me?
Hunter, would you discern?
Consult healers of the ear and eye
Who reside in black anthill

or isolated baobab
in that mysterious country
where stars are bleached
before, encrusted with sky,
they are set into circulation.
I know the initial temperature of waters
I know the nature of stars
I know their destiny
I know the secret of the moon
in its sickle phase when it pierces the clouds
in its spring fullness when, turning night to day,
it boasts of clotted milk.

Enter, those who have been through!
Those who have been through, enter!

(Fulani)

VOICE OF THE KARAW

(1)   *Bursts of twilight's frantic wing-beats, submit to me, I am*
            Yori
         I am as the arching sky, as encounter of crossroads in space
         Green savanna, entirely fresh, green savanna entirely
            outstretched
               where no dog may scavenge
         Hornbill of deaf-mute village I am deaf-mute chief.
         What sort of a thing is this? *Come, old tearers-to-shreds,*
            submit to me, I am Yori.
         Astonishing! What we are learning now existed already,
            arriving from beforehand: rhythm
         I entered the flow and found it was transformation—
         Rhythm, beginning of all beginning speech, was the
            crowned crane's:
               I speak, said the crowned crane,
               meaning I know I speak.
         Oh, if I here misspeak, may heat of error be sufficient
            to pardon my mistake;

If I omit, may omission be forgiven that anticipates!
Old knives, having been sheathed, cannot transpierce the
　　mystery—
　　　　come, old tearers-to-shreds, submit to me,
　　　　I am Yori
I am as the arching sky, as encounter of crossroads in space,
I am as the unique sun!
Cock's head of night's transformation, Father of my
　　instruction,
　　　　see, my arm is bent behind my back as you wish;
Memory itself is to blame for all mistakes,
　　　　memory which makes me stumble, if I do
As for oblivion—blame inattention of spirit;
Perhaps a running knot will form along the cord of my
　　speech;
　　　　but all cords are corridors leading to embrace
And all antechambers lead to our common origin: Mande
All having derives from another's possession
　　　　To have you come, you arrive by means of instruction;
Transformation, where true possession takes place,
　　　　even moderate insight
　　　　anticipates penetration.
His word has been translated exactly!
Transformation, all transformation, man's furnace, crucible
　　of patience,
　　　　I say all waiting is pure patience
If these words be spoken at the crossroads of space!

(2)　　Shake, shake (things of the world, if you would elicit speech
　　　　of)
　　　　　White savanna!
Last bursts of twilight, you are as animals:
　　　　behind them—obscurity
　　　　before them—obscurity
You are as a blind hippo hedged by inescapable bush,
A powerful hippo hoisting itself on a small animal,
　　　　hoping to penetrate inaccessible bush;
How may the blind see? How maintain cadence of the gait?

The furnace has spared us, Father of our instruction,
Sky, bend; earth, open! O white clearing,
O abandoned bush, deserted forest,
Nothing is left aside; all is encompassed;
the furnace has spared us.
Bursts of twilight's frantic wing-beats, submit to me, I am
Yori;
I am as encounter in space, as the arching sky.
Father of my instruction, elder *kara,* your word is ancient
I say: from the cradle of Mande to the luxurious corridor
of transformation to the straw hat of the ignorant
This is the *kara,* unsheathed, erect, pure concentration;
You are the awaiting heart. Aardvark knows this;
falcon is ignorant;
The meaning, truth itself is a mystery porcupine defends,
but cannot pierce, nor aardvark unearth;
But I'm forgetting the white falcon!
Whatever I know, I had from someone;
This is the *kara;* now you need no longer call Him—
deaf-mute hornbill, deaf-mute chief of deaf-mute
village.
If I be mistaken, call error itself to task;
what I have forgotten, may it be pardoned by omission.
Yori, my father; Yori, my mother; Yori behind me,
transformer of my descendants,
Yori of transformations,
come, transfigure the entire person;
Come, fellow sky-shredders,
let us distribute the weight of this burden;
Each pupil's attention partakes of the master's
perseverance;
If you be mistaken, captive spirit of mine,
may error do me no harm.
Transformation! Bursts of twilight's frantic wing-beats,
calm yourselves here; I am Yori
I am as the arching sky, as encounter of crossroads in space!
Night's obscurity is not void; it contains—
whatever I know I had from Someone.

(3)　　*Be at peace, old tearers-to-shreds, here am I, Yori,*
　　　　As handle of spear I am, as the arching sky
　　　　I am as the unique sun,
　　　　You there, slapping the face of twilight,
　　　　　　calm yourselves; here am I, Yori,
　　　　I as the arching sky, I as the unique sun
　　　　Deaf-mute hornbill, fire which spared the bone,
　　　　　　chief of deaf-mute village,
　　　　I say mumble mumble, I say caw-caw the cacophonous,
　　　　Sheathed, sheathed are the old knives. Yori, my father,
　　　　　　Yori, my mother, Yori, my ancestor,
　　　　　　I have gone to question our founder.
　　　　The old man as if seized by uncontrollable itching
　　　　　　scratches his head; thoughtfully rotates his jaw
　　　　　　as if pestered by a piece of gristle;
　　　　　　then hastens to Ségou to consult the sages;
　　　　For some things may be found in the enemy's house
　　　　　　that the friend's house lacks;
　　　　　　and that which is lacking makes enemies friends;
　　　　Founder, my father, my friend, exacerbation of questing
　　　　　　is calmed within; there the true task begins;
　　　　　　but transformation is arduous, arduous.
　　　　Come, what we are learning now existed already;
　　　　　　let us accomplish the rhythm:
　　　　All cords are corridors leading to embrace of origin.

(4)　　*Bursts of twilight's frantic wing-beats, submit to me, I am*
　　　　　Yori
　　　　I am as the arching sky, as encounter of crossroads in space
　　　　Green savanna, entirely fresh, green savanna, entirely
　　　　　outstretched
　　　　　　where no dog may scavenge
　　　　Hornbill of deaf-mute village I am, deaf-mute chief;
　　　　I say mumble mumble, I say caw caw the cacophonous;
　　　　Come, old tearers-to-shreds, submit to me, I am Yori,
　　　　As handle of spear I am, as the arching sky, encounter in
　　　　　space.

What sort of a thing is this? *You, there, slapping the face*
    of twilight, calm yourselves!
Let us be off to question the old women. They who have
    lived say: Nothing could be more arduous.
Let us be off to question the young virgins. They in their
    innocence say:
What seems to resist wishes to yield, wants
        ecstasy.
Come, what we are learning now existed already,
And some things may be found in the enemy's house
    that the friend's house lacks.
I have gone to question our founder, father of my
    instruction,
And he, vexed and perplexed as by gristle and fleas,
        made haste to Ségou to consult the sages;
But the teaching of *kara* cannot be unraveled without
    reflection;
Nor can there be strands of thought without illumination;
Nor can crepuscular rays strike unless there be mast,
        unless there be pennant unfurled from apex of spirit.
Brother tearers-to-shreds, I turn for your explication;
But alas, in a sack are hidden such strands of illumination!

> (Bambara)

EIGHT ORISHA

ESHU

First born
Known to everyone
Anger prompting retaliation out of all proportion.
Sharer in sacrifice
Turner of right into wrong, who makes the innocent guilty.
He went as far as Ijebu
    but returned the same day;
He went no farther than the gate of our compound
    and didn't return for many years.

If he has left his cloth behind
    he rips off the cloth-seller's;
If he leaves his wife behind
    husbands go searching for their spouses;
If there be no drums
    he will dance to the pounding of mortars.

Standing alone in the entryway, like a stranger's son.

[song]
Take a cowrie shell, present it to *'Bara*
Buy two kolanuts
Cut midrib of the oil palm for Eshu
When you awaken, they'll say, "Eshu is going to support you"

Latopa
Eshu, sharp as a razor, supports for nothing
Lalupon
Eats his yam [exclusively] with a small snail.

OGUN
The day Ogun came down from his hill
He was clothed in fire
And wore a garment of blood;
Then he borrowed palm fronds from palm trees;
Attired in fresh palm fronds, he entered Ire
And was immediately proclaimed king.
Owner of two machetes:
    with one he prepares the farm
    with the other he clears the road.
One does not break covenant with Ogun.

[chant]
Ogun korobiti korobiti
Ogun, huge [as a mountain]
Ogun, in the house
Ogun, in the fields
Ogun, at the town gate.

BABALUAIYE
Spotted prowler, you know the country
Powerful danger
Bees swarm: the farmer is playing
Impatient, the sufferer tramples his tormentors
Prowler
Dry wind
Bringer of many children.

[song]
Obaluaiye—with regard to the snail
Gently, at the right time—with regard to the snail
Owner of many little medicine gourds—with regard to the snail
You who wash your face with palm oil—take a look at the snail
May you be gently forthcoming—in the manner of the snail.

YEMOJA
Queen who lives in water's depths
Yemoja smooths bush into path-surfaces
Yemoja stoops on calabash-brink, sipping effervescence;
She waits seated, even in a king's presence.
Yemoja rises, eddies, when tornado enters the country;
Dissatisfied, she ruptures bridges;
Mother-of-fishes eats in the house as well as in the river.
Mother of weeping breasts
She has grown a thicket about her private business
And is tight as a dried yam.
Deep-swelling queen of the world, she heals like medicine;
Old woman of the sea
Flute-girl, who plays for the king's awakening
Woman who gently bears the swimmer to rest someplace.
She doesn't wish to respond on land
But on the surface of the water she speaks rapidly.

Iya mi Awoyo

SHANGO

He dances savagely in the courtyard of the impertinent
He sets fire to the house of the man who lies
Owner of the destroying ax,
He sounds his maracas like iron handbells.

With eyes white as bitter kola
Cheeks puffed out with kola nuts
The masquerade who emits fire from his mouth
The god who frightens cats.
Elegant and leisurely husband of the kola-seller;
If someone is brazen-faced to you
Shango will teach him a lesson;
With eyes white as bitter kola
Shango, fierce lord!

[song]
Red and white beads
    worn by the adept
Red and white beads
    worn by the adept
Little children: red and white beads
Elder with grown children: red and white beads
Shango, no noose tied around my neck!
Red and white beads. . . . [repeat 2×]

OSHUN

Ruler of riverbed
Great wealth is pleasing;
She dances, and takes the crown
She dances without asking permission
She keeps her own counsel.
She who has children listens for their crying
So she may take them up, tranquilly.
She who is laden with brass ornaments;
She eats costly gumbo without asking for credit;
City woman
If a woman like this moves onto the road, man flees;

Come to the dance: she clinks her bracelets;
Owner of the swamp dances to the drum at dawning
She dances in the depths of richness
She casts a calabash into marsh water as though it were sky
She casts a plate into marsh water
As though her soap were the open road!

Ore yeye-o Ore yeye-o Ore yeye-o

OBATALA
He is patient, he is not angry
He sits in silence to pass judgment
He sees you even when he is not looking
He stays in a far place, but his eyes are on the town.
The granary of heaven can never be filled
The old man full of life-force.
He kills the initiate
And awakens him to let him hear his words;
We leave the world to the owner of the world.
Death acts playfully, until he carries away the child.
He rides on the hunchback;
He stretches out his right hand
He stretches out his left.

Obatala, who turns blood into children
I have only one cloth to dye with blue indigo
I have only one head-tie to dye with red camwood
But I know that you keep twenty or thirty children for me,
Whom I shall bear.

Iba oriṣa nla

OYA
O mother, Oya-o
It's not from today that she is honorable
[but from long ago]

O mother, Ọya-o
May you not be received rudely

The one who enters witch's house dragging muddy feet

O mother, Ọya-o
May you not be received impolitely

Ancestor, owner of the whip, elder Egun

O mother, Ọya-o
May you not be received improperly

Mighty, mighty Orisha who dares confine the elder to his room
Authority in the house who uses truth to terrify the wicked person

O mother, Ọya-o
May you not be received disrespectfully

Customs officer in charge of the life/death frontier

Reaching an agreement with parent of a child, she never breaks it

O mother, Ọya-o
Customs officer at the frontier

Wife of Ogun picked up the drum and played it on her vast chest

O mother, Ọya-o
When she's got her eye on something
she never changes her intention

She slipped under the Odan tree and the Odan got itself uprooted

O mother, Ọya-o
When she's got her eye on something
she never changes her intention

Person who causes lightning to rip through the house
She patrols the compound around around, waiting for Olodumare
    to show up
If he arrives, he won't find the culprit inside

> *O my lady of power*
> *When she's got her eye on something*
> *she never changes her intention*

Oya has no home, no special road
The person who thinks about is unlikely to encounter her

> *O my lady of power*
> *When she's got her eye on something*
> *she never changes her intention*

When she fights with you it's never her fault
When she fights with you it's without remorse
Everything she does she gets away with

> *O my lady of power*
> *When she's got her eye on something*
> *she never changes her intention*

If her group is performing, if bembe drums are playing
She dances bembe, dances shekere

> *O my lady dances*

Who's that dancing to the bata drums?

> *O my lady dances*

Wife of Ogun, she's been performing Egungun a long, long time
Oya turned around and became Orisha
She guards the road into the world, guards the road to heaven.

[chant]
Oya, strike debt from my head, toss it away
Oya, shake death off my head, shake death off my head
Oya, cleanse loss from my head, completely
Oya, shake trouble off my head: no more punishment!

(Yoruba)

TO THE EARTH (1)

The earth does not get fat
    It makes an end of those who wear the head plumes
The earth does not get fat
    It makes an end of those who act swiftly as heroes
Shall we die on earth?

Listen, O earth; we shall mourn because of you
Listen, shall we all die on the earth?

The earth does not get fat
    It makes an end of the chiefs
    Shall we all die on the earth?
The earth does not get fat
    It makes an end of the women-chiefs
    Shall we die on the earth?

Listen, O earth; we shall mourn because of you
Listen, shall we all die on the earth?

The earth does not get fat
    It makes an end of the nobles
    Shall we die on the earth?
The earth does not get fat
    It makes an end of the royal women
    Shall we die on the earth?

Listen, O earth; we shall mourn because of you
Listen, shall we all die on the earth?

The earth does not get fat
    It makes an end of the common people
    Shall we die on earth?
The earth does not get fat
    It makes an end of all the animals
    Shall we die on earth?

Listen, you who are asleep
    Who are left tightly closed in the land
    Shall we all sink into the earth?
Listen, O earth, the sun is setting tightly
We shall all enter into the earth.

(Ngoni)

TO THE EARTH (2)

Earth, condolences
Earth, condolences
Earth and dust
Supreme Being
I lean upon you
Earth, when I am about to die
I lean upon you
Earth, while I am alive
I depend upon you
Earth that receives dead bodies.
The Creator's Drummer says
From wherever he went
He has roused himself
He has roused himself.

(Akan)

TO THE RAIN

Bringer of wealth
Feeder of orphans

Fall gently
Come and feed us peacefully
Oh, fall gently.

(Acoli)

THREE TOROU

MOUSSA GOURMANTCHE Right bank of the Niger

In front, a hump
Behind, a dune
Above, a stick
Below, a serpent
If you go up, the stick will strike you
If you go down, the snake will bite you!
Iron bow, if the sun is hot
You can't carry it on your shoulder
Or it will break your last little rib;
If you carry it on your head
It'll boil your brains!

HAUSAKOI Left bank of the Niger

He lost a cowrie
So he burned Tombuctou;
He threw ash to the winds
So blazed up Yaouri;
Ash to the wind, turning back
He found his cowrie;
They said, What made you do it?
He answered, That cowrie was my friend!

FARAM BAROU Rippling water

Faram Barou is crying for her pretty bird
Dada-ase, the little red and yellow one;
All you others better go look for it
Or the village won't be peaceful.
On your feet, everyone, Torou included

To please Faram Barou
Crying for her own lost little one!

(Songai-Zarma)

THE BORI CALLED BATUREN GWARI

We are the end
We are meningitis
We are all the other illnesses
We own the bit of earth behind the hut
Laughing one, there's no cure for this illness
Reveller, there is no rejoicing without us.

(Hausa)

CALLING THE WATERSPIRITS
*"We've reached the place, we have
arrive' (at Bolo Island)"*

(1)   Son of water-people, O my father, all happiness
    languishing far away, Nembe waterside, sea . . .

    Pulling riches from the sea, my waterspirit lover
    gently, gently drawing nearer to me

    Amgbiri entered the canoe; Anji entered the canoe
    Python, colored like the rainbow, entered the canoe seven
        times

    Amgbiri inhabits his watery world
    Rainbow python descends from the skies

    When the python coils, and remains coiled, he's angry
    Coiled in still water, Python's poised to attack

Ambaya is the spirit we are seeking
  shoulders shimmying with desire *ya ye o*
Kikiya is the spirit we are seeking
  shoulders shimmying with desire *ya ye o*
Anji-o is the spirit we are seeking
  shoulders shimmying with desire *ya ye o*

Anji, we cannot resist, you are too handsome
We lust for you, lust for you, lust for you

(2)   Only Anji can outspin the top
Anji alone dances whirling on one foot
Nonstop, whirling faster than faster, only Anji

Alaye son of Adumuya, my beloved, come home
O Seki, crocodile masquerade, come home to play
I'll even fetch salt water for you, O Seki

Fine cloths coming to shore, gliding gently gliding
Shining bells chiming bells, gliding to shore gently
Bearing riches on its way, the marvelous masquerade
    arriving in our own town, gliding gently

Tingling bells, shimmering reflections, waterspirits arrive
Arrayed in beauty, Ogwein the mermaid approaches

Ogwein, floating masquerade, when the time comes round
  to play
If your carrier won't display you, he will die

(3)   Hollow bamboo drum, I'm hearing it speak-o, bamboo drum
Small membrane drum, I hear it sounding-o, membrane
    drum
Wooden dugout drum, I'm hearing it call-o, slit drum
Wooden clapping sticks, I hear them clapping-o, wooden
    hands

Singers, take your seats, come eat biscuit
Waterspirit chorus, come quickly, we're calling you now
Singers, we're about to begin, come enjoy tinned biscuit

Sons of waterspirits, come quickly, come
Okputuya, quickly quickly
We are calling you, Adumuya
Kikiya, quickly quickly
We are calling you, Otoboya
Aleleya, quickly quickly
Ogwein's sons also, come, come quickly

Okpengbe, we call him, talkative waterspirit
  he's shaking the water, shaking the whole place
Okpengbe, Okpengbe, nonstop talkative spirit
  rattling his shield, shaking the ramparts
Okpengbe, wagging his tongue like a leather fan
  whipping up a stiff breeze, whitecaps answer
Okpengbe, boastful chairman of the churning waters

Ogbiki-o, angry, angry waterspirit
Ogbiki-o, waterspirit full of anger, waterspirit
Fertile tortoise, full of anger
Son of Akilala, wrathful waterspirit
Belonging to Nembe—partly, belonging to Kula—partly

Son of Awiri, agèd waterspirit, O destiny
Waterspirit, ashamed of his exploits
Son of Akilala, agèd waterspirit, O destiny

Beat it, beat this special drum for us
Drum beater, call the dark cloud

Ikonibo, this merman is strong *ye ye ye*
Ikonibo, this merman is sexy *ye ye ye*
Aleleya, Obiriye, Wabiriye [many names, many wives]
Ikonibo, plentifully, on land and in the water

Waterspirit world, working us too hard
The players have reached the crowd, let's call it a day

(4)   Waterspirit world, waterspirit world: difficult for humans
He comes to you, you say, "No, I don't want to carry you
     today"
You call, you pour drink, he may refuse possession

That day a call went out, message received:
you would not be awakening me in the night
Fiancé, forgive my disappointment

Aburuya, a call went out, message received:
you would not be coming to me in the night
O waterspirit lover, forgive my disappointment
                                        (Ijọ, Okrika dialect)

ODO MASQUERADE

May the congregation here listen,
Listen, for it is Odo hearing the market din
The Odo who lives near Nkwo market
Speaking his mind—his eternal mind:
I say to you
No other Odo gnaws into my trunk
And into my branches
Except Hornbill
Who thundered and ate his visitor;
I am the Odo who feeds on the market din—
I, Ogene-the-bell, who summons to conferences
I, the beaked singer, who rips open the maize cob
I, mysterious tripod used for cooking
So the pot can stand erect;
Two of my three legs give way
And the pot falls off, rolling
Seeking the eternal cook.

I ask the creator-scatterer of locusts
Please to retreat a pace
For almighty Odo is girded with cloth
And is going in peace—
If soldier ants advance, person advances
If they retreat, person retreats
He who has a basket should bring it to the wilderness
For the numberless locusts
Are a hovering host in the wilderness.

I, the *Ozo* who killed an elephant
I, the *Ozo* who wore palm leaves and rejected the hoe
I, the *Ozo* who took his title on *Eke* day
And performed in the village square on *Olie* day;
I, the beaked Singer
I, thorny weed never used as a carrying pad
I, the branch of the *Iyi* tree that becomes a medicine—
The killer of other trees.

Hornbill.
I am the woodpecker
That destroys trees;
The tree we consecrated
Has ever been my walking stick—
Ha Ha Ha Ha—

I am the Odo that flew straight
And touched everywhere in Igboland
The Odo living in the courtyard of the King of contentment
The Odo whose gate is the *Ngwu* tree;
I am like the child who accomplished a hard journey quickly
And was said to have raced under supernatural influence
I am the craftsman of the spirit world.

I am a gong:
The gong is inspired
And begins to talk
I am the gong with a melodious voice;

The crowd is thick here
The white ants are fluttering in clusters;
My *uturu*-bird voice
Is singing in the Odo fashion;
I have come, I have come, I have come
Son of the Almighty Odo;
The scribe cannot pick up
All that flows from my voice
What I am singing
I, the warbler.

(Igbo)

TRIPTYCH

NYIKANG (1)
The wind will blow, river's son
Foretelling rain, the wind will
    blow;
River's son, do not withdraw
O face of the progenitor!

NYIKANG (2)
On this bank, on that bank—
Royal, do you know it, River's
    son?
The black-splotched cow has
    broken
Whole grass blades!

JUOK
It is from the one side spirit
It is from the other side spirit
But from front and back it is body.

(Shilluk)

COMMENTARY

When speaking of African religions it is difficult to draw the line be-
tween what we mean in English when we say "spirit" and what we
reckon as "divinity," or between these and "power" or "force" or
"animating principle." The African world is animist. Even prosely-
tized people remain so, *au fond*. Animist: This means that every thing
contains an active or activable soul-essence. And because these in-

dwelling principles are lively, they can decide, or be enticed, to take up new habitations—either long-term or short-run. An ancestor may be ritually established in a forked stick, in an altar stone, in a masquerade; it may possess a person or be reincarnated. And according to the way things are, reflected in the African world's insistence on polyvalence, supernatural forces of various kinds and degrees of intensity may be present in different forms simultaneously.

Praise-words are one way of provoking divine presence in the way the human community at the moment wants it. Praise-words may also encourage whatever or whomever not to unleash its destructive potential. But invocation and placation are not the only forms of spirit-praising. Sometimes it is the supernatural power personified that speaks. And again, since the boundary between dramatic presentation and possession is flexible, sometimes both states of consciousness seem to manifest themselves simultaneously or to slide back and forth from one to the other almost imperceptibly. That is, when the word has been efficacious, how can we tell the dancer from the dance or from the *danced*?

VOICE OF THE DIVINE HERDSMAN. This is an excerpt from part one (or "the first clearing") of a Fulani initiation text: A. Hampate Ba and Germaine Dieterlen, *Koumen: Texte initiatique des Pasteurs Peul,* (Paris-La Haye: Mouton 1961), pp. 32–35. The authors collected this material from Master Ardo Dembo, encamped near Linguère, Senegal, who had his best pupil, Aliow Essa, recite it as proof of learning.

Who is Koumen, "the enchanter," who later praises himself as "master of sacred spells"?

The Fulani believe themselves to be consubstantial with their cattle. According to myth, the world emerged from a drop of milk that contained the four elements to which correspond the four basic bovid colors and the four directions (fire-yellow-east; air-red-west; water-black-south; earth-white-north). These elements, which also are affiliated with the four Fulani clans, having formed the earth, proceeded to coalesce into the great hermaphroditic bull-cow, symbol of the universe, whose secret name is an incantation for bovine fertility. The first herds emerged from the sea and journeyed, under the tutelage of the great serpeant Tyanaba, from the mouth of the Senegal river

to Lake Debo in Mali. Their sinuous course may be seen today out-
lined by the Senegal and upper Niger rivers. Tyanaba's assistant dur-
ing this first transhumance of the Fulani cattle was Koumen, the
herdsman; and it is he who knows and transmits the pastoral secrets,
stage by stage, to qualified initiates. The text in question recounts the
initiation of the first of these, whose name was Silé Sadio.

Each subsequent postulant must follow in Silé Sadio's footsteps.
That is, as he learns progressively about the structure of the universe
and about the ritual techniques necessary to achieve an enlightened
pastoral competence, the candidate passes through twelve "clearings,"
undergoing the ordeals appropriate to each stage, and at the end must
unravel twenty-eight (lunar) knots of higher knowledge. Presumably,
memorization of this text proceeds apace, along with absorption of
its more esoteric meanings. The first stage ("clearing") presents Silé
Sadio's initial encounter with Koumen. Looking for a lost cow, the
herdsman hears a voice: "My voice! My voice!" and so on. After the
self-praise given here, a narrative passage tells us, "This is what Kou-
men said when Silé Sadio surprised him lying under a tamarind tree
beside Toumou pond." Thinking Koumen to be a baby (he is in the
guise of "divine child"), Silé Sadio is preparing to pick him up; but
instead, the divine herdsman (now suddenly bearded like a patriarch)
seizes the initate and questions him about his spiritual intentions!

"kelli," "nelbi," "delbi"—Part of the instruction has to do with the
virtues of plants.

"Hurr hurr hurr"—These two lines are an incantation; the second
line is an English approximation based on Mme. Dieterlen's notes.
The words evidently refer to an act, divinatory chicken sacrifice. The
headless chicken beats the dust this way and that. How it finally rests
determines whether or not the important sacrifice to follow will be
accepted. In this case, it clearly is.

"Seventh sun"—Worlds upon worlds—this is the final one. The sys-
tem is comparable to that of medieval planetary regions as depicted
by Dante.

"When my disciple sucks my tongue"—This is done during initiation so that the moisture containing the word may be passed from teacher to pupil. Afterward the word is uttered aloud.

"Enter, those who have been through"—This incantation is addressed to initiates who have already passed through the first stage successfully and may now return to instruct others. Those who wish to arrive at final knowledge/illumination immediately, without going through the progressive stages, are by implication excluded.

VOICE OF THE KARAW. Here the divine voice (italics) alternates with the all-too-human voice of the initiate as he attempts to recite this sacred text exactly.

The *karaw* (singular *kara*) are initiatory masters of the Bambara Kore society. This is the last of a sequence of six secret societies, that in which man realizes mystic participation in divine being. *Karaw* are also straw mats that are rolled into cylinders when stored and may be unrolled to form temporary enclosures. Hence, an enlightened man is one who may unroll knowledge of our relationship to divinity. Thirdly, *kara* is the name of a spatula-shaped plank of decorated wood—an emblem both of the enlightened and of the enlightening word. During *karaw* recitations this standard (some eight or nine feet high) is set on the ground. At mouth level (as though it were a flat, elongated mask) the *kara* has an opening, through which the spokesman puts the three central fingers of his left hand—tongues of the sacred utterance. And finally, the *kara*—the sum of words recited— is divinity itself, synonymous with Yori, who begins by demanding absolute submission.

Yori repeats this demand several times as the discourse unrolls. He characterizes his mouthpieces as last-sunset-rays-attempting-to-penetrate-the-gathering-obscurity-of-the-mystery. They rip up and tear to shreds old misconceptions and spurious hypotheses. What seems twilight to them (they are at one point pictured as impatiently slapping the face of the setting sun) is in reality dawning, a new illumination announced by cockcrow. What has intervened is the dark night of the soul. One must be reborn into knowledge. The cock announces transformation, a process compared to the transmutation of matter in a smith's furnace. West African smelting takes place in a womb-shaped crucible out of which the liquid ore runs through a clay pipe into a trough. This structure and its function (as well as its symbolism) are compared throughout the four-part cycle to a clay hut of similar shape (although roofed with straw) called the *Blo*. This little house, located in Kangaba (on the Niger below Bamako) is the national shrine of all who speak Malinké dialects, of which Bambara is one. The *Blo* is called the "cradle" of Mande. To this spot every seven years all the clans pilgrimage to perform sacred rites of unification. Tribal unification is compared to sexual union. The initiate awaiting transformation and fusion with the divine essence is like a lover waiting in the antechamber while his mistress prepares the mat inside; he is like the penis beginning to enter the corridor.

But the corridor is also a cord connecting the initiate to the truth. Instead of leading in and out of a labyrinth, this thread is to be unknotted. Strands of thought, compared to crepuscular rays that lead to final insight, strike the erect, concentrated intelligence by divine grace—an illumination compared to the sudden unfurling of a gonfalon atop a standard. One can almost see it atop the *kara* itself as the speaker utters his divinely inspired words. "Deaf-mute" means not-revealing himself. This condition, by the end of the fourth stanza, is seen as having altered. Nonetheless, the language of the *karaw* to a certain extent must retain its obscurity. The texts ends, metaphorically, in a *cul-de-sac*!

This material was collected, transcribed, translated into word-for-word as well as literary French, and published with full commentary by Dominique Zahan in his *Sociétes d'initiation Bambara*, vol. I., *le n'domo, le Korè* (Paris-La Haye: Mouton, 1960), pp. 257–277.

EIGHT ORISHA. These examples of praises to eight of the most important Yoruba Orisha bespeak a relationship to divinity which must strike the reader as radically different from that of the Sudanese Fulani or Bambara. The following statements could apply to Zarma practitioners of the Holé cult, to Hausa devotees of Bori, as well as to Orisha and Vodu worshippers:

The initiate has a double personality . . . that acquired in his [contemporary] social context . . . and the other [manifested] in trance, which may be considered, from the orthodox animist point of view, as ancestral personality reinculcated according to ancient social traditions.[1]

To each divinity corresponds a behavior pattern, a schema of incarnation, an archetype in the etymological sense of the word. In the course of ritual possession there is a total fusion between the personality [of the initiate] and a mythological being.[2]

There is considerable debate over the question of similarity between the two personalities thus "fused." When possession occurs, the soul-essence of the human being is replaced by that of the entering divinity, and the character now seen dancing or prophesying may behave in a manner totally different from that of the initiate under normal circumstances. Or, the possessed may seem an expanded version of himself or herself. In psychological terms, possession may flood consciousness with a repressed aspect of the personality, or it may simply remove inhibition and allow an integrated personality to express itself creatively. Sometimes it is the hidden *anima* or *animus* that is disclosed in a trance state. And thereafter, a male worshipper will learn to cultivate the river goddess within, a woman to realize the commanding aspects of her thunder-god personality, and so on.

Praises to the Yoruba Orisha are chanted and sung on various occasions—sometimes, of course, in order to induce the divinities to benefit the community by descending upon the heads of their adepts; but praises, interspersed with songs, may also be performed during the weekly celebrations modestly offered each of these passionate archetypal temperaments in the compounds of those who "own" them. The orisha with whom one has established a profound relation may also be approached at any time with standard salutations followed by personal expressions of need, perplexity, and gratitude—in turn followed by intimate conversation. In order better to convey the intimacy of personal relation as well as the social liveliness of orisha-praising, a few songs have been included in this edition—or, if not a

---

[1] Pierre Fatumbi Verger, "Role joué par l'état d'hébétude au cours de l'initiation des novices au cultes des orisha et vodun," Institut Français d'Afrique Noire, *Bulletin* XVI B 16 (1954), p. 338.

[2] Louis Mars, "Nouvelle Contribution à l'étude de la crise de possession," *Mémoires*, Institut Français d'Afrique Noire (Les Afro-Americains), 1953, p. 218.

song, at least a conventional salutation for each orisha. Finally, to conclude the sequence: a verbatim excerpt of a live performance, whose disproportionate length might also be deemed "traditional"; for in a pluralistic religious universe, it is obligatory not only to respect the others but to intensify and extend the votive range of one's own by praising it to the skies whenever the occasion arises.

Eshu. Sources: All lines but the last are taken from Joan Wescott's "The Sculpture and Myths of Eshu-Elegba, the Yoruba Trickster," *Africa* XXXII (1962), pp. 336–353 passim. The last line, which emphasizes Eshu's presence at transitional points, liminal sites and liminal states, is from Pierre Verger's "Notes sur le culte des orisa et vodoun," *Mémoires*, Institut Français d' Afrique Noire (Dakar), 1957, p. 296. The source of the appended song is Ayodele Ogundipe, *Esu Elegbara, the Yoruba God of Chance and Uncertainty: A Study* (Ann Arbor, MI: University Microfilm International, 1980), vol. II, p. 68. The singer of the song was Baderinwa Esubunmi.

Ogun. Source: E. Bolaji Idowu, *Olodumare, God in Yoruba Belief* (New York: Praeger, 1963), pp. 86–88 passim. This is the Orisha worshiped by Yoruba hunters, blacksmiths, and warriors, among others. The first time Ogun came down he was too terrible to behold, so he put on palm leaves. According to a fascinating article by Robert G. Armstrong, "The Etymology of the Word 'Ogun' " in *Africa's Ogun: Old World and New*, edited by Sandra T. Barnes (Bloomington: Indiana University Press, 1989), pp. 29–38, proto-Ogun was in all probability a ritual cleansing of killing and its maddening effect on the killer of a person or fierce animal with leaves and water used to cool wrought iron in the forge. The appended praise-chant is traditional. Before Adeleke Sangoyoyin of Iragbiji, Nigeria, taught a dance for Ogun in a studio here in New York, he insisted we recite it, ending with "ode" (out-of-doors) rather than "bode" (town gates), a reputable alternative, recorded in Aja Were (Republic of Benin) by Pierre Verger.

Babaluaiye. Source: Verger, "Notes," p. 296. "Father-of-the-world" is a pseudonym for the divinity of suffering, whose real name is considered too dangerous to mention. One of his manifestations is disease, in epidemic proportions, particularly those maladies brought by dry winds and registered by the skin (like smallpox) or by disoriented mental behavior. In recent times, AIDS has fallen under his patronage. Verger collected this praise in Dassa Zoumé, Republic of Benin. This song was taught a group of us by Adeleke Sangoyoyin on May 5, 1993. He and Mei Mei Sanford drafted transcriptions and brief explanations of the various verbal materials presented in his workshops, whose participants, however, were fortunately free to tape them. To wash one's face with palm oil instead of soap would give it a bloody appearance and implies a hot temper.

Yemoja. Source: Verger, "Notes," pp. 297–298. This praise of the great mother of the waters was collected in her "home town," Abeokuta, Nigeria. Yemoja is also mother-of-all-the-Orisha, and the Gelede masquerades dance for her as mother-of-witches.

Shango. Sources: The first stanza is from Verger, "Notes," p. 363, and the second, a praise of Shango by his wives, from the libretto of Duro Lapido's folk opera *Oba Koso,* in R. G. Armstrong et al., *Occasional Publication No. 10,* Institute of African Studies, University of Ibadan, Nigeria, 1968, p. 41. Shango, the Yoruba thunder god, was a legendary king of Oyo. Source of appended song: Adeleke Sangoyoyin, May–June 1993. Because Sangoyoyin is a honey-voiced child of Shango, we sang this one repeatedly!

Oshun. Source: Verger, "Notes," pp. 426–427. This praise was collected in Ilesha, Nigeria. Oshun is goddess of the river that bears her name. She is also the most beautiful of Shango's wives. Oshun is associated with child-bearing, healing, witchcraft, social relatedness, and cowrie-shell divination. Yoruba diviners are expected to marry Oshun priestesses, from whom presumably they have many secrets to learn!

Obatala. Source: Ulli Beier and Bakere Gbadamosi, *Black Orpheus,* Special Edition on Yoruba Poetry (1959), p. 14. Obatala is also called Orisha(n)la, the great Orisha, or sometimes simply Orisha. He made human beings by forming them out of clay; then the Creator himself breathed life into them. Because Obatala made a few "mistakes" under the influence of palm wine, his priests may not drink it; and deformed people like hunchbacks, congenital cripples, and albinos are sacred to him. Divinity of the white cloth, Obatala is as all-encompassing as life and death.

Oya. These praises were sung on Oya's day of the week by the women who worship Oya in Ogbomosho, February 15, 1977, and published, along with the Yoruba text, in *Oya: In Praise of an African Goddess* (San Francisco: HarperCollins, 1992), pp. 8-9. My thanks to Afolabi Epega for help with the text and for numerous clarifications. Oya has a variety of strenuous portfolios: Strong winds escalating into tornadoes, the river Niger, lightning, and the transition between life and death, death and life. She is considered to be the mother of progenitors of lineages who return to perform as Egungun masquerades. Mythologically, she had two husbands: first Ogun, then Shango. Originally Oya (like Ogun) was a purification ritual, not of the individual killer but of the community as a whole: a whirling masquerade ritual performed in times of social dissension, blight upon crops, infertility of women—all these imbalances attributed by male elders to female witchcraft. The brief ritual chant appended to the Ogbomosho performance should be performed by moving both palms across the top of the head, from front to back, followed by a flicking gesture with each wrist. Repeat continuously while chanting. Source: Adeleke Sangoyoyin, May 29, 1993. The formulaic willing away of evils is a component of other Yoruba chants. Oya certainly doesn't own the format, but the gesture and the vigorous verbs in this version bear the stamp of her personality.

TO THE EARTH (1). Source: Margaret Read, "Songs of the Ngoni People," *Bantu Studies* XI (1937), pp. 13-15. This song is accompanied on the *igubu,* a musical bow with a gourd resonator like the Brazilian berimbau.

TO THE EARTH (2). Source: R. S. Rattray, *Ashanti* (Oxford, England: Oxford University Press, 1923); see notes on Beretuo clan praise above, p. 59. At every commemorative Adae ceremony the royal drummer thus addresses the earth. Throughout Africa, when one drinks one pours a little libation on the ground for the ancestors.

Rarely does the earth require sacrifices other than those she naturally receives.

TO THE RAIN. Source: Okot p'Bitek, *Horn of My Love* (London: Heinemann, 1974), p. 174. Elemental forces respond to praise whether or not they are personified or anthropomorphized!

THREE TOROU. These are praises from the Holé possession cult of the Sonrai and Zarma people of the middle Niger. They belong to the repertoire honoring the Torou, most noble of the Holé spirits. All seven Torou are associated with the river. Their "mother" is Harakoi Dikko, for whom I don't have a praise beautiful enough. These divinities are summoned by the *godje*, a single-stringed violin, backed up by an orchestra of three calabash-drums. The *godje* player begins with an obbligato air that states the Holé's leitmotif, then moves into another and perhaps a third expression of it. As he plays he begins, at first almost imperceptibly, to sing the words . . .

Moussa Gourmantche. Source: Jean Rouch, *Essai sur la religion Songhay* (Paris: Presses Universitaires de France, 1960), p. 104.

Hausakoi. Source: ibid., pp. 104–105.

Faram Barou. Source: Personal communication from Dauda Sorko, translated into French by Damouré Zika, Simiri, Niger, April 1977.

THE BORI CALLED BATUREN GWARI. Source: Mary Smith, *Baba of Karo* (London: Faber and Faber, 1954), p. 228. I would like here to quote Baba's account of the singing of this song:

Twenty days ago Fagaci [the District Head] forbade *bori*-dancing in the town. Then Tanko's wife went to Fagaci's compound to greet his wives, and as she came out from the women's quarters she had to pass through the room where he was sitting. She and her three co-wives knelt down to greet him, and as she was kneeling down the *bori* came and possessed her—it was Baturen Gwari, the European from Gwari country. "Imprison me, bind me, call the police and lock me up! Isn't there an order forbid-

ding *bori?* Very well, look at me, I have come. Lock me up then!"
When the spirit was quiet for a little the women pushed her out
and took her home—she went on and on. She sang this "praise-
song" right before Fagaci. (p. 228)

In a note, Mary Smith, Baba's interlocutor, gives the following
comment:

This incident illustrates the clash of different cosmological prin-
ciples. The District Head upholds Islam and bans *bori* sessions;
the spirits reply by possessing a woman in his presence and
threatening calamities if the order is not revoked. As women
cannot be punished at law for these *bori* practices, or disobedi-
ence to the D.H.'s orders, the D.H. cannot effectively prohibit
or suppress *bori*. The incident was relished by the women in the
town, particularly since the spirit concerned was one of the
"Europeans" who have appeared among the traditional *bori* spir-
its of recent years, and are presumably not subject to the Native
Authority (p. 287)

CALLING THE WATERSPIRITS. In the Niger Delta Ijo-speaking
women who are consistently "worried" by the waterspirits may even-
tually decide to heal themselves by ritually marrying the one at the
source of all their troubles. Menorrhagia, infertility, inability to carry
the pregnancy to full term, or a succession of infant mortalities are
core problems, which are likely to be accompanied by other symp-
toms, such as dysfunctional marriages (usually involving physical
abuse of the woman), severe depression (including extended bouts of
crying, periods of being unable to get up out of bed), financial diffi-
culties, and all-around bad luck. Such marriages take place following
a period of seclusion called "going into the fatting house," during
which time the woman is waited on, fed delicious meals, and painted
with indigo designs (*burumo*) attractive to her waterspirit lover. Except
that it is an individual rather than a group process, the fatting house
experience duplicates on another level of implication the seclusion
format of young girls on the verge of marrying real men (rather than
spirits)—a coming-of-age ritual more honored in the breach these days

than the observance. Learning songs is part of the novitiate in both instances.[3]

Young girls are thought to be enamored of waterspirits to whom they bid an ambivalent farewell in their songs on the eve of social and sexual maturity. The songs of the women for whom reproduction has not worked out are full of sexual longing. If they continue to be married (and some men are actually supportive of the process), these women will set aside special nights during the week for communion in bed with their waterspirit husbands.

These representative songs in the Okrika dialect were recorded August 11, 1988, in Ngowuka Nsaru's house in the island township of Bolo by a group of eight "waterspirit-carrying" women friends of Ngowuka's. They were sung a cappella with hand clapping according to a call-and-response format in which the entire song is repeated by the chorus and the resulting structure reiterated many times. Chief Allision Ibuluya transcribed the tapes two years later and made a word-for-word literal translation, from which these English versions gradually evolved. This is their first publication. Of the thirty-six songs sung that night, twenty-four have been arranged in groups according to mood and subject matter. In the second section the women are praising waterspirits in their masquerade guise. The third section evokes all the drums used in waterspirit possession ceremonies and masquerade displays, with the pointed exception of waterpot drums, to which the waterspirits themselves are most likely to respond. The "players" of the last song of this section are probably male masqueraders, although a woman who gives a possession performance (which includes costume and makeup but no mask) for her waterspirit husband and affiliates is also considered a "player." The epigraph is the title of a song by another woman named Ngowuka, also from Bolo, who records her own topical songs commercially on local labels.

ODO MASQUERADE. Source: Romanus Egudu and Donatus *Nwoga, Igbo Traditional Verse* (London: Heinemann, 1973), pp. 23–25. Generally, ancestor-masks of Africa—to which an entire section might

---

[3] For a repertoire of those learned by a small group of girls in Ogbogbo village, Okrika, see Judith Gleason and Chief Allison Ibuluya, "My Year Reached, We Heard Ourselves Singing. . . ." *Research in African Literatures*, vol. 22, no. 3, Fall 1991, 135–148.

well have been devoted—control communities at the same time as they amuse them. The dead come back to life as dancers in outlandish costumes, often topped by carved masks of animals, mainly, it would seem, to ensure that women behave themselves. Vowed enemies of witches, masked ancestral forces nonetheless give vent to their own kind of obstreperous antisocial behavior, showing no more respect for constituted village authorities than their true probity warrants. By satirical performances (displays of virtuosity in dance and mime) or by subjecting offensive members of the community to nocturnal ordeals, by exacting tribute from all, masquerades manifest the moral order, force a clean sweep, then disappear again into the ground or forest.

In the Nsukka region of southeastern Nigeria, each village and often each lineage formerly had its own Odo cult. It was Odo's habit to arrive, fully costumed, from the spirit world every three years and live among men for seven months.[4] For a while he resided in the grove, site of his initial appearance, then he moved into the home of an Odo priest. His arrival coincided with the planting of seed yams; and during his residence everyone's good-tempered behavior was considered necessary, not only to avoid Odo's ire but to ensure the success of the crop.

Odo always visits every compound in turn to receive gifts and to check up on conduct, especially that of wives and daughters. After the harvest of corn and new yams—of which he receives a "first fruits" offering—Odo sadly dances out of town. He will be back.

In this praise-song Odo is presumably announcing his arrival. He is a masquerade who has taken title, the *Ozo* being a most prestigious male honor society. His voice, disguised by a spider's-egg membrane stretched over a mouthpiece, probably sounds more like an eerie kazoo than like the local nightingale; but he looks like a giant bird, emissary from the "above" as well as from the "below."

TRIPTYCH. The Shilluk of the upper Nile, so Godfrey Lienhardt tells us, divide the universe into three parts: earth, sky, and river (which reflects the other two). "It is the single person of Nyikang which gives

[4] C. K. Meek, *Law and Authority in a Nigerian Tribe* (Oxford, England: Oxford University Press, 1937), p. 76. What follows is based on Meek's account.

all three regions their coherence";[5] for he belongs in part to all. Nyikang, first divine Shilluk king and an active spirit still, was born into the world as the son of the river-principle, Nyakaya, who sometimes materializes as a crocodile, and of a father who either came from the sky or was created *ex nihilo* in the form of a cow. Behind and beyond Nyikang is Juok, an omnipresence reflecting and particulate in many beings, most naturally associated in an abstract way with sky and with invisible wind. As Juok cannot be reached by precise thought, so words in his case are unavailing. It is to Nyikang that one turns in distress. He can control the rain-bearing wind. But—and this is the question the second of his poems asks—can he do anything about death? Source: Livio Tescaroli, *Poesia Sudanese* (Bologna: Editrice Nigrizia, 1961), pp. 18–19. Tesaroli explains that there is a Shilluk riddle beneath the surface of *Nyikang* (2). What lies on this side and on the other side of (but not in) the river? Answer: Sleep, foreshadowing death, here personified by a certain type of cow marked as though by foreboding.

The center of the "triptych" is a metaphysical statement made to Fr. Wilhelm Hofmayer by one of his informants and quoted by Lienhardt ("The Shilluk," p. 155). This comment on the human experience of divinity was not intended to be a poem, but its structure and its remarkable condensation make it one. Some things have more Juok in them than others. The very statement conveys it in verbal form and might well be applied, *mutatis mutandis*, to a person possessed by a god or to a mask or to the wooden plank raised when transmitting the voice of the *karaw*, or to any presence of spirit.

[5] Godfrey Lienhardt, "The Shilluk of the Upper Nile," *African Worlds* (Oxford, England: Oxford University Press, 1954), p. 150.

IX : *Palm Nuts and Bones*

SOTHO PRAISES OF THE DIVINING BONES

INVOCATION

You, my white ones, children of my parents
Whom I drank from mother's breasts!
And you, many-colored cattle
Whom I knew when carried on my mother's
    back
You from whose hooves these chips were cut
Hooves of cattle, yellow, black, and red.

Oh, the evildoers—
Such men rob, steal, injure;
They can slay an elephant with a slender
    stalk
And did so, only last summer;
But rain is preceded by thunder!

It is they who seek the love of the female
    serpent
Who will fight among themselves for her
    affections
Who struck our cattle suddenly last summer;
Thieves are they, preying on harmless
    people.

But rain is succeeded by flooding of
    embankments!
The hides are a dark brown dog who belongs
To diviners of the dead and the living.

PRAISING
INDIVIDUAL
BONES

More o moxolo: Ox-hoof
Spreading tree, great medicine
Mighty chief! Hear how he threatens!
Saying: My anger is aroused;
What I gave, I take back again.

Mmakxadi: Horn-piece of ivory
Friendly queen, praised by all!
One who shuns the light of day
Who traveled here by night
Contemplating evil: in vain!
Witches, you err
You who feast in darkness.

Selumi: Ox-hoof, young warrior
You who warn me on my way
Come now, whisper in my ear.
No man, unwarned, is left to perish
For you, Selumi, know the place
Where the sharp-toothed leopard crouches.

Thswene: Anklebone of Baboon
Monkey's son, who makes us laugh:
Once his father cut his finger
On sugarcane. Such painful aching—
Who would not have amputated?

Returning, with a full basket
I slipped and fell:
Food all mixed with dirt—
What's gone does not return!

Had I, Baboon, the lion's strength
Who would venture on my territory?
Tladi: Toe-joint of flamingo
Thunderbird of river banks
Basking in the sun whose rays
He throws back again:
Red javelins, fiery spears!

Phuti: Anklebone of duiker
Duiker feeds at dawn
Then hides in the ravine;
Hunters lose the ax-shaped spoor:
No quarry!

PRAISES OF
VARIOUS FALLS

The swimming of the sunbird
Sunbird, secret and daring
When you take a bit of straw
And say you imitate the hammerhead
You are imitating the inimitable!
It is the bird of those who put on
A new garment in the deep waters.
It is building above the pools
Taking little bits of straw, one by one.
The little sunbird should not fall—
Phususu it sounds, falling into the pools.
It is the patient one sitting at the drift:
Sins are passing by and you see them.
Reed of the river is mocking reed of the plain;
It says, "When the grass is burning . . ."
Reed of the plain is mocking reed of the river;
It says, "When the waters are swelling . . ."

The famous fall
Of the wild orchis of the Matebele
Of sharp horns of the buffalo—
They pierce, they tear out.

Driving them to the pools—
Who can drive winter buffalo?

Rise of the Cobra
He fell on the rock
But picked himself up again,
Shaking off the dust.
White hair
Adorned with black and white tassels
From tails of mountain rabbit
Is the envy of ancestors.
Be cautious.

Fame of the lamp
Of the sight of the female elephant:
O elephant, I have become blind;
Do not enter secretly!
In the path of such deception
Blood ran;
Tracks yawned into graves.
Shake your ear, stampeding elephant
That others may grow to your size
That your name be remembered with favor!

The heavy stones of the night
We have crushed the wicked
Who devoured the stranger's ox
And buried the carcass in straw!

IFA SUITE: IN PRAISE OF THE YORUBA ORACLE
In memoriam, John Ogundipe

(1)   Ifa, I wake to greet you in the morning
Ifa, I wake to greet you in my full regalia
Ifa, I wake to greet you with my entire army
Ifa, I wake to greet you with my six titles, six retainers

With my good character I greet the one most worthy of
　　honor.
I greet divinity of the white cloth
I greet master of the sacrificial knife
I greet house where I live
I greet road
And, finally, open space
Who is big enough to take everything upon its chest.
Ifa, such is my awakening.

(2)　　Ifa is master of today
Ifa is master of tomorrow
Ifa is master of day-after-tomorrow
To Ifa belong all four days of the week
Created on earth by Orisha. . . .
On the day Death is coming to seek me
You are the one to shield; shelter me
As a big leaf wraps my cornstarch pudding
As water plentifully covers sand in the river.

(3)　　Water drags sands, *gerere*
Water has no legs
Water has no hands
Along the slope of riverbend
Water drags sands, *gerere*
Saying over, over again
My life will never end,
Water drags sands
No legs
No hands . . .
The meaning has finally gripped me!

(4)　　Road of interminable memory
Made Ifa for the lord of divination:
What road brings, night can carry away—
May all good things remain with me!
Come, everybody—
Travelers, suppliants, slaves

Join me on the road,
Come, share my good fortune!
Sacrifice, be efficacious!

(5)   One great poem of Ifa deserves another
Important medicinal remedies are for swapping
A good deed might elicit two thousand cowries—
These three divined for God-of-the-sea
On the day all bodies of water backed up against him.
The client was asked not to neglect the earth-spirits,
And a certain sacrifice was proposed to him.
After he had performed everything, Eshu
Put the mouths of all bodies of water together
And shoved them toward the ocean
Who began to dance, who began to rejoice,
Praising the priests, who were praising Ifa.
Ocean opened his mouth
And out flowed this song:
Olokun is older
Olokun is older
All you bodies of water,
Defer to God-of-the-sea-O
Olokun is older!

(6)   Slender as a needle
Grimy and frayed as clothesline
Shiny as fool's gold
Full purse clunks to the ground
Encumbered net slumps down
Two cocks young play tag-and-tease
Two cocks old bedraggle themselves along
Bony buttocks fall with a thud
All these made Ifa for My-thoughts—
Heavy as a waterbuck—
Who worshiped Our Mother of Waters at Ido
On the day he was using the tears in his eyes
To hunt for the good things of life.

Can he prosper when everything seems to elude him?
They said, You must bring a crayfish
Eight pigeons, and eight bags of cowries.
My-thoughts sacrificed;
They cooked the crayfish with "leaves-of-wealth" for him,
Cast Ìrẹ̀tẹ̀ Méjì and mixed
The dust-writ into the potion
Saying: Drink, eat.
He began to grow rich;
Soon his compound was filled with wives, with children;
And as he began to build for all of them,
My-thoughts sang:
Exactly as the diviner said:

Slender as a needle
Grimy and frayed as clothesline
Shiny as fool's gold
Full purse clunks to the ground
Encumbered net slumps down
Two cocks young play tag-and-tease
Two cocks old bedraggle themselves along
Bony buttocks fall with a thud
Made Ifa for My-thoughts,
Heavy as a waterbuck,
Who worshipped Our Mother of Waters at Ido
On the day he was using the tears in his eyes
To hunt for the good things of life.
What about the wealth I've been looking for?
It was crayfish told all good things to come in.
What about the children I've been yearning for?
It was crayfish told all good things to come in.
My slender body filled to the brim?
It was crayfish told the tides to flow in.
What about land? I've been wanting to build on it.
It was crayfish closed the holes of the sieve.
I cast my hopes to the neap tide and then
All the good things of life flowed in.

(7)   O closer of roads, close well
          Toward death, toward disease
          O closer, close these roads well.
          O closer, don't bar the road to riches
          Don't obstruct the way to women
          But close the road to all bad things
          Road-closer.

          Now what remains to be done for divination?
          There remains the casting of palm nuts
          Releasing the freshness, they said
          There remains the creator of song and heroism.
          It's up to you to start casting.
          If it's up to me to begin
          Where, then, is the chorus?
          Who will join in?
          No stranger knows how
          To respond to the sound
          Of our song in Ile Ife. . . .
          Little aerial roots
          Where did you hang my death?
          On Albizza tree with sixteen branches
          Eight of which are stiff
          Eight flexible.
          I can see my death is well hung!
          There remains casting the palm nuts
          Releasing the freshness
          There remains creator of song and heroism:
          May you begin!
          If I begin
          Who will know to join in?
          Little aerial roots
          Where did you hang my death?
          On Kola which can be split
          Into sixteen segments—
          Eight dry, eight fresh.
          I can see my death is well hung. . . .
          There remains casting the palm nuts

Releasing the freshness
There remains creator of song and heroism:
May you begin!
If I begin
Who will know to join in?
Little aerial roots
Where did you hang my death?
On Palm tree with sixteen branches
All of which are wet.
This time you have hung my death very well indeed!
Go, fetch me unbroken pepper
Bring whole kola and foaming wine
For whoever eats alligator pepper with us
Whoever eats kola with four eyes
Whoever drinks guinea-corn wine with us
Shall not perish.
In the calabash of Odu we shall drink guinea-corn wine.

O closer of roads, close well;
Block the road to death
Block the road to ill health
But open the way to all good things.
Greetings for the sacrifice,
May the sacrifice be efficacious!

(8)   It was the Lord of Heaven
Laid the hand of darkness
On Blue Touraco;
It was the Lord of Heaven
Laid the drizzly-grizzly hand
On Leopard's back
(So that it shimmered
As light rain falls
On the puckered surface of a pond).
He gave the calabash of mud
To Python; but it was Egret
Who carried the calabash of chalk.

(9)   May darkness obstructing the path of their vision
       Like tangle of creepers
       Dissipate into infinite shadows
       Cast by shade trees on tilled soil.
       May darkness of the pitfall behind them
       Creep out upon the savanna.
       All are forgiven.
       May my children move freely now in the land of Ife;
       For on the day goat is delivered
       On that very day kid's eyes are opened;
       Sheep gives birth, ewe's eyes open early;
       So humankind, once born, start seeing
       Twice born, start seeing:
       Said Orunmila.

       O Opener, open my eyes
       That I may look freshly upon the world
       O Opener, help me clear
       My path of vision.

COMMENTARY

Divination is an integral part of religious and social life in traditional African societies. It is also a form of primary health care. Both oracular pronouncements by entranced, inspired individuals and divination by the manipulation of lots are widespread. Less ubiquitous forms are "friction" oracles (which answer rather in the manner of the Ouija board), divination by animal tracks or by the deployment of insects, ordeals of various sorts (including the imbibing of poisonous concoctions), and water-gazing. Praises associated with two forms of lot-casting have been selected to serve as an introduction to this rich area of symbolic formulation.

Casting lots, one moves from sign to symbol to synergic, therapeutic, and revivifying behavior. The manipulation of certain consecrated objects produces a set of signs, which in turn point to an equivalent set of symbols—images and ideas expressing synchronistically the state of cosmic affairs with regard to a human questioner. That is, for a quandary or murky, disordered state of affairs is substituted, in accordance with the rules of the divining game, an ambiguous message capable of interpretation—at least by an expert whose innate mental disposition, arduous training, and experience render him capable not only of activating and interpreting the oracle but of eliciting full psychic participation on the part of his clients.

SOTHO PRAISES OF THE DIVINING BONES. Sotho divination bones (called *litaola*) consist of four major pieces and (in principle) forty-two minor ones. Two of the major pieces are cut from cattle hooves and two from horns. The hoof-pieces, when thrown, may land on one of four sides. The ivory pieces are flat and therefore capable of but two positions—up (walking, showing its face, or smiling) and down (resting, sleeping, or dead). The other pieces are bits of anklebone from various animals (male and female representatives of each) sacred to the several clans of the Basotho, and a few special counters like the toe joint of the flamingo (lightning bird), helpful in weather prediction or sorcery detection (when lightning has been used as a weapon), and a stone found in the entrails of a goat. Having swept the ground where the bones are to be thrown, the client shakes, then tosses them; the diviner chants the "praise of the fall" and then interprets the configuration in accordance with what he intuits the question to have been.

The sources of the material presented here are three: The praises of the bones, uttered by the diviner before the seance begins, are from W. M. Eiselen, "The Art of Divination as Practiced by the Bamasemola" *Bantu Studies* VI (1932), pp. 1–19. (The Bamasemola are a Sotho group who migrated to the Transvaal long ago from Swaziland.) The last two lines of the invocation, however, are from two sources: S. M. Guma, *The Form, Content and Technique of Traditional Literature in Southern Sotho* (Pretoria: J. L. van Schaik, 1967), p. 148, and "The Praises of the Divining Bones among the Basotho," by Father F. Laydevant, *Bantu Studies* VII (1933), p. 344.

Following the invocation, three of the major pieces are eulogized here, and three of the minor ones. In some Sotho sets the second hoof-piece is feminine (taken from a cow) and the horn-pieces are masculine and feminine. Here both the hoof-pieces are feminine and the horn-pieces are masculine. The praises of the falls are from Laydevant's article, pp. 349–373 passim. Two of them—"Fame of the lamp" and "Rise of the cobra"—occur also in Guma's book, and in these cases I have synthesized the parallel texts.

Note the recurrence of animal praises (and the nourishing-cattle poems) in a divinatory context. The bones are metonyms of animal spirits.

"The swimming of the sunbird"—A note by Laydevant explains that sunbirds falling into water are girls undergoing circumcision rites. The reeds represent village in-fighting. The hammerhead, a bird of power, is closely affiliated with the thunderbird. The diviner's explanation of these lines: People are jealous of your good luck and wealth. Someone wants to kill you by sorcerous lightning. Protect yourself with medicine made with a feather of the hammerhead or of the sunbird and with a flamingo feather as well!

"The famous fall"—Interpretation: Your own relatives, jealous of your power and wealth, have bewitched you. Using medicine borrowed from (or learned from) the Matebele people, they have made you ill. Your cure must involve medicinal use of a certain type of wild orchid.

"Rise of the cobra"—Old age is the envy of the ancestors. It is a venerated condition all hope to attain. You nearly met with a bad accident and managed to escape.

"Fame of the lamp"—A chief is secretly spreading discord among his own sons. His plots are poisoning the people, who must be inoculated with medicine. "Lamp" is a homonym in Sotho for a type of straw with yellow flowers used for medicinal purposes, as part of the concoction smeared on small pegs stuck on every path leading to the village.

"The heavy stones of the night"—If this is a case of illness caused by witchcraft, the cure must include the stones-of-fumigation, which induce sweating when heated. However, the "heavy stones" in these verses are generic. If the trouble diagnosed by the doctor-diviner is not the above-mentioned, the stones will be set down as impediments to evildoings of various sorts.

IFA SUITE: *In Praise of the Yoruba Oracle.* Palm nuts are the sacred counters used to cast configurations of the Yoruba oracle. In practice, however, it must be said, a divining chain called Opele is more generally used because with "chattering" Opele the figures come quicker. The results obtained by either means are inscribed in the wood-dust that diviners sprinkle upon the divining board or tray (*opọ́n Ifá*), which can be as small as about eight inches or as large as about eighteen inches in diameter. Each oracular configuration, known as *odù* (calabash), is the product of sixteen times sixteen possibilities, which means that when the diviner ("father-of-secrets" or *babaláwo*, in Yoruba) casts for you, any one of 256 signs may appear. Further, each of these signs has many roads radiating out from it. To these roads are attached verses (*ẹsẹ*), which are legion. When a certain Odu shows up on the board, the diviner will begin to recite some of these verses. When what he is saying seems to apply to your case, then a correct determination of the road has been made. Depending on what this is, a particular sacrifice is indicated, the ingredients of which are built in to the recitation. These ingredients may be expensive, and the client is free to refuse; but if he wants things to come out well for hm, he had better comply. With each Odu are associated certain medicinal leaves, which the *babaláwo*, aware by now of the client's situation, will use in the treatment—assuming, of course, that the latter is willing to go through with it.

Although often highly lyrical and obscure in their references, the various divination verses operate on a common-law principle. That is, they tell of a precedent, of a certain client who once consulted the oracle in a certain state of disequilibrium and with a certain eventual result. Some of these "clients" of the past have metaphorical names, like "My-thoughts"; others are divinities, like Olokun; others may be chiefs of real places, animals, or things. The standard form of these case histories begins by naming the diviner or diviners involved, then gives the name of the client and describes his quandary, recalls the prescription given by the configuration in question, and states whether or not the oracle's injunctions were obeyed, and with what result. If the fictional client did what he was supposed to, then the verse will end with his grateful rejoicing, most often preceded by a reprise of the earlier sections, or a part of them. Into this texture, songs and praises expressive of the "character" of the Odu may be woven, as well as symbolic digressions on the meaning of the oracular system itself.

Ifa is the name of the system and of the divinity presiding over it, although the latter is usually personified as "Orunmila." By means of the oracle, cosmic as well as terrestrial forces are regulated. Ifa provides an opportunity briefly to see and thence to put oneself in tune. Various Yoruba divinities (Orisha) speak through the configurations of the oracle and make known their demands on the client. Indeed, it is through Ifa that one's ruling spirit is disclosed, that one's destiny is given in code form.

Praising is integral to the process of Yoruba divination. Not only is the literature filled with clients singing and dancing and extolling the virtues of the strangely named diviners who treated them so successfully, but the names of these diviners themselves may be seen as praise-names of the configurations. Thus, "Slender-as-a-needle" and its associates are part of the meaning-continuum of the figure known as Ìrètè Méjì. Further, Ifa itself is praised throughout the divination corpus. And, finally, the entire verse recited may be seen as an epical tribute to the divine spirit, or supernatural force, which each Odu really is. Time and again the diviner begins his recitation by saying, "Now it is Òbàrà Méjì we want to praise," or, "Now it is Ògúndà Ogbè," or whatever—these being among the 256 windows through which the cosmos is glimpsed, each a shining fragment of Ifa's truth.

This "suite" is composed of bits and pieces from a very few recitations, mostly from those I collected from the late Awotunde Aworinde of Oshogbo, Nigeria, in 1970. But because, as both Ifa priests and Ogotemmeli say, it is good to exchange the word, I have included two selections from the magesterial work of 'Wande Abimbola. Ifa is the verbal computer in which is stored the wisdom of the Yoruba. Like that of all great philosophical systems, the truth of Yoruba religion is dialectical. Its own version of yang-yin is epitomized by the comings and goings of the living and the dead within a continuum of forces. But if it is vibrantly flowing (dancing with no legs, no arms), it is also in continuous evolution. At one pole, the Yoruba's is a no-nonsense way of life. Passing through stages of initiation to the other pole, one moves toward illumination. Morally and emotionally, Ifa is a rhythmical opening and closing of the floodgates. It is with this process in mind that these selections were chosen, in praise. A *juba ojo, a juba o* . . .

(1) From Èjì Ogbè, first in rank of the sixteen major or "twin" figures, road of roads, the beginning of all rebeginnings. Source: Judith Gleason, with Awotunde Aworinde and John Olaniyi Ogundipe, *A Recitation of Ifa* (New York: Grossman Publishers, 1973), p. 26.

(2) The figure is Ògúndá Méjì. This major Odu is, often, the voice of Ogun, god of iron and of hunters, who is a great road-opener. Source: 'Wande Abimbola, *Ifa, An Exposition of Ifa Literary Corpus* (Oxford, England, and Ibadan, Nigeria: Oxford University Press, 1976), pp. 169–171.

(3) Again from Èjì Ogbè. Source: Gleason, *A Recitation*, p. 30.

(4) The conclusion of Awotunde's recitation of Èjì Ogbè. Source: ibid; p. 36.

(5) This charming story, a compact example of the "common law" case method, is from Abimbola, *Ifa, An Exposition*, pp. 58–60. A diviner reciting it might repeat the lines beginning with "One great poem of Ifa" and ending with "sacrifice was proposed to him." The repetition would take place after Olokun opens his mouth and begins to sing, the song itself coming as a coda after "sacrifice was proposed to him" for the second time. My English wording differs from Abimbola's poetically. Òfún Méjì, last of the major Odu on earth, is first in heaven. It is associated with a vast kingly power capable of smothering.

(6) This story is from Ìrètè Méjì, fourteenth of the major Odu. It is a figure associated with witchcraft. Note the illustration of sympathetic magic (the use of crayfish to control tides of wealth). Repetition is included here. Source: Gleason, *A Recitation*, pp. 161–62.

(7) The name of the figure from which this ese is taken is Òdí Méjì—a name very close to that of Odu, the Great Mother, who "con-

tains" the oracle. A Greek parallel: the umbilical mount of Gaea at Delphi. This selection is from a long sequence having to do with the origin and propagation of the divination system. Everything is reversed in this system, here symbolized by the aerial roots hanging down from the tree/sky. Death becomes life. Source: ibid., pp. 76–78.

(8) This lyrical passage occurs at the beginning of one of the *ẹsẹ* for the mixed figure *Òfún Òyẹ̀kú*. Actually, this is an extended (praise) name for the diviner of the case. The two calabashes are of the highest ritual and metaphysical importance, as are the colorings given from above to the first two animals. These colorings represent the contents of the other two calabashes. Together the four contain the *prima materia* of transformation. Source: ibid., p. 277.

(9) From *Ọ̀bàrà Meji*, an Odu of rather frightening extremes and intensities. Source: Gleason, *A Recitation*, p. 106.

X: Leaves and Days

A YORUBA HERBAL

"PLANK-
BUTTRESSED"
MIMOSA

(1) *Àgbọnyìn:* Praising wisdom.
If death sees my hoary head
May death be unable to kill me;
Innumerable,
A little child cannot count
The leaves.

Live long!

TURNSOLE

(2) *Agogo igún:* Attention, Vulture
If death sees me
May death be unable to kill me;
When Beak-of-vulture bears fruit
Its mouth turns the other way.

Turn back, evil!

FALSE THISTLE

(3) *Ahọn ẹkùn dúdú:* Leopard's-black-tongue
Leaves of Leopard's-black-tongue,
Do not bring me harm,
Carry harm to my enemy!

Witch, lose
your grip!

RED SORREL   (4)   *Àmukan:* Maker-of-sourness
It makes the forest sour,
Sours the bush;
Let the mouth of death be sour
On my body, Maker-of-sourness!

Insect, don't
nibble me!

"FOUR-   (5)   *Àrìdan papa:* Long conjure.
WINGED"   [Fruit] with four ridges
MIMOSA   [Two tough, two sweet]
Cast a spell on someone!

Come, money!

RAUWOLFIA   (6)   *Àsofẹ́yẹjẹ:* Fruit-for-birds-to-eat
My fruit is not for the witchbird,
Not me; my fruit is not
For witchbird eating.

Madness,
leave me!

RAUWOLFIA   (6a)   *Ọrá igbó:* Lost-bush.
Don't make me mad
Fruit-for-birds-to-eat.
Someone vanished in the bush.

Don't drive me crazy!

STAR BURR   (7)   *Dágunró:* To stop war.
We eat wild spinach
We dare not eat Stop-war—
Inedible!

Child,
teethe gently!

FODDER- GRASS	(8) *Éran:* Remember. What I was going to forget Memory grass reminds me of; Now it's very clear to me. Remember!
ROUGH BRISTLE-GRASS	(9) *Emòn eiye:* Bird's gum Doesn't stick to human bodies; Bird's gum doesn't lime humans. Child, remain on earth!
SPEAR-GRASS	(10) *Èkan:* Countdown. I am next It's my turn— Good for number one, Me only! Husband, fight with wife!
LANTANA	(11) *Èwòn agogo:* Chain bell Sounds strong as iron gong. Binding bell Sounds strong as iron gong. Child, remain on earth!
HEMP-LEAVED HIBISCUS	(12) *Idà òrìsà:* Sword of divinity. The sword that is sharp Is Orisha's sword Is the sword that is sharp. Stop, thief!

FISH-POISON
BEAN

(13) *Igùn:* Lengthy.
Death, kills the children of fish
Lengthy, alone in the river
Kills the children of fish;
The day we squeeze it into the river
River becomes angry in its belly.

Draw blood,
Witch!

A DEEP-ROOTED
WEED

(14) *Ìlèkè òpòló:* Frog's spawn.
Frog's eggs are
Abundant beads
Suspended in the river.

Enemy, itch!

A SUCCULENT

(15) *Odùndùn:* Always sweet to the mouth
Be it dry
Or rainy season,
Water's never scarce
Within.

Calm!
Cool it!

A SILVERY
HERB

(16) *Sòkòyókòtò:* Fatten husband.
The vegetable known as
Stretch husband's drawstring
Is in town; if you see it
In the market, buy, bring home
That my trousers may become replete.

Quit coughing!

PRAISES OF THE LUNAR MONTHS:
A SOTHO CALENDAR

The moon has gone into the dark;
The moon is being greeted by apes!

PHAETO

    Morose, outrageous Phaeto
    Of the bleak winds from charred grasses
    Of the black waters, dust-thick
    Thrashing embankments.
    The herdboy weeps. Wait—
    There will be sly underground swellings
    There will be bird laughter.

The grass is showing milk teeth!

LOETSE

    Loetse, gentle moon of anointment;
    He to the upper pastures then
    Goes only for thick cream—
    In his mind's eye the swelling teats—
    Black-nosed the grazers
    Black-nosed the wrestlers.

MPHALANE

    Mphalane of the gleen,
    Of the reed flutes
    Blown by elderly women;
    Broad ears sprouting from bulbs
    Of the healing *leshoma*.

PULUNGOANA

    Pulungoana of the young gnu;
    Dotted like dung on the distant slopes
    He sees afterbirth of the spring buck.

TSITOE
> *Tsitoe tsitoee tsitoeee*
> Listen, it is the ceaseless
> Sweet hiss of the grasshoppers!

Foreseeing, the chief
Orders enclosure
Of winter pastures.

PHEREKHONG
> Pherekhong of the interjoining sticks
> Of marrow and vetch
> Of the plucking of fresh mildew;
> Time to build scarecrow pavilions:
> Greening, the corn shoots;
> Blanching, the grasses.

Hunger season:
When the hen evacuates couch-grass!

TLHAKOLA
> Tlhakola of the wiping-off;
> Watch well!
> It is the unveiling of corn cobs.

TLHAKUBELE
> Tlhakubele,
> It is the exposure of the grains!

MESA
> Mesa of fires kindled by the roadside.

Chilly bird-scarers dare
Roast corncobs openly;
Reckless roasters!

MOTSEANONG
> Bird laughter
> Motseanong: it is the mockery
> Of the firm-toothed corn!

We share in the ancestral beer
Of thanksgiving.

PHUPJOANE
> Sly underground swellings;
> Phupjoane: time to break sod!

PHUPHU
> Mute Phuphu
> Of the bulging roots and stems.

Women, skirt-fiber plant
Of the young girls is blossoming!

> *The moon has gone into the dark;*
> *The moon is being greeted by apes!*

COMMENTARY

A YORUBA HERBAL. Simples are praised to release their healing properties, which depend, of course, upon whether one is using the root or the leaves or scrapings from the bark. Different cultures within Africa have found different uses for different plants: There are pharmaceutical uses and magical uses and those that combine the two approaches (the two chemistries cooperate). When the focus is on the desired effect, the praises of plants are incantations.

The little herbal presented here is but a tiny sample of the medicinal literature of the Yoruba diviners. It is drawn from a collection made by Pierre Fatumbi Verger called "Yoruba Medicinal Leaves" and published by the Institute of African Studies, University of Ife, Nigeria, as a monograph (n.d.). I have selected plants for their aesthetic (verbal) qualities rather than for their medicinal properties.

The use given for each plant is one of several, according to Verger. Indeed, the reader will see from the notes in the right margin next to the plant praise that some effects desired are pharmaceutical and others magical. The words in the latter cases are meant to attack the spiritual cause of the person's malaise—which does not mean that the same plant couldn't relieve symptoms. (These imperative statements in the margin are based on Verger's declarative ones.) On the left a common English name for the plant is given if there is one. Otherwise, to help the reader visualize it, I have given a simple description or tentative English name based on J. M. Dalziel's descriptions in his *The Useful Plants of West Tropical Africa* (London, 1937), or his *Flora of West Tropical Africa*, written in collaboration with J. Hutchinson, 2nd ed., revised by R. W. J. Keay (London, 1954). To arrive at the "scientific" name from the Yoruba I used Verger's notes mainly, checking them with R. C. Abraham, *Dictionary of Modern Yoruba* (London: University of London Press, 1958). When Verger and Abraham conflicted I looked to Dalziel for help. And here I would like again to thank Mrs. Lothian Lynas of the library of the New York Botanical Garden (Bronx) for helping me find these plants in Dalziel. The English name is a literal translation of the Yoruba, which usually contains a pun. But pronouncing these metaphorical praise-names and the extensions that follow would not be sufficient to achieve the curative goal. The diviner in practice would use further incantations stored in the "memory bank" of Ifa, and the plants themselves would probably be combined with other substances and procedures.

(1) *Piptadenia africana, Mimosaceae*—According to Dalziel, this tree is also called *aga-igi* (chair-tree) in Yoruba, probably because of its large plank buttresses. The tree sprouts freely from the stump. The heartwood is termite-proof. The timber, not easily split, is often used for canoes. Properly prepared (Verger doesn't say whether bark, leaf, or heartwood is used), this tree-essence insures long life for the client.

(2) *Heliotropium, Boraginaceae*—As this turnsole turns toward the sun, so a concoction made from it will turn away evil. In some West African languages it is called cock'scomb from the shape of the flowers.

(3) *Acanthus montanus*—Use: to rescue people attacked by witches. According to Dalziel, the plant produces a good cough medicine. Its leaves are sharp; the Ibo call the plant *aga* (needle); no wonder it makes an effective weapon!

(4) *Hibiscus Sabdariffa, Malvaccae*—The description is contained in the plant's praise. It is used against insect bites.

(5) *Tetrapleura tetraptera, Mimosaceae*—The scientific (Greek-derived) nomenclature like that of the Yoruba is based on the conformation of the fruits of this tall (80 feet) forest tree. These fruits are "15 cm. long or more, each valve [of four] with a longitudinal wing-like rather fleshy ridge about 2 cm. broad" (Dalziel, *Useful Plants*). Under the divination sign Ọ̀sẹ́ Òtura this fruit is prepared to secure the client wealth.

(6) *Rauwolfia vomitoria, Apocynaceae*—This member of the dogbane family has traditionally been used by Ifa diviners in the treatment of mental illness, and more recently in western hospitals. Its tranquilizing properties have been known for centuries in India. For the use of this drug by the Yoruba see R. H. Prince, "Some Notes on Yoruba Native Doctors and Their Management of Mental Illness," in *Proceedings of the First Pan-African Psychiatric Conference*, Abeokuta, ed. T. A. Lambo (Ibadan: Government Printer, 1961), pp. 270–288. Both Prince and Lambo have written many articles in medical journals and elsewhere on the subject. Prince, in collaboration with Frank Speed, made an excellent film on traditional approaches to mental illness called *Were ni! (He Is a Madman!)*.

(6a) The divination sign for Rauwolfia is Òtura Ọ̀bàrà. It has two praise-names, both based on the belief that witchcraft is responsible for madness. The familiar of witches is a bird.

(7) *Acantho-spermum Hispidum*—Another common name for this branched herb with pale yellow flowers (Abraham, *Dictionary*) is devil's thorn. Verger lists two uses: to stop war and to help a child teethe gently.

---

(8) *Digitaria debolis, Gramineae* or *Digitaria velutina Gramineae*—The Yoruba text is built on a pun: The word for fodder-grass and the word for remembering or reminding both have the *ran* stem. The scientific names convey weakness and lushness.

(9) *Setaria verticillata, Gramineae*—The action here is "sticking." The grass is used to keep an *abiku* (born-to-die) child from returning to heaven. When a mother loses one child after another she is thought to be losing the same child over and over again. This child is called Abiku. He belongs to a society of his own kind in the spirit world and here on earth impishly tries to return to his friends. An Abiku who survives is usually exceptional: difficult in temperament and gifted in mind.

(10) *Imperata cylindria, Gramineae*—This spear-grass is used to make a husband fight with his wife. Note the weapon: self-centeredness!

(11) *Lantana camara, Verbenaceae*—This red and yellow flowered plant, as all who have grown it know, has a strong smell, rather like sage. It too is used to keep an *abiku* child on earth. I think the strong smell is metaphorically transferred to one's sense of hearing—the plant "sounds" like a warning gong. In this case the action is like belling a cat.

(12) *Hibiscus cannabinus, Malvaceae*—This plant is cultivated throughout West Africa for its fibers. Its leaves are sharp and have a toothed look. Its flowers are bright red. The magical use given by Verger is to find a thief. The Orisha sword mentioned has a mythological history. It was given by Ogun to Obatala.

(13) *Tephrosia Vogelii, Papilionaceae*—Here the plant's spine is used to give someone's blood to a witch. What can stupefy fish can stupefy persons. Its ordinary use is as a fish poison: "The leaves are more commonly used, but in some districts the pods, or both. . . . Usually the fresh leaves or leafy twigs are pounded to a soft pulp to which may be added in some cases flour of some cereal. . . . The persons wading in the poisoned water to drive or catch the fish generally com-

plain either of a dead feeling in the legs or of roughness of the skin.
. . . The effect on fish is due to *tephrosin*, a crystalline body only
slightly soluble in water. . . . A very dilute solution of *tephrosin* is
sufficient to paralyse and kill fish" (Dalziel, *Useful Plants*, p. 264). The
pods (containing seeds far more potent than the leaves) are long:
hence the Yoruba name.

(14) *Commelina Vogelii, Commelinaceae*—The purpose given here is
to make somebody itch. It is called "Frog's spawn" (or, alternatively,
"Snail's spittle") in Yoruba because of mucilage in the spathe.

(15) *Kalanchoe crenata, Crassulaceae*—Verger gives the purpose of this
plant as the procurement of calm. The watery nature of succulents
would be considered cooling. In Ghana, says Dalziel, the leaves of this
plant, boiled or macerated, are used as a sedative.

(16) *Celosia argentea, Amaranthaceae*—Verger suggests that this herb,
by curing your husband's cough, will make him fat. The seeds are also
an efficient remedy for diarrhea.

PRAISES OF THE LUNAR MONTHS. The source of these poems is
an extraordinary article by Justinus Sechefo: "The Twelve Lunar
Months among the Basuto," *Anthropos* IV (1909), pp. 931–941, and
Anthropos V (1910), pp. 71–81. The short praises (ejaculations, or sim-
ply remarks) printed on the left are culled from Sechefo's lyrical com-
mentary on the cycle of seasons. The lines about the dark of the moon
are praise-names for the two days of the moon's invisibility. Apes,
seated on mountain peaks, are believed to see the new crescent before
we can. The first month of the Sotho year (Phaeto) roughly corre-
sponds to the August of our solar calendar. The approach of each
Sotho month is always greeted, says Sechefo, by a compound word,
perhaps extended by a few terse phrases, the whole foreshadowing
the quality of life or epitomizing the activities characteristic of that
segment of the year's flow. Some aspect of nature signals the things
to be done during that month and gives that phase of the year its
name. Thus, in the language of Alexander Marshack, time is poetically
"factored."

Phaeto. The blackness in air and water comes from the charred fields. The chaff has been burned; the farmer begins to plant corn. But the focus of the month is on the herdsman. This is a miserable time for the young man who tends the family herds, so the praise reminds him of happier months to follow. The phrase on the left is used to greet the new grass peeping up through the ashes of last month's brush fire.

Loetse. The word is derived from a word meaning to "anoint with fat." Sechefo says this fat is tenderness. Plants and animals are being carefully tended to. The second, third, and fourth lines chide the lazy latecomer to the high pastures. The herds are black-nosed from grazing in the charred grass for new shoots; the young herdsmen are black-nosed because they have thrown each other to the ground in the exuberance of their spring sport.

Mphalane. The word has a double meaning: The first is "glittering" and refers to the way the fresh green fields look in the sparkling sun. The second refers to the flutes (actually made of corn stalks) that the old women blow about the village to announce the annual beginning of the girls' circumcision rites. But the key sign of this new month is the condition of the *leshoma* plant. Shoots from its huge bulb appear. The herbalist thinks of replenishing his dispensary. Women think of sprouting girls.

Pulungoana. The word is the diminutive of "gnu." The second and third lines of the praise are Sechefo's comment, much condensed, on the signs hunter and herdsman see along slopes of the steep mountain pastures. This is a good time for hunting the female gnu: When pursued she will not abandon her young.

Tsitoe. This month is praise-named after the sound the grasshopper makes in the tilled fields. In its hatched and winged phase this tiny animal endures but one month.

Pherekhong. The word means "to interjoin sticks." Bird-watchers' huts made of plaited wattles and thatch are set up in the fields; but the intense vigil will take place during the month to follow. The subsidiary black bean crop is almost ready and the pumpkin shoots look promising. But there is very little for people to eat. The hen, finding no grains in the courtyard, went to scavenge in the dog grass; now even those seeds are exhausted!

Tlhakola. The word means "wiping off" in two senses. The corn is in its *mohula* phase, meaning the green grains of the cobs have pushed through the leaves of the husks, visible only to the birds, who, if the watchers aren't vigilant, will finish them off before they have a chance to ripen. The human scarecrows shout out the pests' names; if this fails, they add a shrill whistle to the bird praise; and if this fails, they use sticks to beat the enemy away, or as slingshots, tipping them with clay pellets.

Tlhakubele. Now the grains are completely exposed (literally: "corn-in-grains"). The bird-watchers in their pavilions redouble their efforts to save the crop. From the stalks that the seasonal winds have blown to the ground, women make a special strong beer.

Mesa. It is the ninth month of the lunar year. There is frost on the ground as the bird-scarers go forth in the chill of the early morning. They warm themselves by lighting small fires along the way. Upon these they now dare openly roast a few cobs, for it is almost harvest time and fully ripe ears are plentiful. The name of the month is a pun on "to kindle fire" and "to roast." The phrases on the left are proverbial utterances common at this season. The "reckkless" let cobs burn!

Motseanong. Although the word means "bird laughter," it is the corn which now laughs at the birds. The grains are at last too strong for them to peck. Sotho corn is not harvested until the crop has become thoroughly frostbitten. Then the stalks dry up, the grains on the ears harden and do not have to be spread out and exposed to the sun before storing. Kernels shaken loose when the ears are put into baskets are thought to be gifts from the spirits, so they are brewed into a sacred beer. The word for this beer is "the falling."

Phupjoane. The word is the diminutive of "to swell." The enterprising farmer, surveying his fields, tests the sod with his hoe. If he happens to see a certain bulb burgeoning underground, he knows it is time for the strenuous work of sod-breaking to begin. The name of the bulb is "looking-slyly-at-the-tiller." The turned turf must rot before he can put in his corn seeds. But the swelling bulb foreshadows to the farmer the swelling of the seed-corn and therefore pricks his conscience.

Phuphu. The sly bulb swells almost imperceptibly. Now roots and stems alike are more obviously "bulging." The *shoeshoe* plant, from the fibers of whose leaves young girls' loincloths are made, is an early bloomer. As they pluck the *shoeshoe,* old women inevitably think ahead to the month of Mphalane. And the young herdsmen lead the cattle into the winter pastures, providently set aside by order of the village chief at the conclusion of the grasshoppers' singing.

XI: *Modern Times:*
Five Trains, a Gun,
and a Bicycle

TRAIN (1)

The one who roars in the distance
The one who crushes warriors, smashes them!
The one who debauches our wives:
They abandon us, they go to town,
The seducer, and we remain alone.

(Thonga)

TRAIN (2)

He entered, this madman. . . . This thing came in, I tell you,
with face turned upward as if conscious of its own renown.
I'm telling you, the thing twisted its waist, gliding gently
as it entered Bloemfontein station; it did so with much
self-esteem and so effortlessly that it could have come
but a short distance. . . . He entered quickly, this madman,
running on the tips of his toes; this thing swung its head
from side to side and clearly it was now entering a
city of immense size [Cape Town].

—S. Nkoto Sekoai
(Sotho)

TRAIN (3)

Ironware coming from the place of Big-workshops
Tear-the-hands, having torn those of the Englishmen
Rhinoceros, it has no front or back;
Tshukudu, I thought it was going that way
Tshukudu, it is coming this way!
It comes trailing a spider's web
Or a swarm of gnats.
Having been sent on its way by the point of a needle
Black beast, coming from Bump-against-tear-the-hands
Out of the big hole of the mother of gigantic women,
The umbilical cord is shining iron.
I encountered such a woman-of-the-track
Swerving along the banks of the river;
I thought I would snatch her at the bridge;
I said, "Get out of my way, you there at the teat!"
Team of red and white pipits
It gathered the track unto itself
So spotlessly clean!
Tshutshu of the dry plains
Tshukudu of the highlands
Beast from the south, it comes along steaming
It comes from place of Big Workshops
And from Tear-the-hands.

(Hurutshe)

TRAIN (4)

I am the black centipede, the rusher with a black nose
Drinker of water, even in the fountains of witches
And who do you say will bewitch me?
I triumph over the man-devouring sun
And over the impenetrable darkness
As carnivorous animals drink blood day and night.
I am the centipede, the mighty roarer from within;

My people have named me "I'm-still-going-south";
But I have changed, I am no longer a carrier of goods;
Black calf of the south
I am the black witch
Black witch of day and night;
I am a traveler, the vigorous rapid one, fed up with the road;
I am the one who kindles fire in the stomach;
I have defeated the horse.
When we raced, I was the fastest;
Sand filled the air, and I passed, I the black calf;
I arrived where the circumcision drum was beating;
When they asked me, I told them I came
From a place nobody knows, from a faraway country;
They asked me what kind of provision I would take;
And I said, No provisions for my journey,
Unlike those cowards of yours
I sleep without food, I, the omnivorous.
I shun the veranda where Ramaesela is married;
If I were found on the veranda an outcry would be heard
Like the great outcry when the tiger has seized the royal animals!
At my home they've given up hope of finding me;
I am not a house-child
I am the centipede who praises the wide open veld;
I am not delayed by hunger
Nor am I delayed by sore feet;
But I am delayed by steep hills and mountains,
And so to pay tribute I pray to them
For I do not want to die for the sacred
Children of the wild, who belong to nobody.
My people never should have allowed me to become a deserter;
Whole villages would not have been taken into captivity;
For I, the brave, when the village stands alerted to danger,
And the countryside says: Where shall I hide them, these cowards?
I remain with my feet on the road
And go on sliding, sliding into the dry ravines;
I imitate a river in flood
Carrying away whole villages of the black man;
What can they do to me, owners of the mines, of the roads

To me, the black centipede
That rushes for schedule times?

—Demetrius Segooa
(Sotho)

TRAIN (5)

The train
Carries everybody
Everywhere.
It carries the men
It carries the women
It carries me, too
A blind boy.
Wherever it carries me
Alas, I meet distress
And knock against it
With my knee.
It carries the men
It carries the women
It carries the blind boy
To his distress.

(Iteso)

GUN

I met Galuak at the dance
where my gunshots are always heard
with the rounds from Rath Tumbil's rifle
and the shots of Gac, Bol Deang
and Cuol Tungcuor.

We carry our rifles like those of Waldeth,
like the cavalry, like the Congolese army,
like the Anyanya guerrillas. Girls run away,
smoking like cigarettes when we fire.

Smoke from poor guns smells like exhaust.
Girls hate these guns like they hate
the monitor lizard. The dance is ruined
even if everyone keeps the beat.
Girls hate these guns like they hate
the monitor lizard.

The belly of an ox, Bil Rial,
is the color of the skullcap of an Arab.

The belly of an ox, Bil Rial,
is the color of the skullcap of an Arab.

His hide is like the sun itself:
he is the ox of moonlight.
Whenever I find that ox, a bull comes along.
It's true, Tuitui, the ox is like moonlight.
Whenever I find that one, a bull comes along.

Tunyang, this gun, a rifle with two shots,
made a man back down. Nyang Nyakong
and Nyang Nyankaat, I make men anxious
like those of the town "To be anxious,"
strutting with my rifle like an Egyptian.
The gun is a tawny thing like my ox
whose horns meet overhead.

> —*Sung by Daniel Cuol Lul Wur*
> (Nuer)

BICYCLE

My frail little bicycle,
The one with the scar,
My sister Seabelo,
Horse of the Europeans,
Feet of tire,

Iron horse,
Swayer from side to side.

                                                              (Hurutshe)

COMMENTARY

"The assimilative wisdom of African metaphysics recognizes no dif-
ference in essence between the mere means of tapping the power of
lightning—whether it is by ritual sacrifice, through the purgative will
of the community unleashing its justice on the criminal, or through
the agency of Franklin's revolutionary gadget" (Wole Soyinka, *Myth,
Literature and the African World* [Cambridge, England: Cambridge
University Press, 1976], p. 49). With the introduction of western tech-
nologies and their attendant symbol-systems, the "word" begins to
carry new semantic loads. The masquerader substitutes dark glasses
for a raffia face-veil, or puts on an army surplus gas mask. When his
dance is performed off-season or in a place different from that origi-
nally prescribed by sacred fiat, it becomes "theater" only and not the-
atrical ritual. A woman walks gracefully to market with enamel
"calabashes" piled on her head. A young man may be seen head-
carrying a box-spring mattress instead of a rolled mat, while behind
him effortlessly walks the principal of the school he attends, or per-
haps is beginning to teach in. As his parishioners dance their dona-
tions to the collection plate, an Aladura minister in Port Harcourt
acrobatically jumps for joy. A white-gowned Seraphim "dashes" her
pastor by plastering a five-Naira note on his glistening brow. African
world without end . . .

The arrival of the steam engine, like a new species of animal or
cataclysm or ogre, has elicited much praise-comment. Even the Yo-
ruba oracle has not been unaffected, as witness the following two
"parodies" collected by William Bascom:

(1)   Road is very straight, it does not turn
        Cast Ifa for Reluwe [Railway] on the day he was going
            down river to trade with Whiteman.
        They said all Whiteman's loads would belong to Reluwe.
        They said he should perform a sacrifice. . . .

Reluwe refused to make the offering.
From that time on, whoever puts his load into Reluwe's
  belly
Takes it out again when he alights from the train. . . .

(2)   Road is very straight, it does not turn
    Cast Ifa for Reluwe on the day he was weeping because he
      had no followers. . . .
    Reluwe offered three shillings and the cloth from his body,
    But did not offer the three cocks [also prescribed]. . . .
    Reluwe began to become a person with followers;
    They entered but, when it became evening,
    His followers got out, everyone going to his own home. . . .[1]

Train praise-poems allow us a vivid picture of the process of compo-
sition. A new symbol is born, attracting to itself a constellation of
attitudes and images. Praised by analogy to the familiar, the railway
carries emotional charges resulting from the social changes of which
it is both harbinger and instrument. And its cow-catcher catches old
anxieties, perpetual dissatisfactions, reckless, restless terrors and
ambitions.

TRAIN (1). Source: Henri A. Junod, *The Life of a South African Tribe*
(1912; reprinted. New Hyde Park, NY: University Books, 1962), vol.
II, p. 197. This praise was collected well before World War I. The
praiser worries about the women. Fate was to carry half the male
population of BaThonga country away to South African and Rho-
desian mines.

TRAIN (2). In 1951 Paramount Chieftainess 'Mantsebo Seeiso set off
for England, personally to congratulate King George VI on the out-
come of World War II. A member of her entourage, S. Nkoto Sekoai,
later wrote a book, in Sotho, about this journey. He called it *Travel
Broadens the Mind* (English translation). His description of the rapid
Orange Express entering first Bloemfontein station and then Cape

[1] William Bascom, *Ifa Divination* (Bloomington: Indiana University Press, 1969), pp.
560–562.

Town is in the traditional epic-praise style. Source: Daniel P. Kunene, *Heroic Poetry of the Basotho* (Oxford, England: Oxford University Press, 1971), pp. 146–147. "At the base of all this," says Kunene, "is ANIMATION."

TRAIN (3). Source: D. F. v.d. Merwe, "Hurutshe Poems," *Bantu Studies* XV, 4 (1941), p. 335. "Big-workshops" and "Tear-the-hands" are praise-place-names, here referring to a single unspecified location (Kimberley or Johannesburg?). *Tshukudu* is a double image, aural as well as visual. It means "rhinoceros" and it sounds like a steam engine. The smoke reminds the poet of both a spider's web and swarming gnats. The lever, setting the train in motion and controlling its speed, is referred to first as a "needle" and later as a "teat." The context of the latter identification is the remarkable comparison of the train to a great woman, whom the poet at one point attempts to embrace. (The engineer is his rival.) Power is mother, cow, and lover whose flowing hips seem tantalizingly graspable at the bridge. But the spotless red and white coaches fly off on the straightaway like carefree larks. The origin of this train is fantastically obstetrical.

TRAIN (4). Here a restless, displaced young man at a training college *is* the train; its rebellious energy realizes his. Source: H. J. van Zyl, "Praises in Northern Sotho," *Bantu Studies* XV, 2 (1941), pp. 133–135.

TRAIN (5). This beautiful poem was published by Ulli Beier in his anthology *African Poetry* (Cambridge, England: Cambridge University Press, 1966), p. 35. He gives as his source "Gerhard Kubik, verbal communication." I wish I knew who spoke it to Gerhard Kubik and under what circumstances.

GUN. Source: Terese Svoboda, *Cleaned the Crocodile's Teeth: Nuer Song*, Greenfield Center (New York: Greenfield Review Press, 1985), p. 19. This *tuare* ("improvised autobiographical song-segment") uses the convention of cattle praise to praise a gun, worth a cow in bridewealth settlement. According to Svoboda, "Waldeth" is a Nuer settlement (presumably fashionably armed). "Anyanya" are guerrilla fighters organized during the first phase of the Sudanese civil war, which started up again a year or so after she left the country in 1976, and continues.

BICYCLE. Source: v.d. Merwe, "Hurutshe Poems," p. 336. The "scar" is a thin tool bag attached to the frame. The operation completed, off we go down the road. . . .

XII: (You) Praise to the End

FOR THE BEST IN PAPERBACKS, LOOK FOR THE

In every corner of the world, on every subject under the sun, Penguin represents quality and variety—the very best in publishing today.

For complete information about books available from Penguin—including Pelicans, Puffins, Peregrines, and Penguin Classics—and how to order them, write to us at the appropriate address below. Please note that for copyright reasons the selection of books varies from country to country.

In the United Kingdom: For a complete list of books available from Penguin in the U.K., please write to *Dept E.P., Penguin Books Ltd, Harmondsworth, Middlesex, UB7 0DA.*

In the United States: For a complete list of books available from Penguin in the U.S., please write to *Consumer Sales, Penguin USA, P.O. Box 999— Dept. 17109, Bergenfield, New Jersey 07621-0120.* VISA and MasterCard holders call 1-800-253-6476 to order all Penguin titles.

In Canada: For a complete list of books available from Penguin in Canada, please write to *Penguin Books Canada Ltd, 10 Alcorn Avenue, Suite 300, Toronto, Ontario, Canada M4V 3B2.*

In Australia: For a complete list of books available from Penguin in Australia, please write to the *Marketing Department, Penguin Books Ltd, P.O. Box 257, Ringwood, Victoria 3134.*

In New Zealand: For a complete list of books available from Penguin in New Zealand, please write to the *Marketing Department, Penguin Books (NZ) Ltd, Private Bag, Takapuna, Auckland 9.*

In India: For a complete list of books available from Penguin, please write to *Penguin Overseas Ltd, 706 Eros Apartments, 56 Nehru Place, New Delhi, 110019.*

In Holland: For a complete list of books available from Penguin in Holland, please write to *Penguin Books Nederland B.V., Postbus 195, NL-1380AD Weesp, Netherlands.*

In Germany: For a complete list of books available from Penguin, please write to *Penguin Books Ltd, Friedrichstrasse 10-12, D-6000 Frankfurt Main I, Federal Republic of Germany.*

In Spain: For a complete list of books available from Penguin in Spain, please write to *Longman, Penguin España, Calle San Nicolas 15, E-28013 Madrid, Spain.*

In Japan: For a complete list of books available from Penguin in Japan, please write to *Longman Penguin Japan Co Ltd, Yamaguchi Building, 2-12-9 Kanda Jimbocho, Chiyoda-Ku, Tokyo 101, Japan.*